THE LAST WEEKEND

Born in Skipton, Yorkshire, Blake Morrison is the author of two bestselling memoirs, *And When Did You Last See Your Father?* and *Things My Mother Never Told Me*, two novels (most recently the acclaimed *South of the River*) and a study of the Bulger case, *As If*. He is also a poet, critic, journalist and librettist. He teaches creative writing at Goldsmiths College, and lives in south London.

ALSO BY BLAKE MORRISON

Dark Glasses

The Ballad of the Yorkshire Ripper

The Yellow House

And When Did You Last See Your Father?

As If

The Cracked Pot

Too True

Selected Poems

The Justification of Johann Gutenberg

Things My Mother Never Told Me

Oedipus/Antigone

South of the River

BLAKE MORRISON

The Last Weekend

VINTAGE BOOKS
London

Published by Vintage 2011

2 4 6 8 10 9 7 5 3 1

First published in Great Britain in 2010 by Chatto & Windus

Vintage
Random House, 20 Vauxhall Bridge Road,
London SW1V 2SA

www.vintage-books.co.uk

Addresses for companies within The Random House Group Limited can be found at: www.randomhouse.co.uk/offices.htm

The Random House Group Limited Reg. No. 954009

A CIP catalogue record for this book is available from the British Library

ISBN 9780099542346

The Random House Group Limited supports The Forest Stewardship Council (FSC), the leading international forest certification organisation. All our titles that are printed on Greenpeace approved FSC certified paper carry the FSC logo. Our paper procurement policy can be found at www.randomhouse.co.uk/environment

Printed and bound in Great Britain by
CPI Bookmarque, Croydon, CR0 4TD

To Kathy

I never found a man that knew how to love himself.

Othello, Act 1, Scene 3

In all matrimonial associations there is, I believe, one constant factor – a desire to deceive the person with whom one lives as to some weak spot in one's character or in one's career. For it is intolerable to live constantly with one human being who perceives one's small meannesses. It is really death to do so.

Ford Madox Ford, *The Good Soldier*

June

You know how it is with friends – the closer you get, the less you see them for what they are. They suck you in. They drag you down. You resist but their allure's too strong. Choked by their needs, you cease to see how mad they are. Or perhaps you see it from the start but choose to ignore it, out of love. Or the madness lies dormant until the chemistry between you sets it off. Who can say? I've only my own experience to go on.

The one thing I have learned is this. When people accuse you of harbouring negative feelings – anger, jealousy, malice, resentment – it's they who're feeling them. I dare say there's a technical term for it. A shrink-word. But you have to be there – enfolded in someone's weirdness – to know what it's like.

It's Ollie I'm talking about. But it could as easily be Daisy. Both were my friends. And both have left me with a sense of guilt, as though I, not they, were responsible.

Would it have been better if I'd never met them – better for them and better for me? I've sometimes thought so, over recent months. But you can't spend your life hanging back. Friendship demands intimacy and intimacy carries a risk. I say friendship but what I mean is love. I did love Ollie and Daisy. No one has ever doubted that.

I've this memory of myself as a small boy, on the beach at

Bridlington, afraid to step into the sea. What's scary isn't the cold but the vastness, the grey-brown water going on and on. My father, holding my hand, tries to coax me – then loses his patience and drags me in. As the waves reach my midriff, I break free, and turn and run, and keep on running till I reach my mother on the warm sand, and bury my head in her soft striped towel. 'Don't cry,' she says. 'What's up with you?' But even when my tears have stopped, I don't have the words to explain it.

At least I'm not that boy any more. I've lived. I've competed. I'm no longer a loser or a wimp.

As to the events of August, I don't suppose I'll ever get over them. I'm the kind of guy who feels guilty even when he's innocent – who expects to be stopped going through customs even when he has nothing to declare. But what happened that weekend would surely have happened anyway. It's not like I'm a rapist or a murderer. Even if I were, I would be honest with you. I'm trying to tell the story, that's all – not to unburden myself or extenuate some offence but to set things straight.

It began with a phone call.

'You're joking,' I said. 'A country-house weekend?'

'In a house,' Ollie said. 'In the country. Over a weekend. But no, Ian, not a country-house weekend.'

'Not white suits and straw boaters and people sipping champagne next to a ha-ha.'

'No.'

'Not even Pimm's and picnic hampers.'

'Not that we planned.'

'Oh.'

'You sound disappointed.'

'Don't be ridiculous,' I said.

It was a Sunday evening in late June and I was sitting in the box room with a heap of exercise books on one side of my desk, a glass of beer on the other, and the computer screen glowing in the middle. Sunday evenings used to be convivial: Em and I would play badminton at the sports centre, grab a curry on the way home, then snuggle up and watch a DVD. Now there was always work to do, especially for Em, whose caseload grew larger by the month and whose colleagues seemed to think Sunday the perfect night to dump their problems on her. I'd been surprised to find the phone call was for me.

'It'll just be us,' Ollie said. 'And you two, we hope.'

'I'll have to ask Em.'

He fell silent, as if I'd been rude not to accept straight away.

'She and I barely speak these days,' I said, jollying him along.

'That bad, eh?'

'When I'm in, she's out, and vice versa.'

'Sounds like you need a break.'

'Absolutely. I can't remember the last time.'

I could remember perfectly well. Lanzarote, at Easter. But I knew what Ollie and Daisy would think of Lanzarote.

I tried making small talk but he cut me short. All he wanted was to hang up so I could ask Em. When something mattered to Ollie, nothing else did.

'Call me back tonight if you can,' he said. 'We don't go to bed before midnight.'

'What's the name of the place again?'

'Badingley. I went there as a boy. You'll like it.'

With the window open, I caught the scent of honeysuckle from the patio, where I'd been watering plants before coming upstairs – the tips of my trainers were still wet from the hose. It was late, nine thirty, but the light was good, and I could hear a thrush calling – I'm always amazed by how many birds there are in our small garden. Was there birdsong in Ollie and Daisy's garden too? Did the sun leave the same faint print, a late remission on a red-brick wall? We'd visited their current house only once but I could remember the sliding glass doors, the wooden decking, the wrought-iron table and chairs. Perhaps Ollie had been sitting there when he called. When he wasn't in chambers, he liked to be outdoors.

'Who was that?' Em called out.

'Ollie.'

'Who?'

'Ollie Moore.'

'God, what did *he* want?'

I went offline and swigged my beer before taking the six steps along the landing. If Em saw the glass, she'd berate me for not offering her one. And if she knew I'd been playing on websites, she'd be cross about that, too.

'He called with an invite,' I said, leaning my shoulder against the frame of the doorway. Em was sitting at the desk with her laptop, the pine double bed beyond heaped with stuff she'd brought home from work – box files, Xeroxes, print-outs, plastic folders. The spare bedroom, which doubles as her office, is bigger than the box room. But her job is bigger than my job. Or so she reckons – there's more paperwork anyway. Sometimes I wonder why we keep a spare bedroom at all. I can't remember the last time anyone slept in it.

'What kind of invite?' Em said, not looking up.

'Don't sound so suspicious.'

'I know you two are old friends.'

'I can tell there's a "but" coming,' I said.

'He's not been in touch for ages. When's the last time you did anything together?'

'Exactly. He said the same thing – that it's time we saw them.'

Now she did look up.

'*We?*'

'You're invited too. Daisy will be there.'

She gave a twisted little smile. 'I assumed it was boys only.'

Years ago, when I first knew Em, Ollie and I had gone off to a stag night in Dublin. Just that once. Yet she makes out our 'boys only' weekends are – or were – a regular occurrence.

'He asked us to stay,' I said, letting it pass.

'In London?'

'On holiday with them.'

'Where are they off to this time? The Caribbean? The Galapagos?' Over the years, Ollie – or rather Daisy – had been dutiful about sending postcards from far-flung places. Em and I saw it as a form of sadism. 'Wherever it is,' she said, going back to her work, 'we can't afford it.'

'They're renting a house in East Anglia. Near the sea.'

'When's this?'

'August. They're suggesting the bank holiday weekend.'

'Which one's that?'

'I'm not sure. The calendar's behind you.'

It was a calendar showing a stag by a loch against a backdrop of purple heather. Em's family originally came from Scotland and her aunt sends her a similar calendar every Christmas, to remind her – now her parents are dead – of her Celtic roots.

'There,' I said, fingering a blank box below the heather, 'we could go on the Friday. Friday the 27th. The last weekend.'

I looked at Em and tried to imagine what I'd feel seeing her for the first time, rather than as someone I've been with for fifteen years. The wide brow, the full lips, the large breasts inside the turquoise blouse: her features were too big to be called beautiful, her gestures too expansive, but I could see why people felt they could talk to her – why they knew she would listen. She did listen, even to me. And though made wary by hearing so many hard-luck stories, she still looked young and naive. But for the lines across her forehead, which deepened on Sunday nights when she went through her caseload, she might have passed for thirty. Whereas I was looking my age these days: receding hairline, hunched shoulders, double chin.

'So what did you say?' Em said.

'I said I'd ask you.'

'You could have asked while you were on the phone.'

'I thought you'd want to discuss it.'

'Since when do you and I discuss things?'

'Don't be like that.'

'I'm not being like anything.'

'So you'd like to go?' I said.

'We're hardly inundated with invites. We're not like Ollie and Daisy.'

The various ways in which we're not like Ollie and Daisy is a conversation we often have. Indeed, we've spent far more time talking about them than in their presence. The essential contrasts, all to our disadvantage, go: large Georgian house in west London vs small modern semi in Ilkeston; Range Rover and BMW vs Ford Fiesta; Mauritius (Florence, Antigua, etc.) vs Lanzarote (if we're lucky); The Ivy vs Pizza Express; Royal Opera House vs local Odeon; Waitrose vs Morrisons; golden couple vs pair of ugly toads. I exaggerate but not much.

'Besides,' Em went on, 'by the end of August I'll be desperate for a break. You get shot of your kids for the summer but mine are at their worst.'

By 'her' kids, Em doesn't mean children she had with a previous partner. Nor is she in a position to talk about 'our' kids, the progenitive being another difference between us and the Moores – they only have Archie, but that's one more than we do. (I say 'the Moores' because it's a habit, but Ollie and Daisy have never married and at work she's known as Daisy Brabant.) No, by kids Em means the problem teenagers she deals with at work.

'As long as they're OK with dogs,' Em said.

The dog was a red setter, Rufus, moulting on a rug downstairs.

'They know we have one,' I said.

'Even so. We can't just take him without asking.'

'It sounds like you're making excuses,' I said.

'I'm being practical. You're the indecisive one.'

'Me?'

'You knew we were free but you wouldn't commit yourself. Be honest: do you really want to go?'

Did I? I'd been so preoccupied with Em's response that I hadn't really thought about it. A long weekend near the sea might appeal to most people, but I'm a townie – grew up in Manchester, did my teacher training in Birmingham, distrust big waves, feel uneasy when there's no concrete. On the other hand, Ollie and Daisy were bound to be staying somewhere comfortable, even grand, and it would be good to get together. I'd begun to think that we might not meet again, ever.

'Ollie seemed pretty keen,' I said.

'The friends they originally asked have cried off, you mean.'

'It'll be fun. We all get along, don't we?'

'It depends who else is around. Remember that time at Primrose Hill?'

Em has more reasons for disliking Daisy than she realises. The one she cites is the occasion, ten years ago, when Daisy and Ollie were living in Primrose Hill, and invited us for the weekend without mentioning that they were having a party and that the guests (more than sixty of them) were mostly their work colleagues and therefore unknown to us, neither of which omissions might have mattered had Daisy not failed to introduce us to people and then treated us like kitchen staff, though as to the last I think the blame lay partly with us since, for want of something better to do, it was we who started passing plates of food around. The fact that two other couples stayed overnight, and that we'd no time alone with the Moores on the Sunday, didn't help. Ollie bore some responsibility, of course. But the real culprit was Daisy. I too had resented her neglect.

'It'll just be them,' I said. 'Ollie said so.'

'Good. Daisy's fine when she's not showing off. And it'll be nice to see Archie. You're supposed to be his godfather, remember.'

'Ollie didn't mention Archie.'

'Archie or not,' she said, letting me know she'd had enough, 'it sounds like we should say yes.'

'Right. I'll call them back.'

'Not now. It'll make us look desperate. Leave it a few days.'

'OK,' I said, leaning down and kissing her.

'Meanwhile . . .'

'Meanwhile you've got work to do, I know.'

'Don't you?'

I did, but not as much as she had, or not sufficient to deter me from going downstairs to fetch another beer. Shutting the fridge, I noticed the back door was open, and stepped outside, and felt the heat of the day still stored in the back step. Ours is a small garden, fifty feet or so, mostly gravel rather than grass. But there's a view of the hills over the houses behind. And the previous owner created a pond, bequeathing us his koi and goldfish. I picked up the canister of fish food, treading on a loose flagstone as I approached. The noise drew them upwards through the weed, their open mouths and feathery tails churning the surface. Goldfish are meant to have a memory span of ten seconds. So how did these ones know, when I trod on that flagstone, they were about to be fed? And why, whenever a heron visits, do they stay close to the bottom for days afterwards? I admired them for living so simply. 'Pond life,' people say, as an insult. Perhaps Ollie and Daisy thought of Em and me as pond life. But they wouldn't have called unless they wanted to see us. They probably liked us for the same reason as I liked the fish.

Drawn by the splishes from the pond, Rufus wandered out to join me, lethargically sniffing the lily pads before shambling back inside. I too was almost panting in the heat, but rather than follow him in I sat on the back step, avoiding the snail trail which shone like spilt semen. The sun was finally setting over the roofs. It seemed too grand a sunset for our street, so triumphant I half expected trumpets, glorious but also brutal, the clouds underlit with blood. How long before the sun went completely? Ten seconds? Twenty? I settled on fifteen and counted it down, to the last orange wisp. Twenty-six seconds. I'd have lost that bet.

The dusk gathered round, heavy and hot. I sat there for a long time. Anything was preferable to marking.

'OK, love?' Em called as I finally creaked back upstairs, meaning would I please get on with my work so that when we'd both finished we could go to bed and do what couples our age are supposed to do once or twice a week. I ought to have felt flattered – to have my partner of fifteen years still desire me – but as I sat in the box room, unable to concentrate, my brow sweating from the beer and humidity, the mouse connecting me to websites, what I felt was chided, for being the lesser, lazier partner in the marriage.

It was different when we first lived together. Then I'd been the one with the demanding job, a young teacher learning to cope with unruly kids, whereas Em was merely in training, for what precisely she didn't yet know, social work broadly, but whether work with the old, disabled, addicted, delinquent or merely impoverished she wouldn't decide until she had her certificate. We were hard up then, more so than now, in a rented flat with dusty carpets and no washing machine. But I assumed the pattern of our lives would stay the same, with me at work all day and Em a dilettantish part-timer. I'm not the kind of man who expects his wife to have the dinner on the table when he gets home, but even when she qualified and began her first job it seemed only right that Em took on the bulk of household duties – preparation for when children came along. They never did, or haven't yet. And as the prospect of them has receded, so Em has begun to immerse herself in other people's children, her daily dealings with kids who have been damaged in some way – through abuse, neglect, violence, malnutrition and all the other charming hand-me-downs – compensating her for the non-arrival of ours.

Her work is hard. Harder than mine. A weekend away would do her good. 27 August. 2, 7, 8. Three lucky numbers of mine. I put the date in my diary.

Procrastinating, I retrieved an old road atlas from under my desk and looked up Badingley. I wasn't surprised it didn't appear in the index: there isn't room for every small village or hamlet. What was frustrating was to turn to the relevant page and find it torn out. No worries: I could always google. But the missing page seemed faintly ominous – as if the whole area had been wiped from the map.

Despite Em's discouragement, I was tempted to call Ollie back that night, so we all knew where we were. In the event, he saved me the trouble. The phone rang just as I'd finally settled to my marking.

'I hope it's not too late,' he said.

'Not in the least.'

'Good, because –'

'I've talked to Em,' I said, leaping in to keep it brief. 'It's sorted. We're free. You're on.'

'Right. Good. Only, I'm sorry, this is awkward, but I was hoping you hadn't talked to Em so we could change the date – it turns out Daisy has already asked someone else for the bank holiday, without telling me. You're not free the previous weekend by any chance?'

'I don't know,' I said, though I did. 'I'll have to ask Em.'

'If that's not a nuisance. I don't mind waiting.'

'She's in the middle of something. I'll call you tomorrow.'

'So it could be difficult.'

'I don't know. But we need to discuss it.'

'Just a sec,' he said. I could hear footsteps in the background and the sound of a door closing. I was too taken aback to feel angry, but I knew that was how I ought to feel and irritably drummed my red biro on the desk. Had he not consulted Daisy before he called me? Had she now ordered him to dis-invite us? I imagined her losing her temper with him on the leather sofa in their drawing room: 'For God's sake, Ollie, how could you be so stupid? We've asked the Fitchinghams that weekend, they and the Goades are chalk and cheese.' Em was right about Daisy: our small-town ways were an embarrassment to her; Ollie might feel some lingering attachment to his old mate, but she didn't want us around. I threw my biro down and drained my beer. Jesus, this was insulting enough without Ollie expecting me to hang on indefinitely while he wandered off somewhere.

'On no account ask Em anything,' he said, returning in a

newly hushed voice. 'I should never have called you back. It's just Daisy thought if you'd not spoken to Em . . . But you have, and that's fine, so let's leave things as they are. I'd much rather you came on the bank holiday weekend – it'll give us longer.'

'But if you're double-booked . . .'

'It's only one of Daisy's designer chaps. He can come another time.'

'Really, if it's difficult, I'm sure we could switch.'

'Enough, Ian. It's settled. Come on the Friday morning. Come as early as you can. Let's make the most of it.'

I hung up and tried to concentrate: ten minutes' marking and I'd be done. But Ollie's call – his second call – was all I could think about. There he was, crossing the floor of his study (not a box room like mine, but a high-ceilinged, book-lined sanctum, with sash windows overlooking the garden) in order to close the door, so that Daisy wouldn't overhear him talking to me. Why? Their relationship had always seemed enviable and nobody envied it more than I did. But if they'd reached the point where one made arrangements without consulting the other, was something wrong? I suddenly remembered the last time we'd seen them. Three years ago, at half-term – they were passing through with Archie on their way to a holiday in the Lakes, and we had lunch in Matlock and went for a walk, during which Ollie wandered off and failed to rejoin us till we reached the car park an hour later. No great drama: he'd spotted some sort of roadside display in the distance and by the time he established what it was (a floral memorial to a dead cyclist) he had lost sight of us and then turned right where we'd turned left – a simple enough explanation, but I recall Em saying afterwards that Ollie and Daisy seemed out of sync in some way.

I felt sad to think their marriage might be in trouble – sad but excited. Partly responsible, too: I was the one who'd introduced them to each other all those years ago.

I went online again, hoping a spin of the wheel would distract me. But Ollie was too much in my head. He'd always lived with a manic kind of vigour: if the weekend didn't include a five-mile run, a dinner party with fellow lawyers, a concert or exhibition, a game of tennis or squash, a skim-read of a new political biography and three hours preparing his latest case, then it wouldn't be an Ollie weekend. But he was in his mid-forties now, when men begin to lose their edge. And he hadn't sounded his old self on the phone. Was he going grey? Had he finally put on some weight? I saw him cross the room in blue cotton trousers, a white polo shirt and navy sailing shoes, but I couldn't make out his waistline or his face.

Hearing Em get up from her desk, I quit the website with a mixture of frustration and relief.

'I'm off to bed,' she said, in the doorway. 'Who was that?'

'Ollie again.'

'He must be keen.'

'He is.'

'It's sorted, then?'

'Yes.'

I didn't mention the business over dates because it would have annoyed her. If we were going to spend a weekend with Ollie and Daisy, it was best she go into it with an open mind. I was protecting Em from herself – but also, if I'm honest, protecting Daisy. She and I go back a long way. I knew her before she met Ollie. And there are episodes which, misinterpreted, might prejudice Em against her.

Couples should be honest with each other. But when being honest causes trouble, tactful omissions are kinder. That's how I see it – though Em would certainly disagree.

The light was fading beyond the window but street lamps

kept the dark at bay. It's a good street to live in. A street free of knife attacks and muggings. A street where the handmade posters pinned to trees are messages about missing cats, not missing children. A street which *has* trees, enough of them for estate agents to call it 'leafy'.

As I returned to my marking, with Em waiting in bed, the phone rang again.

'Ian,' Daisy said, like an alarm going off, 'I am so, *so* sorry.'

For a moment I thought she must want to change arrangements again. I braced myself not to show anger or hurt. What did it matter whether or not we saw them? They were gone, people from the past, strangers.

'Ollie ballsed it up,' she went on. 'He missed the point completely. I don't know what's wrong with him these days. Am I forgiven?'

How could I not forgive her? What was there to forgive?

'We've been planning this for ages,' she said. 'You suggest it every year on your Christmas card. Well, finally we've got round to it. I'm so glad you can come.'

I got the whole story then. How Ollie had forgotten that she'd asked a client of hers called Milo to stay over the bank holiday ('His wife is going to the States for a month, he has two young kids to look after, for me it's more duty than pleasure but the least I could do was offer'). How she would see if Milo could do a different weekend, but if not it didn't matter, he was lovely, we would like him and there was loads of room, the house had five bedrooms. How she hoped Ollie hadn't given the impression that she was putting us off. Nothing could be further from the truth. It would be lovely – *lovely* – to see us.

'Ollie's been under a lot of pressure lately. It will do him good. And anyway, well, I don't have to tell you.'

It was one of her old phrases. She didn't.

I held the phone tight and possessive to my ear. Was she in bed yet? I could imagine the silk nightdress and the hair falling to her shoulders. The intimacy of her voice made me feel special. But that was a trick of hers. Whoever she talked to was, at that moment, the most important person in the world. She and I went right back. But friendships have to go forward. And ours hadn't moved for years.

'How's Archie?' I said.

'Sixteen next month.'

'Will we see him?'

'I doubt it.'

When she didn't elaborate, I asked if we could bring Rufus.

'You know I'm fond of dogs,' she said.

I knew she wasn't fond of dogs – that she was allergic to certain types of dog hair and that there'd been some sort of trauma with an Alsatian when she was little. But after the earlier embarrassment, she didn't object.

'So are things OK with you?' she said. 'No news?'

When Em's mother used to ask her 'No news?', what she meant was 'Aren't you pregnant yet?' Daisy wouldn't be so crass. She assumed either we were 'waiting for the right moment' (at thirty-eight, Em still has time) or that we'd decided against kids. Both assumptions were fine by me.

'Nothing major,' I said.

'Nothing major our end either. Except for Ollie losing the plot. Oh, and there is one bit of news. But we're saving it till we see you.'

The bell of her voice rang in my ear. What would count as news, when we saw them so rarely and knew so little of how they lived? In her job as a headhunter, Daisy mixed with artists and designers as well as company execs. Had she ever fallen for one of them? She'd always said that Ollie was the love of her life. But a lifetime's obdurate monogamy seemed too much to expect of someone so attractive. The same went for Ollie: at university there'd always been girls eager to sleep with him. But if either of them had had affairs, it wouldn't be news they could relay to us (or even each other). Perhaps they were buying a second home. Or retiring early. Or Ollie was becoming a High Court judge. It was bound to be something feel-good or trivial. Why the mystery?

'You've got me intrigued,' I said.

'It's a ruse to make you turn up.'

'You don't need a ruse for that.'

Light flickered on the horizon. Thunder grumbled far off. Was a storm brewing in London too? I pictured Ollie in the shower, rinsing off the humid day, while Daisy sat there in her nightdress, the sheets drawn up to her knees.

'I'll let you get to bed,' she said, as if to confirm it. 'Love to Em. Oh, hang on a sec – here's Ollie again.'

Doubtless emerging, a white towel round his waist, from the bathroom, before kissing her bare shoulder and silently demanding the handset. She would have to slide over to make room for him, the black silk creasing and shimmying as she did.

This is weird, I thought, as she passed the phone to him: no contact for years then they call us three times in one night.

'I meant to say earlier,' he said. 'Remember to bring your gear.'

'What?'

'Your weapons. Your clubs. Don't forget them.'

'If I still have them.'

'And get some practice in – that's if you're serious about the bet.'

'I don't know what you're talking about,' I said.

'Don't worry. There'll be no rough stuff.'

I told myself it was just banter and forgot about it as soon as I'd hung up.

'Ollie again?' Em called from our bedroom. I could hear her drawing the curtains, the wooden rings clattering along the rail.

'Yes,' I said, not untruthfully.

'The man's possessed,' she said.

'Barking,' I said.

'Coming to bed?'

'In a minute.'

I had a last few tests to mark. And one final splurge on the Internet to make up for my earlier disappointments.

'Remember to turn the lights off,' Em said, as she always does at bedtime. Not 'Make sure the front door's locked' or 'Check the catch on the living-room window' but 'Put out the lights'. Energy-saving has become her passion. An intruder might break in and murder us in our beds, but to Em that would be the lesser catastrophe. What price our own deaths compared with the death of the planet?

'Will do,' I answered, as I always do, and dutifully descended, my hand riding the banister. The lights were all off downstairs but lightning flickered on the horizon, and there were street lamps, so it didn't feel dark. I stood by the garden window, brooding on Ollie and Daisy, and wondering about the fish. Did they hover there after darkness, asleep? Or keep on swimming all night? I was tempted to go outside and look. But the strangeness of the evening had made me weary. I crossed the dark green carpet and climbed to bed.

Friday

I'm a primary-school teacher. Did I tell you that? With most people I just say 'teacher', so they assume I work in a secondary school or sixth-form college. Own up to teaching young children and the reaction is suspicion (am I a paedophile?) or contempt (could I not find a proper job?). People like Ollie and Daisy are more benevolent but still bemused: they wonder how someone so 'intelligent' could have ended up doing what I do, as though children would be better entrusted to the stupid. I'm a little touchy on the subject, as you can see.

I have done the state some service and they know it – nearly two decades working for a local authority. In fact, since the age of five I've spent only six months outside an educational institution. That was the year after qualifying as a teacher when, disenchanted by my experience of teaching practice, I began making other plans – to start my own business, join the civil service, become a fitness instructor, manage a casino or make a fortune on the stock market. The plans didn't get very far. Mostly I lay in bed, or on my parents' sofa, reading books or watching the racing channel. I'd had glandular fever in my last year at university and my lethargy may have been related to that. Or perhaps it was ME, 'yuppie flu', just then being discovered and given a name. It could even have been depression. What I remember, aside from my mum being anxious ('Are you running a temperature, love?') and my dad his usual bullying self ('There's nowt wrong with you that a boot up your arse wouldn't cure'), was a recurring dream from which I'd wake in a pool of sweat. In the dream I was running. Or rather, failing to run. There'd be an earthquake or erupting volcano, and I'd almost have reached safety when my legs would stop working. I'd look down, bemused, and they would be flippers. Or fishtails. Or frogspawn. In the worst and last dream I dreamt I woke and pulled back the bedcovers to find my legs had turned to water – then really woke and found I'd pissed the bed. It was that dream which finally scared me into getting off my butt. It isn't healthy to live with parents after twenty, especially parents as wearing as mine, and I knew once I got a job – which I did, thirty applications and seven interviews later – I would stop feeling trapped. Work liberated me. But the real source of my freedom, and the reason the dream stopped recurring, was Em.

I was twenty-eight, and still feeling my way as a teacher. A boy in my class had been acting strangely, inserting pointed objects (pens, twigs, crayons, sticks of chalk) into his own and other children's orifices. Concerned, the head contacted social services, and a senior social worker came to interview the boy, along with Em, then a student trainee on a temporary placement with the child protection team. We got talking over a cup of tea in the staffroom. Thick specs, black leather boots and gypsy blouse: I wasn't sure what to make of her. But she was slim, and laughed a lot, and after the lies and mystifications I'd encountered in other women her straightforwardness was refreshing. As a student, she had no authority in the case, but she came to observe the boy as part of her training and sat in on some of my classes. Eventually I asked her out for a drink. Then a meal. Then back to my flat. I thought of myself as an outsider and tried to think of Em as one too. In reality she wasn't, as I found when she introduced me to her friends.

That others liked her came as a shock to me, not because she was difficult to like, but because I thought (a lover's delusion) that I alone had discovered her. She was puzzled by my reaction: what was wrong with having friends? Didn't I have friends? I mentioned Ollie and Daisy. But I was in no hurry to introduce her to them – until I felt more secure, less afraid of being dumped. We were sleeping together by then, with mixed success: she was too slow, and I was too quick, the usual problem inexperienced lovers have, the problem we had anyway. In time we fixed it, and though there were things sex didn't fix, Em gave me a confidence I'd not had before.

At work she kept her surname, because she thought that more professional. Emily Grace Barber she was, until I lopped her. I knew the word 'em' from my Uncle Jimmy, a compositor at a printworks in Salford for thirty years until new technology arrived. I used to hear him with my dad, talking printers' lingo in his wheezy voice – picas and leading, cross heads and Elrods, widows and ems. He suffered from emphysema, which as a kid I thought was an industrial disease caused by working with ems. By the time I married, Uncle Jimmy was long dead, reduced to ash, like all those fags he'd smoked at the stone. But I'd felt closer to him than to his brother, my bastard dad, and abbreviating my wife was a memorial to him. It sat better on her, too. She might be Emily to her parents (who'd chosen a name that would raise her from the backstreets) but to me she would always be Em: the inverse of Me and the least egotistical person you'll ever meet.

Two weeks after Ollie's phone call, we celebrated our thirteenth wedding anniversary. Apart from some field trips I'd been on with the school, and a couple of residential training courses for Em, we had barely spent a night apart in all that time. There's no easy way to measure the success of a marriage but ours seemed to work. And though Em had been under stress and my summer wasn't the break it should have been, both of us felt good the day we set off to Badingley, hoping for a simple weekend with old friends.

To judge by the caravans and people carriers, the entire country had taken Friday off. We had barely left town, past the chained-up schools and sapless parks, when we hit our first queue. We crawled, we stalled, we stewed in exhaust fumes, as the temperature gauge rose towards red. At every junction and slip road, more cars joined the race to freedom, only to find it a cortège. White smoke sailed serenely from the vast industrial vases of the Midlands. But for us, grounded and gridlocked, there was no escape.

We don't have Satnav in the Fiesta, but the route seemed an obvious one: from Ilkeston, follow the ring road round Nottingham, keep on the A52 till it hits the A1(M) at Grantham, then south as far as the A14, which takes you east again, after which you continue eastwards or drop down to exit 8 on the M11 – either way, you end up on minor roads for the last thirty miles, which I imagined would be the torturous part of the journey, not guessing it would be torture from the start. We kept the sun visors down and the air conditioning on MAX, but nothing could repel the heat. Every few minutes a blue siren pulsed past, away to a pile-up or gorse fire. Blue was the colour – of the sirens, the sky, the fields of lavender and linseed. I wanted England back, grey, drab, dark clouds squatting like toads.

Near Peterborough, the tarmac melting around us, Em suggested we re-route and head across the Fens. She was the map reader, and I knew it made sense. But seeing the tailback for the next exit, I kept on south, unaware of the roadworks up ahead. Em was furious. In an hour we moved four hundred yards. The air was tarred and sulphurous, its furnace vapour clogging our throats.

'I thought we were sharing the driving,' Em said.

'We need to put some miles on the clock,' I said. 'You're slower.'

'If I'm slow I should be driving now – we're barely moving.'

'We'll swap at the next exit.'

'Why not here?'

'We're in the middle lane of a motorway.'

'So? I've seen other people get out of their cars. How long would it take? Ten seconds?'

I eyed the cigarette lighter in its ring of fire on the dashboard, and wondered how it would feel to plunge it in Em's arm.

'You're a control freak, Ian. And a sexist. Anyone ever told you that?'

'You have. Often.'

'Not often enough, obviously.'

Had the cars around us not been stationary, our row might have passed unnoticed. But their occupants had a grandstand view. Not that most of them weren't rowing, too, every car crammed with kids whose thirst, hunger, boredom, need to pee or lack of battery life for whichever game they'd brought had now reached crisis point. By the time we got off the motorway, Em and I weren't speaking. Any solicitude was reserved for Rufus, who lay panting in the back.

Somewhere east of Thetford we finally swapped, and Em, behind the wheel, cheered up. She liked the landscape, I could tell: wheat fields, windmills, water towers, pantiled farms with weatherboard outbuildings. I tried phoning ahead, to warn Ollie and Daisy we would be late. But neither of their mobiles seemed to be working. Sweat ran down my back. Em's sunglasses kept misting up. Slow driver though she is, she was flashed by a speed camera in a deserted village. It was one of those days when nothing goes right.

'Fucking hell,' I said, at a temporary traffic light in the middle of nowhere.

'I know you're stressed, Ian, but –'

'Who wouldn't be stressed?'

'You've a lot on your mind. The tribunal's soon and –'

'I don't want to talk about it.'

'I'm not going to talk about it,' Em said, squeezing my hand, 'but you could at least be friendly. OK?'

'OK,' I said, as the light turned green.

The roads were minor and seemed to meander everywhere but east. Where were we exactly? On the plane home from Lanzarote at Easter, a map of England had been displayed on the overhead TV set, with odd, arbitrary towns picked out: Chatham, Kidderminster, Darlington, Morecambe. The map in my head was similarly bizarre, effacing the principal towns of East Anglia in favour of a single hamlet, Badingley. It was too small to feature in our road atlas. But Ollie had emailed directions, and I'd fantasised about it so often since June I felt I knew it already – the village green, the duck pond, the low-raftered pub, the old forge with cartwheels outside, and then the asphalt drive to Flaxfield Grange, a Palladian mansion set among copper beeches and horse chestnuts.

'I don't see it as a Palladian mansion,' Em said. 'More a Georgian rectory.'

'Or a luxury bungalow on stilts above a fishing lake.'

'Or a Californian eco-house with acres of glass.'

'With a swimming pool and sauna,' I said.

'And a fresh stream running by, and green willows.'

'And a tennis court.'

'And red deer roaming the parkland.'

'Which Rufus can chase.'

I looked at Em's hands on the wheel. They seemed bigger these days, more knobbly about the knuckles, less tapered towards the tips. Her mother used to suffer from arthritis. Would Em go the same way?

'Did I tell you about Magda?' she said. We were following a slow tractor, easily passable before the next bend, but Em just sat there on its tail.

'Who's Magda?' I said, exasperated.

'A new case.'

New? Em's cases were always the same. Misery piled on misery, each indistinguishable from the last. The sixteen-year-old who tried to strangle his mother. The fifteen-year-old addicted to stealing BMWs. The fourteen-year-old who fed her crack habit through prostitution. And those were just the older kids.

'I lay awake half the night thinking about her,' she said.

Please spare me the detail, I wanted to say. But the earlier row made me conciliatory.

'I'm all ears,' I lied, and tried to pay attention.

Magda was a twenty-year-old from Lithuania, now living in Derby, it seemed. She had turned up at Em's office with a split lip, bruised cheekbone and black eye. Em's speciality is kids on probation. But she was duty senior that day and Magda's appearance was so vulnerable (not just the injuries but the torn jeans, flimsy T-shirt and nylon jacket) that Em – overhearing her broken conversation with the reception clerk – invited her into one of the 'consulting rooms' (a windowless cell with bulletproof glass). It was only then that she realised the girl had a baby with her, silent in a pushchair. Em was struck by how well dressed the baby was, unlike its mother. How well cared for, too. What's she called? Em asked. Anna. How old is she? Seven months. She's a beautiful baby, Em said. Yes, but I need fossilhelp. Fossilhelp – what do you mean by fossilhelp? To have my baby. To *have* your baby? To take from me. You want someone to take your baby? Yes. You want to place your baby for adoption? I do not understand.

Nor did Em understand, but over the next hour – between tears and cups of tea and nappy changes and mangled syntax – she slowly got there. It was a complex story involving a baby whose arrival made Magda's boyfriend angry and violent. Distressed, Magda had gone back to Lithuania for a month, but her family didn't want to know. Reunited with the boyfriend in Derby, she tried to make a go of things but then . . .

It was hot in the car and to be honest I dozed off, though I did hear the explanation of fossilhelp.

'Foster care,' Em said. 'Someone had told her about it. So I explained about a child being placed in care and how in time it might be returned to its mother, but there was no guarantee, and so the best thing Magda could do was . . .

The next thing I knew was Em prodding me.

'Completely unprofessional of me, right? Ian? *Ian?*'

I sat upright and rubbed my eyes.

'Like I say,' she said, 'I'm in the leaving care team, not the fostering department: I should have referred her and let them deal with it. Instead of which I scrambled together fifty quid of emergency funds, got her a place in a hostel over the weekend, handed her an extra twenty quid out of my own pocket, gave her my mobile number so she could call me any time, and told her to come back and see me on Tuesday.'

Handing out twenty quid was certainly unprofessional – and generosity we couldn't afford. But this wasn't the time to say so.

'You did the right thing,' I said. 'You helped her.'

'I could see she loved the child and shouldn't be rushed into something she might regret.'

'Absolutely,' I said, stroking the back of Em's left hand as it rested on the gear lever. I was wide awake now and wondered, since I'd listened nicely, would she let me take over the driving again.

'And the story of the rape was appalling,' she said. 'Her parents accused her of bringing shame on the family but, Christ, it was hardly her fault. You suffer one kind of nightmare and then the bastards put you through another.'

Was the baby the product of a rape, then? I'd been asleep for that bit.

'You were moved by her story,' I said. 'That's understandable.'

'I hear terrible stories all the time. Usually I'm detached. Why wasn't I this time?'

The lanes had narrowed and we were stuck behind a lorry carrying sand. The tailgate was loosely bolted, so that every time the lorry hit a bump the flap tipped open and spat out sand grains.

'Stop beating yourself up about it.'

'I asked a question, Ian.'

She kept her eyes on the road rather than look at me. We were passing a tower block of straw bales in an empty field.

'Because she's a woman and most of your cases are young men.'

'That's not the reason.'

The dotted white lines crawled beneath us. Badingley could take hours with the sand lorry in front of us. There was no getting round it.

'Because of the baby,' I said.

'She couldn't be left there. The boyfriend's too much of a risk.'

'Absolutely.'

'Magda needs support, till she sorts herself out. But good short-term carers are hard to find. It made me think.'

'Think what?' I said, walking straight into it.

'That fostering's an option for us. Or adoption. I'm sure they'd fast-track us. If that's what we wanted.'

What I wanted was for Em to fast-track us past the sodding sand lorry. But there was a Land Rover with a flashing light ahead of it, and ahead of the Land Rover was a combine harvester – red, rusty, a relic of the agricultural revolution – taking up most of the road.

If I'd been honest, I'd have said it wasn't Em's job to take in waifs and strays, let alone the progeny of rapes. That I got enough of kids at school. That I liked the silence of the house, the vacancy of the rooms. That to me silence and vacancy signified potential, not failure.

'It's a big step,' I said.

'I knew you'd say that.'

'Well, it is. How could we cope with a baby when we're both working? We don't even know this Magda.'

'You're missing the point.'

'How am I?'

'I'm not suggesting we foster Magda's baby.'

'What then?'

'I was talking about fostering in general. But even the thought of it seems to send you into a panic.'

Had I been so obvious?

'Having our own kid is different from taking on someone else's,' I said.

'But what if it comes to that?' she said. 'If you don't want children, I ought to know.'

'Of course I want them, if you want them.'

'But do you want them for yourself? I sometimes wonder how committed you are. I'd like you to think about that, Ian.'

I stared at the tailgate of the sand lorry, as sand grains fell useless on the road.

'OK,' I said, 'I'll think about it. But this weekend's meant to be a break. If Ollie and Daisy start asking questions . . .'

'I won't say a thing.'

'Promise?'

'Promise.'

We squeezed hands, closing the discussion. I'd been let off. This time.

Out in the sticks, with all four windows down, the heat seemed different – syrupy, poppied, medicinal. I turned to stroke Rufus, who was still panting heavily in the back. It was early afternoon now, the sun high in the sky.

'How far now?' Em said.

'Ten miles maybe. Not that we'll ever get there,' I said, nodding at the vehicles ahead.

As soon as I said it, though, the combine and Land Rover pulled over into a lay-by and the sand lorry miraculously turned off. 1.27. The first bit of luck all day. With Ollie's emailed directions to guide us we made good progress – until we reached a pink pub with a thatched roof and (as instructed) turned right, right and right, which brought us to the same pink pub again.

'One of those rights must be a left,' Em said, pulling up in the pub car park.

'Or a straight on,' I said.

Rufus began to bark, thinking we'd arrived. We got out to stretch our legs and give him some air.

Outside the pub an old man was sitting on a bench, a stick beside him, his face purple as heather, and a handkerchief knotted on his head. When I asked him the way to Badingley he said he'd never heard of it.

Em suggested we enquire at the bar, but I was for pressing on and grabbed the driver's seat before she could. After a sequence of experiments with lefts, rights and straight-ons we found ourselves by a peculiar flint house called the Hexagon. If we turned left there – so Ollie's emailed directions said – we would arrive in Badingley directly.

So it proved. We were at Badingley in no time. And remained in no time till we left.

I met Ollie in my second term at university. At school, French, maths and history had been my A-level subjects, and I would have been happy to take any of them as a degree, but my dad said they wouldn't 'lead to anything'. Neither he nor anyone else in the family had been to university (Uncle Jimmy was the nearest, with his Higher Certificate from Salford Tech). But ignorance never stopped my dad from having an opinion. And though I almost talked him round to letting me choose maths – with all his betting, he respected numeracy – in the end I succumbed and applied to do law. 'It's a proper career and you'll earn a good whack,' he said. 'I can just see you in a wig,' my mother added. I was offered a place but from the start I hated law. The courses were mechanical, the lecturers unimaginative, the books indigestible. There'd been a lot to memorise at A level, but French verbs and the dates of battles seemed to sink in, unlike tort law. I tried to change subjects after six weeks but the university discouraged it, telling me I'd have to repeat the first year. My parents were no help, either. 'You're a bright lad, just give it time,' my mother said, while my dad read my unhappiness as slacking. 'Them that can't stick owt don't get nowt,' he said, with his usual half-baked logic.

Law was not the only reason for being miserable. Eager to make friends, I tried to look cool. But smoking Gauloises and reading French novels had no cachet in the law department. And though there were a couple of girls in my tutorial group, neither seemed to notice me. The one consolation was Ollie.

To begin with, the two of us moved in different circles: I didn't really have a circle – my circle was me. But I was aware of him sitting in lectures: with that brooding intensity, and those sooty Spanish features, you couldn't miss him. Not that he was literally dark-skinned, but in the absence of black or Asian students he looked exotic. (In the eighteenth century, he once told me, the Moore family had been involved in the slave trade: 'I'm probably descended from a half-breed.') He stood out for another reason – wearing sports jackets, cord trousers and collared shirts while the rest of us had jeans and T-shirts. When he wasn't carrying a briefcase, you'd see him with some boot, ball, club or racket bag, the different shapes of which suggested an awesome range of sporting activities. I knew from school that the old cliché about boffins versus jocks is rubbish: the boffins *are* the jocks, and the ones who get the girls too. Ollie proved the point. He was smart, sporty, funny, handsome and popular – the antithesis of me.

It was sport, ironically enough, that broke the ice between us. One February night in the foyer of the library, he hauled himself across to me on crutches and we got talking, not least about the plaster cast on his left leg, which was there because he'd snapped his Achilles tendon.

'Does it hurt?' I asked.

'Only when I think of all I'm missing. The rest of the rugby season. And cricket next term. Basically I'm fucked till September.'

'Then take up something else.'

'Like what?'

'I don't know. One-arm wrestling. Hopscotch. Kick-boxing.'

'*Kick*-boxing?'

'No one will challenge you with that on your leg. You'll be world champion in no time.'

He looked at me suspiciously, as if I was taunting him,

then laughed and suggested a drink in the union bar. He cut a sorry figure as we made our way there – Pegleg Ollie, with his crutches – but once we sat down he cheered up and insisted on paying for several rounds.

'Were you at the ethics lecture?'

'I slept in,' I said.

'It wasn't till two.'

'Even so.'

'You missed a treat. It made me realise why I'm studying law.'

'I wish I knew.'

'Lawyers are the agents of morality. Their job's to establish the truth.'

'Their job's to represent their client,' I said. 'Truth doesn't come into it. Anyway, there's no such thing as objective truth.'

A statement of the obvious, I thought, but he seemed shocked by it, and we began to argue, less about law than about deception.

'If you tell a lie, it's a lie, even if the person you're telling believes you,' he said.

'No, the only issue is whether you're *caught* lying.'

'Exactly: once a man is caught lying, no one believes him any more – that's why being truthful is important.'

'So if an ugly woman asks you if you find her beautiful you'll be honest and say no?' I said.

'I'd probably fudge it for fear of hurting her.'

'You believe in white lies, then.'

'I might use them for the purposes of social harmony,' Ollie said, 'but I don't believe in them ethically.'

'What are ethics for if not to create social harmony?' I said.

'I give up,' Ollie laughed. 'Get us another beer, will you? Here's a fiver.'

'I enjoyed that,' he said, when I brought back the drinks. 'You're cleverer than I thought.'

He could be a patronising bastard. But I liked to provoke him and he enjoyed being made to think. Soon our debates became a ritual. Every Thursday I'd get up in time for the ethics lecture and after it we'd head for the student canteen, piling our trays with pizza, milkshakes, fruit and chocolate, and face each other across a table. Abortion, the death penalty, apartheid, capitalism, one-day cricket – Ollie could defend any corner with equal conviction (a skill that has since served him as a barrister), but I'd unsettle him by countering his legal arguments with philosophical ones: what did he mean by 'good'? what did he mean by 'reality'? if 'logical deduction' was as infallible as he claimed, let him logically deduce man's purpose on earth. It was a chess match with no pieces, table tennis without a ball. And to me the high spot of the week.

With his sports buddies deserting him, or Ollie finding it too painful to be around them, I soon became his sole companion. We'd go out to the pub or engage in competitive activities, or non-activities, in his room: chess, draughts, whist, Scrabble, even tiddlywinks (if I could persuade him to play for money, so much the better). All games were alike to him, their sole purpose being for one person – Ollie Moore – to win. *You can't touch me*, he liked to crow. We cannot all be masters, and mostly I was content to come second. But once when he was winning at darts, his triumphalism got to me.

'There's more to life than winning,' I said, as he aimed for double top.

'That's rich coming from you,' he said. 'You love winning.'

'Me? I'm just here to keep you company.'

'So you won't mind if I sink this and make it five–nil.'

'Why should I? We've not finished yet. It's best of eleven.'

He laughed and slapped me on the back before throwing the dart home.

Whenever I wonder what Ollie saw in me, it's his laughter

I remember. At school I'd survived by mimicking the teachers. Busty Mrs Anders, lisping Mr Witchett, hunchbacked Mr Moody – it didn't take much to send them up, but my classmates seemed to enjoy the parodies. With Ollie, too, I played the court jester. If nothing else, it helped him forget his gammy leg.

On all our outings, it was Ollie who paid. I would protest, before we went, that I couldn't afford whatever it was (a film, a gig, the pub), and he would tell me not to worry, he'd foot the bill. I told him I felt bad about it, and privately I was resentful: whereas I watched my pennies but got into debt, Ollie spent freely but still had money left over. Though the beneficiary of his largesse, I hated the system that made it possible. When we debated politics, I used to argue for the abolition of inherited wealth.

'I suppose you're a socialist,' he said.

'And proud of it.'

'You want to clobber the rich.'

'No, liberate the poor.'

'Socialism is envy rationalised,' he said.

In retrospect, it all sounds pretty trite. But Ollie was a couple of years older than me and seemed to *know* stuff, exuding an authority which his height and build – he was six foot three, and lean – perfectly matched. The word 'military' came to mind. I attributed that to boarding school, but during one late-night conversation he revealed that he'd spent a year at Sandhurst, training to be an officer cadet. (He told me about it in confidence, perhaps fearing his fellow students would denounce him as a fascist if they found out.) At some level he'd always known that the army wasn't for him, he said. But he felt he owed it to his father, who'd been an officer during the war, to give it a go, and he stuck it out as long as he could. The fact that his father was dead only increased his filial piety. He had died in a tragic accident, Ollie said, adding (his jaw quivering as he spoke) that if ever I met his mother I must be sure not to mention it in front of her. How crass did he think I was? 'Just because I'm working class doesn't make me an idiot,' I was tempted to protest. But I kept my lip buttoned. In truth, I envied him the drama of having a father who'd died tragically rather than one, like mine, who never moved from his chair in front of the television. I also envied him having a mother who indulged him, rather than one whose mission was to stop her son from getting above himself. It seemed that Ollie had done well out of losing a parent, better than I'd done from hanging on to both of mine.

(I'm sorry to sound mean about my mum and dad. But if you had them as parents, you'd understand.)

In the May of my first year at university I began looking for somewhere to live from September, when I would no longer have a room on campus. Ollie, ahead of the game, had made plans to move in with three of his rugby friends. But in the event those plans fell through and we went to see a house together – a three-storey, five-bedroom slum which we signed the tenancy for, along with three Japanese postgraduates who had responded to the same advert. I was frankly surprised to find myself in the position of Ollie's housemate and best friend. But at the end of an otherwise unhappy first year I took comfort from it. He had the edge on me in almost every way and that's what made our friendship work. Prole and Nob, Little and Large, Tortoise and Hare. We were the ideal couple.

Ollie was out to greet us even before I'd parked the car. He looked leaner than when I'd last seen him. *Too* lean, with that stringiness characteristic of long-distance runners, the hollow cheeks, matchstick legs and wafer stomach. I wondered if he might be ill, but he came at us so swiftly through the heat, like a greyhound out of its trap, I set the thought aside. Hopping from foot to foot, he semaphored for me to reverse into a space by the barn. I'd never seen a man look so impatient. Though Rufus was the one yelping as the engine cut, it might have been Ollie.

'You took your time,' he said, opening Em's door.

'Sorry, awful traffic,' she said, accepting his kiss.

'We were starting to think you'd never get here.'

'Wherever here is,' I said, climbing out. 'If it weren't for your directions we'd still be driving round.'

We shook hands, then – as if a handshake were too stiff – held each other closer for a moment, eyeball to eyeball, his hand on my upper arm, mine on his right elbow.

'How are you?' he said.

'Grand,' I said, 'apart from the journey.'

'Come on, you must be hungry.'

It was Ollie who looked hungry. He reminded me of a photo I'd once seen, of some artist riddled with angst or tuberculosis. Middle-aged barristers aren't meant to look that way.

'I hope you didn't wait for us,' Em said.

'It's only salad. Daisy's inside somewhere. I'll show you round. The barn used to be a coffin-maker's.'

We'd been expecting something posh, and the grass-seamed drive between iron railings had promised as much. But Flaxfield Grange was a serious disappointment. 'A converted eighteenth-century farmhouse,' Ollie called it as he led us through the back door, but unconverted outhouse looked nearer the mark. A wood-panelled corridor led past a cramped dining room, dingy snug and gloom-lined study; the three rooms must once have been loose boxes or cow stalls, I decided. Beyond them lay the kitchen, with broken floor tiles. The contents dated from the forties or fifties (no dishwasher or microwave), which would have been sweetly nostalgic had the chunky wall cupboards been less lopsided and the whitewashed walls less flaky from damp. From the kitchen we turned right, under a thick stone lintel, into the living room. The rafters and cross-beams suggested a hayloft, and Ollie clearly expected us to admire it. But the conversion had sacrificed the charm of the original without putting comfort in its place. The old brick floor beneath the tasselled carpet reeked of earth mould and the beams were noosed with spiders' webs. Along the mantel-piece were three dusty photographs (a woman in a hat and two boys in school uniform) interspersed with porcelain dolls: the glazed expressions of the humans in their frames made the dolls look animated. The dolls and photos were reflected in the yellowing mirror behind, scarred and mottled with skin disease. Strangest of all was the display over the fireplace: a pair of swords X-ed below a mounted badger head, like a skull and crossbones.

'So what do you think?' Ollie said.

'What do you think they think?' Daisy said, stepping through the French windows behind us. 'They're trying to be polite.'

It's always a shock to be reminded how short Daisy is, five foot two at most. In my memory I obliterate this, as though the space she occupies in my head makes her physically large as well. But the real shock was her hair, which she'd grown again: it was almost as long as when I first knew her, falling halfway down her back.

She kissed Em first, then me. Her pebble-blue eyes were less implausibly bright these days but she smelled of almonds, the same as ever.

'Well, *we* like it,' Ollie said, gesturing towards the high ceiling.

'Ollie likes it,' Daisy said.

'No television. No phone. No DVD player or hi-fi system. It's wonderful.'

'It's a nightmare,' Daisy said. 'We have to drive to the main road to get reception on our mobiles. I'm amazed there's even electricity.'

'Who needs mod cons? We're on holiday.'

'Yeah, on holiday in a hovel. Come outside while Ollie gets the drinks.'

As we followed Daisy, I wondered if Em was thinking what I was thinking: that we'd only been asked because they were too embarrassed to ask their posher friends.

The garden was a slight improvement on the house. The French windows gave out onto a terrace laid with stable bricks and, beyond, a round pond, palisaded with irises, a stone man fishing in the middle. The lawn was a decent size and, knowing Ollie, I half expected to see croquet hoops or a badminton net. But the grass was too rough and tussocky for games. And the eucalyptus tree at the far edge had shed its leaves, which crackled like tinfoil under our feet. We crossed into the orchard – apple and pear trees with lichened trunks, and raspberry bushes overwhelmed by bindweed. Beyond the orchard lay a stubbly cornfield, with bright yellow bales like giant cotton reels strewn round its edges. A solitary tree stood in the middle, bare limbs thrust out in shock. We stayed there for a minute in the heat, leaning on the fence and sucking straws, like farmers surveying their harvest.

'There's shade over here,' Daisy said, leading us to a metal table, chairs and parasol set out below a high brick wall – the north side of the house. Above us, the orange pantiles had slipped from their batons, exposing black felt.

'You poor darlings, you look exhausted,' Daisy said, as we sat down.

'Terrible journey,' Em said.

'Let's not talk about it,' I said, brusquely. To hear Daisy *poor darling* us got up my nose. I wouldn't care but her background's no different from mine. In the old days she used to call me 'love' and 'chuck'.

'Looks like someone's been enjoying the sun,' Em said, nodding at the tube of suncream on the wooden lounger.

'The house gives me the creeps so I lie out here,' Daisy said.

'Topless usually,' Ollie said, appearing with olives and champagne. 'The neighbours have been having a field day.'

'Rubbish. It's completely secluded. I hope you'll join me, Em. You're looking so *well*.'

Had Daisy noticed that Em had put on weight? Did she think that she was pregnant? Or was the compliment an insult in disguise, drawing attention to her own slim body? If Em inferred a subtext, she didn't show it. While Ollie opened the champagne, and Em described her fear of skin cancer, I studied Daisy's hair. It had always been the core of her being – her pilot light. I remembered its shimmer under street lights. How it snagged on buttons. Or tickled your nose if you got too near. It wasn't just her it enfolded – it was you.

'What a treat,' Em said, taking a glass from Ollie. 'Normally at this time I'm seeing my ASBO boys.'

'Your what?'

'My juveoffs. My teenage criminals. My kids in care. A good pep talk on a Friday stops them doing something daft over the weekend. That's the theory anyway.'

'You're so brave, Em,' Daisy said, patting her arm. 'I could never do a job like yours.'

'No danger of me getting bored, anyway.'

'I'm going to make sure you take it easy while you're here. You too, Ian. We haven't planned a thing.'

I doubted that as much as I doubted the sincerity of Daisy's solicitude. But it was hot, and the champagne tasted good, and I sat back.

In a corner of the orchard was a fruit cage, its wire netting festooned with black ribbons – I thought of the dead crows I'd once seen strung from a gate on Cleckheaton Moor.

'Paradise, eh?' Ollie said. 'Sun, cornfields, butterflies, waves breaking in the distance.'

The sea couldn't be less than ten miles away. But there was no point arguing with Ollie. If I couldn't hear the waves, that was my fault.

The bare tree in the middle of the field was dead, I realised. Had it been hit by lightning? It looked that way, as if suspended at the moment of impact. Like the photo of an electrocution.

'How did you find the place?' I said.

'On the Internet,' Ollie said. 'Funny story, actually.'

'Not funny,' Daisy said. 'Just weird.'

'Em and Ian will find it interesting.'

'You tell them while I sort out lunch,' Daisy said.

'Let me help,' Em said.

'It's only a matter of putting dishes out.'

'I'm finding it too hot here,' Em said, standing up.

'OK then, but bring your glass with you. Two minutes, boys. We're hungry.'

They walked off, Em overdressed in a black knee-length skirt and white high-collared blouse, Daisy light and easy in a short blue cotton dress.

The sun glowed whiter than phosphorus. I sat there dazed behind my sunglasses, the heat lapping my face like a dog's tongue.

'I was talking to my ma one day,' Ollie said. 'Before she broke her hip and went gaga, this was – she's in a nursing home now.'

'I'm sorry.'

I wasn't *that* sorry, having met her only the once, but I let him witter on about her dementia and what it's like when your own mother doesn't recognise you.

'Anyway,' he said, his voice washing over me, 'before she lost it we were discussing the holidays we'd had when Pa was alive, and I asked her the name of the last place we went to, in the summer of '76. Badingley, she said. So last Christmas I went online, and among the entries for Badingley was a house for holiday lets. I recognised the place from the photos.'

'The village?'

'The actual house. Flaxfield Grange. We stayed here.'

'That *is* weird.'

'When I emailed I found it was free in August. So here we are. The owner lives in Belgium. A woman from the village looks after it. A real battleaxe. Talking of which – Daisy will give me hell if we don't go in.'

'Why a battleaxe?' Em said, when Ollie repeated the story. There was a metal picnic table on the terrace but we were in the dining room, because of the heat. The room faced east and felt dank. We were told to help ourselves. A simple salad, Daisy called it – smoked salmon, tiger prawns, Parma ham, pâté, vine tomatoes, rocket, fennel, watercress, Roquefort, Cheddar, ciabatta, New Zealand Sauvignon, sparkling water. That's not how we do simple salads in our house.

'The old bitch obviously resented us coming at all,' Daisy said. 'It chucked it down all the way here – remember rain? – and took us four hours, so you can imagine how we were feeling when we finally arrived. It looked like no one had stayed here for years. You'll see when you go upstairs – there are weapons hanging on walls and the wardrobes topple over if you open them. Plus I'm sure there's a ghost. To be honest, I was all for getting straight back in the car.'

'I carried the luggage up,' Ollie said, 'and there was Daisy, in the bedroom, ranting that the owner should be paying *us* to stay here, not the other way about. When I went downstairs again, blow me, the bloody woman from the village was there – she'd come to see if we needed logs for the wood-burner. As if anyone would need logs in the middle of summer.'

'Mrs Banks, she's called,' Daisy said. 'She was due to come in yesterday to change the sheets but she didn't turn up.'

'You frightened her off.'

'We decided to stay the night then go back to London next day. But the sun was shining when we woke, and it's been shining ever since. We either sit in the garden or go to the beach – so the state of the house doesn't seem to matter. I'm sorry it's uncomfortable. I was going to call you to warn you but Ollie stopped me.'

'Who needs comfort?' Ollie said. 'Holidays should be an adventure.'

'It's certainly that,' Daisy said. 'Cheese, anyone?'

'When the wind gets up, you can hear the timbers creak,' Ollie said. 'It's like being at sea.'

Even without the wind, I could hear movements above our head.

'They didn't bother with foundations in the 1700s. They built straight onto sand or earth. It shows.'

He pointed to the walls. Three were plastered and had long cracks. The fourth was a flint wall backing onto the corridor, with several large fissures and holes.

'Let's hope there isn't an earthquake,' Daisy said.

'The house has been standing for three centuries,' Ollie said.

'They didn't have global warming then.'

'They had gales and floods, just the same as us,' Ollie said. 'All this talk about climate change is hysteria.'

Em raised an eyebrow my way. I lowered mine in discouragement. I couldn't face arguing with Ollie when we'd just arrived.

'What about the village?' Em said. 'Has it changed much?'

'The shop has closed down,' Ollie said. 'Otherwise it looks the same – no housing developments, thank God.'

'The place is in a kind of time warp,' Daisy said.

'That's what I like about the countryside, it's ten years behind.'

'More like fifty. Some places don't even take plastic.'

'Sounds rather fun,' Em said.

'Fun till you try to buy something, but you've no cash, and the nearest ATM is ten miles away.'

They to-ed and fro-ed while we listened politely, Ollie lauding the beaches and fresh air while Daisy bemoaned the lack of designer shops and delicatessens.

'I've ice cream if anyone wants it,' she said, standing up. 'Coffee? Herb tea? No?' She sat down again. 'I don't mean to whinge. But this time last year we were in the Maldives, in a five-star hotel.'

I threw Em a surreptitious here-we-go look as Daisy ran through their recent holidays – the cities, deserts and mountains they'd seen during travels from Aleppo to Zanzibar.

There were more thumps from upstairs. For a minute I thought it might be Rufus but he was lying under the table, waiting for scraps.

'Though in some ways Madagascar is nicer, of course,' Daisy said. 'I wanted to go back but Ollie insisted on a *British* holiday.'

I stared at the tablecloth, which had tiny peasant women in colourful costumes embroidered round the edge.

Another loud creak from above.

'Is that your ghost?' I asked, interrupting Daisy's holidays.

'More likely Archie. We should have said – he came with us. His plans for the summer fell through.'

'Oh, good,' Em said. 'Good for us, I mean. We're dying to see him.'

'How's he doing?' I asked.

'Oh, you know, typical teenager.'

'Still in bed, then,' Em said.

Ollie and Daisy looked embarrassed.

'Actually –' Daisy began.

'He's not at his best,' Ollie said, cutting her off. 'I dare say you'll see him later.'

'No hurry,' Em said. 'The food was delicious by the way.'

'Are you sure you don't want dessert?'

'Not me.'

'Ian?'

'I couldn't.'

'Let's go in the garden, then. It should be cooler now.'

We stood up, scraping our chairs across the brick floor.

'You go in the garden,' Ollie said. 'Ian and I should make a move.'

'For God's sake, Ollie, let Ian relax. He's only just got here.'

'You did bring your clubs?'

'Yes, but –'

'And shoes?'

'Sorry, should I have?'

'There's a dress code.'

'I didn't realise.'

'Of course not,' Daisy said. 'You've had a long drive. It's boiling hot. And you'll be late for supper if you go. Forget it, Ollie, it's ridiculous.' She turned to Em. 'We thought we'd eat out tonight, if that's OK with you. Ollie knows this seafood place.'

'We could just play nine,' Ollie said, 'if Ian's up to that. You can wear what you like on the short course.'

'Nine is OK by me,' I said, 'if Daisy and Em don't mind.'

'We'll be relieved to get rid of you, won't we, Em?'

'Mightily,' Em said.

'You're to be back by seven,' Daisy said.

'No problem,' Ollie said.

'Take Rufus with you,' Em said. 'He could do with some exercise.'

'They don't allow dogs,' Ollie said.

'*We'll* take him for a walk, then,' Daisy said. 'He'll love it by the sea.'

Golf? I know. Like you, I hate it – or hate the associations, anyway. It's a nob's game, a snob's game, not a sport for the likes of me. But friendship demands compromise. I was doing it for Ollie.

At secondary school I'd worn glasses and been put in the lowest set for ball games, on the grounds that I lacked hand-to-eye coordination. Golf, so I learned from Ollie, was preferable in that respect: the ball stayed motionless until you swung your club at it – sometimes even then. He taught me to play that first summer at uni, when exams were over and his cast came off. Until his Achilles healed, he was banned from more strenuous sports, so we spent every day on the golf course. I deplored the accents, the dress code, the inane rules about shouting 'Fore!' or replacing divots. But over time I took pleasure in beating the middle classes at their own game. Not that I played with anyone other than Ollie. And not that I beat him more than once or twice. But I did slowly learn the rudiments of the game.

'You're not bad, you know,' he said, on the occasion of my first birdie (my drive over water had hit the back of the green then rolled down to within six inches of the hole).

'I got lucky,' I said.

'You should have a go at other sports.'

'Good idea. Polo, say. All I need is a horse. And riding lessons.'

'I mean it.'

'So do I. What do they call those clubs they use – chukkas?'

'Mallets.'

'There you go. I'm good with mallets. I used to knock in the tent pegs when we went camping.'

'I'm serious, Ian. Get in shape and have some lessons over the summer and you could be good.'

'At what?'

'Whatever you choose.'

I told him there was no chance of it – that my summer job back in Manchester, in a jam factory, would take all my time. '*Make* time,' he said, and, though I scoffed at the idea, once home again, driven mad by my parents, I took his advice. Every evening after work I'd head for the local sports centre, to work on exercise bikes or weights. I also signed up for squash and badminton lessons at weekends – the more middle class the sport, the better. Those three months were a revelation. What I'd assumed was lack of skill turned out to be lack of application: once fit and focused, I did OK.

My mother found my enthusiasm hard to believe.

'You've always hated games,' she said, heaping bol onto spag in our steamed-up kitchen, 'ever since that time in the park.'

'Don't remind me,' I said, though what I meant was don't remind my father, who luckily couldn't hear us over the television.

'But it's true, pet. I'll never forget it.'

It was a story she liked to recount, even though she'd not been present. I must have been about five, and my dad was teaching me to ride a bike in the local park. Unlike most kids, I wasn't allowed stabilisers: 'The more you fall off,' he said, 'the faster you'll learn.' That didn't prove true, of course, but I'd finally got the hang and was wobbling along a path beside the rec, near one of the goals, when a ball came from nowhere, smacked me in the face and sent me flying. 'Come on, son, you're not dead,' my dad said as I lay there. Between my howls, I was aware of a teenager in football shorts approaching sheepishly. I waited for my dad to shout at him or beat him up. Instead he picked up the ball and handed it back. 'Not to worry, lad, it were an accident.' The hurt of that made me howl louder. I was still howling when we got home. 'You take the fucking little wimp,' my dad said, handing me over, 'I've had it with him.' My mother sat me in her lap and wiped my face with a kitchen towel. 'There, there, sweetheart, whatever's happened?' Eventually my sobs ebbed and I told her.

The episode convinced my mother that I was too 'sensitive' for rough games. We began making trips to the local library – a place of sanctuary, unlike the park. Though no great reader herself, she encouraged me to think that I was. Each week we'd borrow some new title – an encyclopedia, picture dictionary, *I-Spy* book or hobby guide – to satisfy my supposed intelligence. While other kids played cricket and football in the street behind our house, I sat at the kitchen table making cardboard pirate masks or reading about the Incas. Later I moved on to Airfix kits. And there were always jigsaws, the pieces growing smaller as I grew bigger. I remember one puzzle which showed racehorses jumping over a high fence – an especially difficult puzzle, because of all the browns (brushwood, saddles, manes and tails). Finally I cracked it and showed it to my dad, thinking the subject might interest him. 'Very good,' he said, without looking up from his paper.

The only close friend I had in those years was Rod, who turned up halfway through primary school: he'd come from a village somewhere down south and my mother approved of him because he said 'please' and 'thank you'. She might have been less approving if she'd known about his penknife. Rod was keen on wildlife and found it wherever we went: in the park, by the lock-up garages, down at the canal. In truth, the wildlife he was keenest on was dead: a rubbery fledgling tipped from its nest, a pigeon milling with maggots, a flattened tomcat. He used his penknife only to dissect corpses, not to create them, but he was adept and had a strong stomach, stronger than mine. Over time, I too saw the appeal of things that were dead, which couldn't bite or sting or hurt you. I was sorry when Rod went away again, as suddenly as he'd come; my mother thought his dad must have got a job somewhere. I was sadder still because we'd had an argument, down by the canal, the last time I saw him: I'd asked to borrow his penknife overnight but he wouldn't let me and we started fighting. After Rod's disappearance I went back to books, jigsaw puzzles and Airfix kits. Later I was given a Rubik's cube, a Christmas present from Uncle Jimmy, which I keep on my desk to this day.

At primary school the other kids didn't seem to care when I came top in maths and spelling tests: the worst they called me was 'swot' and 'teacher's pet'. But at secondary school being a clever clogs became a major liability and I sometimes got things wrong deliberately. Sport might have been a way to gain some kudos. But the games teachers didn't give me a chance. And when the bald little gym instructor, Mr MacPresley (MacPress-Up as we called him) sneered at my lack of co-ordination, I was happy to join the ranks of the obese, skeletal, myopic, couldn't-be-bothered and last-to-be-picked – a 'spaz' and 'malco'. My mother wrote notes to get me out of swimming lessons, claiming I was allergic to chlorine. But that still left football and cricket, and the torments they brought with them: a wet towel slap-flicked against my buttocks in a wintry changing room, or the slow descent of a hard red ball towards my hiding place out on the boundary. When you've been told you're rubbish at games, you believe it. Not until Ollie's golf lessons, and those summer evenings after work at the jam factory, did I realise that sport could be enjoyable.

The sense of well-being didn't last. When Ollie returned to uni in late September, Achilles heel mended, he had no time for me. Rugby took up his weekends and evenings, and our choice of second-year law courses failed to overlap, so I barely saw him, despite sharing the same house. We did occasionally manage nine holes (my earnings from the jam factory had gone into buying a set of clubs) and even the odd game of squash. But the companionship of the previous term was gone. His bedroom was next to mine but he left early and returned late, without a knock or hello. It was as if he'd thought better of our friendship.

The low point came one Saturday night. Ollie's team (the firsts, of course) had won at rugby that day, down in London, and he got back in a good mood around eight thirty. I was on my own at the house as usual. Taking pity, he asked me to join him for a drink. There was a pub right across from our house, but he insisted on driving us to the university, on the grounds we'd have more chance of meeting girls there. To my knowledge he'd never brought a girl home, but I'd seen how they looked at him and didn't doubt he'd had a few. As he drove he talked about playing the field. 'Play your cards right and we'll both score tonight,' he grinned. I told myself I'd been paranoid about his recent aloofness: here we were, in his Mini, on a lads' night out.

I doubt he knew that the rest of the rugby team would be in the union bar. What I did object to was his behaviour when they called across from their loud and beery table: after a futile attempt to introduce everyone (as if I could possibly recall fourteen names, let alone ones like Slammer, Rancid, Chucky, Stewpole, Oggy and Bean), he sat down to join them, and left me to my own devices. Although there was a seat for me, and one of the team (Oggy, I think) tried to make conversation, it wasn't the evening I'd anticipated, excluding as it did the chance to be alone with Ollie while also meeting girls. It became even less of the evening I'd anticipated at closing time, when the entire team took itself off for a curry. Ollie invited me to join them but I could tell it wasn't a genuine invitation. 'Fine, suit yourself,' was all he said when I declined. Nor did he offer to drive me home again, just left me to walk back alone.

For a few weeks, I didn't speak to Ollie. Not that he was around much not to speak to, but whenever I passed him I let him know with a cold stare what I thought of his conduct. Perhaps it's as well he was so preoccupied with himself that he didn't notice. Over time our relationship healed, like his tendon, and by the end of the second year, we were friends again. To him, we'd never *not* been friends.

'You sound so gay,' Em says, when I talk about that time. 'Anyone would think you were lovers and he jilted you.' She has a point. But though I was hurt by Ollie, then and later – hurt past all surgery – I'm not someone who bears grudges and honestly had no wish to hurt him back. We were friends. We did stuff. We even played golf together.

The first hole at Sandylands is a par-four dog-leg: from the tee, you drive uphill, over an earth mound, towards a narrow strip of fairway, to the left of which is bracken and to the right an alder copse deemed out of bounds; then from the crest (supposing you've reached it) you hit your second leftward and downhill, to a two-level green, the risk being that you'll overshoot and fetch up in the hidden bunker at the back. I had never played there, of course; but during the journey in his MGB Ollie described each hole in detail. He'd not played much lately, he said, but for him, 'not much' probably meant twice weekly. And he had the advantage of knowing the course from years before. He could still remember a thirty-foot putt on the par-three third, and his father's pride and envy when he holed it. He told me this as he drove, with the roof down and the breeze fraying his hair. It might just have been the wind but his eyes watered as he spoke – less from the memory of his father, I suspected, than from recalling the trueness of that putt.

I was wearing the clothes I'd come in: baggy shorts, a T-shirt and trainers. Ollie had shorts, too, but they were tailored. The rest of him – shoes, socks, collared shirt, glove – was impeccably dress-code.

'Your honour, I believe,' he said.

According to Ollie there are four kinds of sportsmen: those who think they're good and are; those who think they're good and aren't; those who think they're bad and aren't; those who think they're bad and are. Though I put myself in the last category and Ollie in the first, he has developed a cautious respect for my game. But to suggest I tee off first, on the grounds I'd won the last time we played, was ridiculous. (Surely he remembered: it was in Surrey and he had beaten me five and four.)

'No, yours,' I said, in the hope that Ollie would screw up.

His ball pinged sweetly, soared two hundred yards or more, and landed perfectly on the hillcrest.

There was no one around to watch me drive off. But my hand shook as I placed the ball on the tee and Ollie reiterated the rules of our contest. Scoring by holes won rather than total shots taken; one mis-hit tee shot to be discarded without penalty; maximum of eight shots on any hole; any putt of less than three feet to be conceded – that's to say a gimme.

They were the rules we'd always played by, and they stopped you missing nine-inch putts or reaching double figures at a single hole. But that didn't make me any less nervous as I settled, or failed to settle, to the ball.

I topped my first drive into the earth fifty yards away. The second sliced into the alder copse.

'OK, *two* discarded drives without penalty,' Ollie said, finally remembering how bad my golf is. 'And I'm giving you a two-hole start, remember.'

He'd always given me a start but this time he hadn't made it clear. Perhaps he'd been waiting to see how out of practice I was before committing himself.

'Sounds fair enough,' I said, and it was, more than fair. But he played (or used to) off a handicap of twelve whereas I wasn't good enough to *have* a handicap. Even with an eight-hole start, I would probably lose.

My third drive flew weak but straight, to land just below the hillcrest, fifty yards behind his.

I lugged my clubs to where my ball sat, while Ollie trolleyed onward to his. A three-iron struck properly would have got me to the green but there was no power in my shot – without the help of the down-sloping, sun-hardened fairway, I'd have reached only halfway instead of ending up a mere thirty yards short. Ollie was less lucky: his ball landed right by the pin but didn't hold up, bouncing and running on into the bunker. From there he wedged his sand shot to within five feet, whereas my pitch veered off wildly, to the far left edge of the green. But my long putt finished close to the hole – a gimme – whereas his short one caught the lip and slipped away. A half, then. Though my five shots were really seven, I didn't argue. I needed all the help I could get.

'Beginner's luck,' I said to Ollie, imagining I'd used my quota. But his arcing drive on the second tee took a freakish bounce into tangled rough, whereas mine kept low and ran on nicely. Two underhit shots from me, and a retrieving slash and perfect six-iron from him, and our balls sat close together on the green. His putt teetered on the brink but failed to drop. Mine, wildly overhit, would have run thirty feet past but, being straight, hit the cup en route, bobbled up and plopped down three feet away. Another gimme. Another half. 'Good stuff,' he said, as we walked to the par-three third.

Ollie's tee shot looked a beauty, heading green-centre, but a sudden gust took it left into a bunker. Mine was under-strength, but the same west wind – now getting up – saved it from a clump of gorse bushes and the grassy mound beyond nudged it diagonally to the nearside of the green.

'What club did you play?' Ollie asked, as I plucked my tee from the earth.

'A three-iron.'

'A three-iron,' he said, giving me a look like one I'd recently had at the gym, when some muscled freak saw how few weights were on my triceps bar. 'It's only 150 yards to the green!'

'You know what I'm like, Ollie.'

'I'd forgotten. But it's coming back.'

I'd always suspected that he liked playing golf with me as a break from serious competition – because he didn't have to push himself to win. Still, as we walked up the third in the late-afternoon sun – the heather simmering with heat haze and bees – I realised I'd got him worried. I heard him cursing in the rough as his first pitch squirted ten feet and his second flew over the green. He recovered well from there, almost holing out with a chip, but meanwhile I'd three-putted, ineptly but safely, for a four. Third hole to me, which because of the two-hole advantage I'd been handed at the start put me three up with six to play.

Even if I lost in the end – and win or lose didn't really matter to me – I was making a game of it.

The fourth was a par five, 450 yards, about 400 yards too

far for my liking. Both our tee shots were lamentable, mine sliced, Ollie's hooked, but he was the less lucky since his ball – which I crossed the fairway to help him look for – couldn't be found. That meant him dropping a shot, as well as playing out of tangled rough, so he was on four before reaching the fairway. For a moment I imagined winning this hole, too. But my second shot was topped, my third found the ditch, and the fourth, fifth and sixth failed to get me out of it, so I was still 200 yards short of the hole when I played my eighth, the maximum number of strokes permitted by Ollie's system. I pocketed the ball. After his wretched start, Ollie's fifth and sixth shots were beauties, and he'd a ten-foot putt for the double bogey that would win him the hole. He missed – just. I was still three ahead.

I began to contemplate winning – not by virtue of my own efforts but because Ollie (moodily silent as I drove off first at the next tee) had lost his cool.

As my drive sailed down the middle on the fifth, I realised how much I loved golf, and how foolish had been my reasons for not playing more regularly. It was time I got over the class thing. The men on golf courses these days were garage hands, factory workers, plumbers, electricians, blokes in white vans. As a primary-school teacher, though, I had another inhibition: that a golf habit, like a pornography habit, would send out the wrong message. In order not to alienate my fellow teachers (all female), parents, pupils and the local education authority, I'd kept my golf a dirty secret, using the driving range in Derby, where no one knew me, or travelling to courses even further afield. Of course, I didn't play often. And playing on my own was no fun. But it had been worth keeping my hand in for the pleasure of playing with Ollie today. As I putted for a half on the fifth green, his moody silence was distracting – but not so much that I missed. Three up with four to play.

A curlew called from a nearby field. The blue sky was faintly skimmed with white. Yellow gorse fringed the sixth tee. I couldn't have been happier. And that was a cue – hubris? complacency? lack of concentration? – for my game to deteriorate.

Perhaps it wasn't that I got worse but that Ollie had finally found his groove. At any rate, he took the next two holes with pars.

One up with two to play: I had rarely pushed Ollie this far. In victory he used to mask his exultation with a polite handshake and 'Well done'. He would not be so condescending today.

Eight's a lucky number for me, and the eighth was an 'easy' par four, so Ollie said. I watched him as he stood over the ball, getting in his own space as he used to describe it, before it became a cliché of sports psychology. 'Watch how I address the ball,' he'd say, tutoring me. 'When I'm in my own head, nothing else counts.' I used to feel patronised and would look away. But now I did watch, positioning myself at the edge of his eyeline. His methods were unchanged in twenty years: two easy, swishing practice swings, then the long readying of himself for the real thing, his legs trembling, his forefingers and thumbs across each other in a double V, his eyes drilled viciously down as though the ball were some hideous offence to nature. But the twitch in his cheek was new. And the pause before he struck seemed too strung out. Surely no one could concentrate so intently for so long. I relaxed, coughed, stretched my legs, expecting him to step away and recommence his pre-shot ritual; I'd seen him do that many times before. Instead, he rushed the club back and crashed it down – an ugly stab, not a smooth swing. The ball flew high and wide, in a steepening curve that sliced it rightwards to the course's one water hazard, where it landed – plish! – mid-pool. He gave me a look as he replaced his tee and set a second ball there.

'Lost ball,' he said, as though it were my fault.

Had I spooked him? Was I still spooking him, since his next shot wasn't much better, fetching up in a prairie of docks and thistles wide left of the fairway? Surely not. If he'd lost his concentration, the problem wasn't me coughing, scratching my nose or shuffling my feet, it was him. Still, I felt jumpy as I stepped up for my shot – for fear not of messing up but of humiliating him. I drew the wood back and hit down and through. The drive wasn't just the best I played that afternoon but my longest and straightest ever, rolling up to within fifty yards of the green. From there, with Ollie marooned behind me in the rough, I surely couldn't lose the hole.

I didn't, though I failed to win it, fluffing my first chip and then three-putting, while Ollie holed a twelve-footer for a half. One ahead with one to play; the worst I could do now was to tie. Ollie said nothing as we walked to the last. I read his silence as fury, not with me but with himself, and wondered how he would manage to get over it – whether the whole weekend wasn't now doomed. But as he thumbed his tee in the ground – 'Still my honour, I believe' – he added: 'I'm not surprised to be losing.'

'Come on, Ollie,' I said, aware that (for the first time in my life) I was patronising him, 'I hardly ever beat you.'

'It wasn't intended as a compliment.'

'Good, I'd hate you to pay me one of those.'

'Don't get me wrong,' he said. 'For someone who says he never plays, you've been excellent. But my golf's been crap. With all that's been happening, it was bound to be.'

'With all what happening?'

'Apart from being given my cards, not much, I suppose.'

'Which cards?' I said.

'Forget it.'

I couldn't forget it. I'd never heard him making excuses for his game before. He'd never *had* to make excuses. And this didn't feel like an excuse but, worse, a reason. Which cards had he been given? Was he being ditched by his chambers? Or divorced by Daisy? Was this the news she'd been saving for us?

Distracted, I got under my final tee shot: the ball flew almost vertically, dropping less than fifty yards away, from where, with my second, I scooted unconvincingly to the right edge of the green, just ahead of Ollie's ball in the rough. For a moment I suspected him of deliberately messing with my head. Though his lie was difficult, a decent chip would see him down in two, to win the hole and halve the game. But he scuffed the shot, hitting the mound surrounding the green, and though his next shot was better the ball rolled past the hole, just missing par. For me it was an easy uphill putt: all I needed was to hold my nerve. And I did, hitting straight and true, but failing to read the slope of the green, which took the ball away left, and more left, and even further left, to end a good five feet from the hole.

'You win,' Ollie said. 'That's a gimme.'

'It's too far away for a gimme,' I said.

'Well played.'

'I ought to putt out.'

'It's a gimme,' Ollie said, picking up my ball and tossing it to me. I might have insisted on replacing it and finishing. But perhaps Ollie was sparing himself rather than being generous to me. The way his luck had gone, my putt would doubtless have dropped in.

Laid-back primary-school teacher though I am, I couldn't suppress a frisson of triumph. No more than a frisson. And not so Ollie would notice. But I glowed like a war hero inside.

My watch showed 18.45.

'Drink?' I said, as we stowed the clubs in his boot.

'I promised Daisy we'd be back,' he said.

'She won't begrudge us a quick beer,' I said. 'What's the clubhouse like?'

'Grim,' he said.

'Anywhere else?'

'There's a pub in the next village. We could try that.'

His wheels churned up gravel as we left the car park.

'Nice wheels,' I said.

'It's the GT model. 1950 cc. Twin choke. They don't make cars like this any more.'

The Buck served real ale but didn't boast about it. We were early and there were few customers.

'Winner buys the drinks,' I said, directing Ollie to a picnic table in the garden. Disgruntled at having to serve me, the barman took an age, but eventually I emerged with two pints of Adnams and two bags of plain crisps. The crisps had blue packets of salt inside.

'So,' I said, chinking glasses, 'what's so serious that it put you off your game?'

'No excuses,' he said. 'You won fair and square.'

'I won because you gave me a two-shot lead.'

'Whatever. One–nil to you.'

'What's this about your cards?' I said, ignoring him.

He paused and drank his beer, almost draining his glass before drawing breath. Several wasps were circling mine.

'Wasps bothering you?' he said.

'It's all right,' I said, though I've had a dread of wasps since the age of six, when I was stung on the neck while eating an orange lolly in our back garden. 'It's your own fault for panicking,' my dad said. 'The little bugger would have ignored you if you'd kept still.' But panicking when there's a wasp about still seems logical to me: I keep reading about people who've died from allergic reactions.

'I've been given my cards,' Ollie said, swatting the wasps away on my behalf. 'By the medics. I'm going to die. Don't tell me we're all going to die, Ian. What I mean is I'm going to die soon. If I'm around to play golf with you next summer, it'll be a miracle. That's it. Finished. So's my beer, look. If the winner's still buying the drinks, I'll have another.'

'Christ, Ollie, you're not saying –'

'Adnams, the same as before.'

I've no memory of going to the bar a second time, or whether the same unhelpful barman was behind it. I only remember that 'My Generation' was playing on the jukebox (funny how kids today go for songs that pre-date them by decades) and that when I got back to Ollie two wasps were trapped inside his upturned glass. I watched them circling, like sharks in a tank. Would they use up all the air in there and suffocate? I hoped so.

'It's not nice,' Ollie said. 'You don't want to know. They found a tumour.'

'Where?'

'A brain tumour. I've had the symptoms for a while. Headaches. Dizziness. Blurred vision and so on.'

'What have they told you?'

'Not much. They won't commit themselves till they've done more tests. But it's obviously malignant.'

'What makes you so sure?'

'I've done the research. I've got all the symptoms. They're doing something called a PET scan next week, when we're back in London. But it'll only confirm the worst. Odds are I've about six months.'

'Jesus.'

He lifted the glass and the wasps flew off. The story he'd

just told no longer seemed to interest him. It could have been happening to someone else.

'Should you be driving?' I said. 'And playing golf? Shouldn't you take it easy?'

'It makes no difference. I might as well be active while I can.'

'God, I don't know what to say.'

'No need to say anything,' he said. 'I didn't plan to tell you. Forget it ever slipped out, OK?'

'How can I? It's terrible. I can't believe it.'

But I could see it added up: the weight loss, the drawn face, the loss of concentration. Could a tumour get worse, burst even, if you pushed yourself too hard? He ought to be home, lying down.

'The weird thing is I don't care,' he said. 'Live, die, so what?'

'Of course you care.'

'No, really, I've been cauterised. Nothing gets to me. Nothing moves me. I've no feelings at all.'

'Rubbish.'

'It's the truth. I could murder someone tomorrow and it wouldn't bother me. I'm evil, Ian. You'd better watch out.'

He laughed, to let me know it was a joke, then furrowed his brow.

'Don't say anything,' he said. 'This weekend, I mean. When we're all together. Don't bring it up.'

'But you have told Daisy?'

He paused, lifted his glass then mumbled something. I caught her name and 'know' or 'no'.

'What?'

He shook his head and I knew not to ask again.

Looking back, I realise I might have misheard. He could have said 'Daisy doesn't want to know', meaning she was in denial about it. Or he could have been begging me not to tell

Em: 'No one *but* Daisy must know.' But what I'd have sworn he said was 'I don't want Daisy to know'. Or possibly 'I haven't told Daisy, no'. Either way, it came to the same thing.

How typical of Ollie to keep the tumour to himself, I thought. *It's my life, my death, and no one else's business*: that was his attitude – repression, stiff upper lip, blind courage, call it what you will. I was astounded, nevertheless. What did it do to hold something so monumental inside you? That he'd not told Daisy was almost as shocking as the tumour itself.

'End of discussion,' he said, draining his glass. 'We're half an hour late already. The girls will be furious.'

As we drove back, I thought of Em's mum, who died of breast cancer last year (her dad died of a stroke three years before). We used to visit her every day at the hospice, or rather Em did – I preferred to sit in the car, reading my paper and watching for the parking warden. On Sundays, when you could park without a ticket, I sometimes went in with her and sat in the lime-coloured room staring at the water jug, the glucose drip, the bedside cupboard. On one occasion Em left me alone with her mum while she went to the Ladies. She was asleep at the time, or seemed to be, but the moment Em left the room she opened her eyes and beckoned me with her taped and tube-strapped right arm. It disgusted me to go near: her eyes were yellow and there were grains of half-chewed tablets between her teeth. But I had to get close in order to hear. 'Make sure to look after my daughter,' she whispered, or something like. You daft old bat, I thought: as if I wouldn't. But I took her hand a second and nodded, to let her know, and I'm sure that eased her passage. She died a few days later, trusting Em would be all right.

Em mostly is all right. But the loss of two parents within three years has been hard on her – harder than the loss of my parents would be on me. She never used to cry. But these days almost anything can set her off: family photographs; television programmes her mum used to watch; the tasteless knick-knacks her parents left behind. There's the baby issue, too: her mum was desperate to have a grandchild, and nowadays Em is desperate too, if only to grant her mother that wish posthumously. Baby or not, it tests my patience to see Em so weepy. Surely a year's more than long enough. I've told her that when the tears dry up I'm giving the house a name as well as a number (it's 27, by the way) and putting it on our garden gate: Dungrievin.

Not funny, Em says. Very little amuses her in her current state. But I know she'll stop moping in due course. And at least she is reasonably healthy. Unlike Ollie, whose tumour I brooded on as he drove us back and insects exploded on the windscreen.

The girls will be furious, Ollie had said. But they did not look furious in the least. They were sitting in the orchard talking to someone, a third girl it looked like, and laughter skirled back at us as we walked towards them. Only Em's face, when she turned round, belied the high spirits. I could see trouble there.

'I'm afraid we've polished off the bottle,' Daisy said.

The third girl had her back to me, but when she turned, the late sun on her curls, it was Archie. Black drainpipe jeans, black sleeveless T-shirt with a skull and crossbones, tattoo on his left shoulder, looped metal chains dangling down his thigh, leather wristband, bead necklace and bare feet – what had happened to my godson? His hair was darker, and he'd either been getting no sleep or was wearing eyeshadow. We have goths in Ilkeston, too, but Archie reminded me more of a guitarist from a 1970s heavy metal band.

He and Ollie ignored each other. But he managed a handshake, from a sitting position, for me. The hand was soft and the face deathly white between the acne. So here was the ghost from upstairs.

'Hello, Archie.'

'Hi.'

'Come and join us,' Daisy said, patting the wooden chair beside her.

Rufus's tail thumped the grass as I stepped past him. The yellow bales out in the field were casting blue shadows. The solitary tree in the middle looked frozen.

'Sit down, Ollie,' Daisy said. 'You're making me nervous.'

'It's nearly time to go,' he said.

'Already?'

'It's gone half seven. The table's booked for eight fifteen.'

'We'd better change then. Come on, Em. Let's make ourselves beautiful.'

Ignoring the girly banter (which I suspected was Daisy's way of soliciting a protest that she looked quite beautiful enough already), Em got up and followed her. The departure made me feel awkward, as if we'd curtailed a cosy chat. I tried talking to Archie but all I got back were monosyllables – sometimes not even those. He kept glancing nervously at his father.

'I need to put a clean shirt on,' Ollie said. 'Coming, Ian?'

'In a minute,' I said.

A weight lifted from Archie once he had gone.

'How's school?' I said.

'Yeah, you know.'

'Never changes, eh?'

'Too right.'

'But they're obviously not too disciplinarian.' He shook his head, baffled. 'I mean your hair.'

'No, they're OK.'

'Personally I think long hair is fine,' I said, and described the policy for dress at our school, where we've kids from many different ethnic backgrounds. Rather than look at me, Archie stared at his hands. I was obviously boring him. Time to go.

'They've not told you, then,' he said, as I stood up.

'Who?'

'Mum and Dad. About me not going to school.'

'That's the way with GCSEs nowadays, I hear – no lessons after Easter, just revision and exams.'

'I've barely been since January.'

I wondered if he was exaggerating so as to shock me.

'Have you been ill?' I said, thinking of his pallor.

'Not really.'

'Did they exclude you?'

'I wish.'

'What then?'

'Ian! Are you coming?'

It was Ollie, from across the garden, barefoot, tucking his shirt into his trousers.

'I'm on my way,' I shouted, but sat down again when he went back inside.

'I just stopped going,' Archie said, fingering his wristband. 'I was bored.'

'What about your GCSEs?'

'The school wouldn't let me take them. They were worried I'd fuck up their position in the league tables.'

'Idiots. You'd have sailed through,' I said, remembering how nauseatingly Ollie and Daisy used to celebrate Archie's achievements in their Christmas round robin: top of the class, captain of cricket team, lead role in drama production, etc.

'I expect you're pissed off with me,' he said, 'what with being a teacher.'

'I'm just sorry things have been bad.'

'Ian!' Ollie shouted again.

'Coming,' I shouted back.

'You're probably not meant to know,' Archie said, as I stood up. 'Don't tell Dad I told you.'

'I'm sure he will tell me. We only got here this afternoon.'

'Still. Promise you won't say anything.'

'I promise. But let's talk, shall we? I'm here till Monday.'

I took his silence as assent.

'So are you coming to the restaurant?' I said.

'Nah.'

'You don't like seafood, eh?'

'Not much.'

'I'm sure there'll be other things on the menu.'

'I promised Em I'd look after Rufus,' he said, stroking his neck.

You may have problems but you're still a good kid, I thought. Here you are, missing out on dinner, in order to do a good turn.

Only later did it occur to me that he hadn't been invited in the first place.

'Close the door,' Em mouthed as I entered the bedroom. 'Have you heard about Archie and school?' she whispered, once the door was shut.

I nodded. She was leaning into the oval mirror of a rickety dressing table to apply mascara. The room was low-ceilinged, with faded gingham curtains and a reproduction of Millais' *Ophelia* over the bed.

'Daisy told me,' she said, keeping her voice down. 'It's been very upsetting for them. For her anyway. Ollie won't talk about it. I'm surprised he even mentioned it to you.'

'He didn't. Archie did.'

I took the least crumpled shirt from my suitcase.

'Daisy wanted to call us when he started truanting, to ask our advice. But Ollie wouldn't let her. Plan B was to get Archie to call us himself. But Ollie vetoed that as well.'

'He'd be embarrassed about involving us,' I said.

'But you're Archie's godfather. And I know about school refusers. We could have helped.'

'I agree,' I said.

'Good. So you won't object if I give Ollie a piece of my mind.'

'I'd rather you didn't,' I said. The guy had a terminal illness, for God's sake. And we were meant to be having a night out. 'What's the point?'

'Apparently he thinks their mistake was not sending Archie to boarding school.'

'I thought he was doing brilliantly where he was.'

'He was. Then the usual happened. He got bored. Fell in with the wrong crowd. Started drinking, smoking dope, staying out all night. Much like the kids I deal with, in fact.'

'A typical Friday afternoon for you.'

'Yes, busman's holiday. Except that Archie's not in trouble with the police.'

'Not yet,' I said, pulling on my trousers, which were black like Archie's but baggy. 'He looks a mess.'

'Daisy says he's better than he was. She's found this college where he can sit his GCSEs in January then do ASs next summer.'

'Some posh West End crammer, eh?'

'No, a sixth-form college down the road from where they live. Archie wouldn't consider anything else.'

'There's my boy – good for him.'

Education has been a sore point between the Moores and us ever since they removed Archie from the local primary school and went private. They spent hours justifying their decision to us – Archie was being 'held back', state education in London was lousy, one's kids were more important than one's principles, and anyway the school they'd chosen for him was liberal and co-ed, etc. Later they didn't even try to justify it – they just knew they'd done the right thing.

'He's friends with a couple of kids who go there,' Em said. 'It's nothing to do with politics.'

'Of course it is. He's against his parents buying him privilege. It's Ollie and Daisy who have screwed him up.'

'He's not screwed up,' Em said. 'He's lost his way for a while, that's all. Most kids do, at some point. Only Ollie can't see that. So tonight I'm going to put him straight.'

'Everyone ready?' Ollie called from below.

Hearing his voice, I felt a pang: how many more times would I hear it? how much longer did he have? The brain tumour was surely a random event. But perhaps he thought the stress over Archie had brought it on or made it worse – another reason he found the truanting difficult to talk about.

'Two ticks,' I shouted down.

I slipped a jacket on, in case it was chillier on the coast.

'Leave it for tonight,' I said to Em. 'Give Ollie a break.'

'What are you afraid of? Ollie can look after himself.'

'I'm not so sure about that.'

'What do you mean?'

I told her what I meant. About the brain tumour. And how he didn't have long. With Ollie at the front door, shouting at us to hurry, I kept it brief. But she got the gist.

He had asked me not to tell anyone. But he could hardly expect me to keep it from my wife.

Em's eyes filled and her lip trembled. I worried she would cry and that Ollie would hear her. Or that her mascara would run and give her away.

'Don't say anything,' I said, as she rechecked her make-up.

'Of course not,' she said. 'Unless they do.'

'They won't. Ollie can't bear to and Daisy doesn't know.'

'*What?*'

'He hasn't told her.'

She shook her head, struggling to take it in.

'Coming!' I shouted, when Ollie called up again.

At the top of the stairs, Em pulled me back and whispered: 'She can't not be told. If Ollie won't tell her, then we must.'

'So it's a seafood place,' I said, as we set off.

'That's right,' Ollie said. 'Oysters from the local creek and fish from the North Sea.'

'We remembered Em's not keen on meat,' Daisy said.

'And that you'll eat anything, Ian,' Ollie said.

As usual they'd got it slightly wrong. Em avoids beef and pork but does eat chicken and lamb. The only fish I like comes in batter, with chips. But we both smiled and said the restaurant sounded great.

I sat in the front with Ollie, Daisy having surrendered the passenger seat on the grounds that I have longer legs than she does – Em, who's as tall as I am, scrunched up with her in the back. At university, Ollie had craved a car like this, with leather seats, a walnut dashboard and a soft top. But it seemed a bit desperate for a barrister with a late-teenage son. Had he bought it knowing or suspecting he was ill – a last indulgence?

'Slow down, Ollie,' Daisy said, her hair streaming behind her, 'it's blowy back here.'

'I'm only doing sixty.'

'It's the last time you buy a sports car,' she said, nearer the bone than she knew.

'My dad used to drive an MGB,' Ollie said, turning to me. 'This could be his, in fact.'

'The same model?'

'The exact same car. They only made about 350. You see the chip in the glass of the oil gauge, there – I can remember that from childhood. That's why I bought it, to tell the truth. Paid over the odds but it was worth it. Me sitting where my father sat – can you imagine?'

I couldn't. But if deluding himself this was his father's car made Ollie feel better, that was fine by me.

He was taking the back roads to avoid speed cameras, he said. All the roads round Badingley seemed to be back roads anyway, as if the budget for road-building had run out twenty miles inland. The landscape changed between each village – from deciduous woodland to pine forest, from scrubby heath to lush farmland, from reed beds to rolling hills. The sun sank in the west over Ollie's shoulder. Side-on, circled by light, he looked like an emperor on a Roman coin. And Daisy, in the back, was a minted empress, her hair flying behind her.

I'd imagined big windows overlooking an expanse of sea. But the restaurant was in a side street, half a mile from the harbour, and our table was a corner table, under low rafters, with a view of a small walled garden run to seed. The tables were imitation-marble Formica, with knives and forks so flimsy a breeze might have blown them away. It was no more Daisy's kind of place than the cottage was, but Ollie, who said he'd eaten here with his parents when they last came, seemed perfectly at home.

'White?' he said. I suggested a New Zealand Marlborough, but Ollie, hogging the wine list, said the only wines worth having were French.

'Let me treat you,' he said, before conspiring in whispers with the maître d', who, despite the modest surroundings, wore a white jacket and black tie. I know nothing about wine but when the bottle was uncorked I turned the label my way: Château Laville Haut-Brion 1986, it said.

'Christ, Ollie, it must be expensive.'

'Not really,' he said, then leaned across in a whisper. 'I don't think they realise what they should be charging.'

'Tastes good,' we all agreed.

I hadn't noticed the other diners till then but they had certainly noticed us. They were mostly couples – men in white shirts and ties (their discarded tweed jackets hanging over their chairs), women in floral dresses with pinched waists and conical bosoms. Why were they staring? Had we made too much noise? Did they consider us underdressed? Or was it just me they'd taken against, a lowlife who didn't belong with the likes of them? I clenched my fists beneath the table – then realised that what they were staring at was the blackboard above my head: Today's Specials, chalked in a looping script. The prawn cocktail and scampi already had lines through them.

'What do you fancy?' I said to Em.

'Guess,' she said. 'I know what you're having.'

'What?'

'The tomato soup to start. Then the tuna.'

I nodded. It wasn't hard for her to guess, since all the other starters involved shellfish and tuna was the nearest thing to steak.

'And you'll have the beetroot salad followed by cod,' I said.

Beetroot salad being the only vegetarian starter apart from the soup, and cod being cod, even if it didn't come with chips.

'Spot on,' Em said.

'God, how sickening of you,' Daisy said. 'I can never predict Ollie.'

'The starter's easy,' Ollie said. 'They have their own oyster beds. You must try some, Ian.'

'Shellfish don't agree with me.'

'Oysters are different. You eat them raw.'

'Yuk.'

'Where's your sense of adventure, man? You'll let him try, won't you, Em?'

'I'm not his boss.'

'Em knows what's good for her,' he winked. 'They're an aphrodisiac.'

'Should I risk it?' I asked Em, ignoring him.

'It's your funeral,' she said.

'Let's order,' Ollie said. 'The service can be horribly slow.'

It seemed unlikely that the service today bore any resemblance to the service thirty-odd years ago. But the frizz-haired waitress in the short black skirt looked as if she could have been around then. And to help the time pass Ollie ordered a second bottle – a Château La Perle Blanche 1976.

'When people talk bollocks about the greenhouse effect, I remember that summer,' he said. 'The heatwave lasted six weeks.'

Em and I exchanged looks. Ollie had doubtless intuited our global warming worries and was winding us up. Or the intimations of his own death made him indifferent to the death of the planet. Either way, I wouldn't be drawn.

'Steady with the drink,' Daisy said, as Ollie topped us up. 'You're driving.'

'I'll be fine,' Ollie said, laughing her off. 'They haven't introduced the breathalyser round here.'

Something else they'd not introduced was the ban on smoking. All around us people were lighting up. Perhaps the restaurant had a special licence, or had reached some tacit arrangement with the local police. And perhaps that's what made it so popular, despite the limited decor and fish-only menu. One woman even had a cigarette holder, as though she were starring in a forties movie.

The waitress arrived with our starters. The tomato soup could have come straight from a can, so when Ollie put an oyster on my side plate I didn't object.

'The Tabasco sauce is optional,' he said.

I lifted the ugly wrinkled shell. The gob of phlegm lodging inside it smelled like a urinal.

'Just tip the shell and swallow it whole,' Ollie said.

'I like to taste my food,' I said, playing for time.

'You will. It's pure ambrosia.'

If oysters are ambrosia, then spare me heaven. The slimeboat slithered down, spilling its cargo. It tasted of snot, marinaded in brine.

'You've still some juice in the shell,' Ollie said. I licked it cautiously, like a cat lapping at a rock pool.

'Wonderful, eh?' He pushed a second oyster at me, sprinkling red sauce on it as he did. 'With Tabasco this time.'

Resisting the impulse to hold my nose, I poured the red-laced phlegmball down my gullet. Instead of an estuary, I tasted fire.

'You'll never make a gourmet,' Ollie said. 'Last one. This time try chewing.'

I offered the shell to Daisy and Em, who shook their heads. I guessed that Daisy had eaten oysters before, and even enjoyed them, but she was indulging us – as if only men had the courage for such cuisine.

I chewed before I swallowed, tasting stringy innards and sand grains, and waiting for some revelation, as though it was mescalin or LSD. Nothing happened. I didn't feel sick, nor did I feel horny. My chief sensation was self-disgust. Oysters, maître d's, fat wankers stuffing their faces – what was I doing here? But this was a holiday. A break from real life. And I owed it to Ollie and Daisy to behave.

'OK, Ian?' Ollie said.

'Grand,' I said.

Outside the world had gone dark. In our low-raftered room the air was hot and smoky. Ollie buried himself in the wine list.

'I think a red now,' he said. 'Even if we are having fish. How would a Château Margaux 1966 be?'

'Astronomically expensive, I expect.'

'The year you were born, Ian.'

'Don't choose it on my account.'

'The 1964, then.'

'A house red would do fine.'

'It's not that pricey. Relax.'

Back home, when we eat out, it's usually a curry and Kingfisher beer, or else rump steak and a Chilean red. Ollie's extravagance put us in a quandary. It wasn't fair to let him treat us but going halves would be ruinous. Perhaps if he paid for the wine, I could cover the rest: honour of sorts.

'It's a special night,' Ollie said, explaining his choices: 1964, the year of his birth; 1976, the year he was last in Badingley; 1986, the year he met me. I felt touched but also embarrassed. Ollie had always been preoccupied with his past. Tonight – robbed of a future – he seemed in thrall to it.

'To old friends,' he said, raising his glass. 'To a great weekend. And to the bet.'

'Which bet is that?' Em said.

'I haven't the foggiest,' I lied.

'We made a bet,' Ollie said. 'Which Ian is winning. Tell them, Ian.'

Em gave me a sharp look.

'Call of nature,' I said, standing up.

It began with one of our lunchtime debates. We'd been discussing chance and probability, and afterwards, on our way across campus, Ollie with his crutches, me carrying his books for him, I recounted a story I'd just read in which two men get into an argument about punishment (which fate is worse, a life sentence or execution?), the first man offering to pay the second a vast fortune if he can survive fifteen years in solitary confinement. I forget now how the story ends or who wrote it (probably some Russian: I read a lot of Russian fiction while bunking off law). But Ollie found it thrilling: to push yourself to the limit like that in order to win a bet. His education had taught him the value of competing. But not that you could do it for money.

He returned to the subject the following day, in order to make a distinction between betting and gambling: a bet involved skill and stamina, he said, whereas a gamble was pure chance. I accused him of playing with semantics: wasn't a man placing a bet on a horse a gambler? Moreover, to bet on a horse was no shot in the dark, I said, but involved judgement and expertise. 'Judgement?' he scoffed. '*Expertise?*' I could have hit him. Betting on horses was something I knew about. My dad has always liked a flutter, and would often send me down the bookie's on his behalf. ('A fiver each way on the Duke of Venice in the two thirty at Doncaster and Honourable Wench in the four o'clock at Chepstow. Got that?' 'Can I have an ice cream if one of them wins?' 'Shut your face and get down there sharpish.') It was illegal for me even to enter the bookie's, let alone place bets. But the man who ran it was a family friend, Micky Cass, and knew the trouble my dad had getting off his arse, so he'd ruffle my hair and say, 'Just this once then.' You can't spend time in such places – among the cigarettes, the television screens, the dingy clothes, the poker faces – and not be tempted. And once I was a teenager, earning pocket money from a paper round, I made errand-running for my dad more tolerable by placing small bets of my own. I didn't win much but nor did I lose so badly as he used to, and by studying form and weighing odds I came to see that betting on horses needn't be a lottery – that judgement and expertise can play a part.

I tried to explain this to Ollie. But it was only by taking him to a betting shop that I was able to prove the point. I'd already located the nearest one, just off campus, which wasn't a smoky cave, like Micky Cass's, but bright as a supermarket. Despite the wholesome ambience, Ollie looked worried, as if we might be mugged or murdered. I calmed him down by suggesting a horse to bet on in the next race: a seven-year-old filly called Mandragora. He shrugged and handed over a tenner, and Mandragora came in at 8–1. That showed him. With the winnings, we kept going for another three hours. By the end Ollie got through forty quid, a small fortune in those days. To me it was money well spent.

There were several more such visits before his plaster cast came off and he decided that betting shops weren't for him. Going to them on my own was unaffordable and less fun. But the experience certainly affected Ollie. Towards the end of our third year, he admitted as much.

'Remember the betting shop? The poker games? And that time you dragged me to the casino to play roulette? I squandered hundreds of pounds.'

'Don't exaggerate,' I said. Our card games had been for modest stakes and I'm sure it was Ollie who suggested the casino.

'What was that shuffle you used to do?'

'The riffle shuffle.'

'You were so fast you could have cheated and I'd never have known.'

'I wouldn't cheat.'

'I know, but you did teach me something,' he said. 'I learned there's only one kind of bet that interests me.'

'Which is?'

We were in a bar at the time. He'd just got a round in. I should have seen what was coming.

'A sporting contest,' he said. 'One man versus another, in a straight fight. You against me, for instance.'

'You against me?' I laughed. 'I don't think so.'

'Why not?'

'Because you'd win, easily. I never beat you at anything.'

'Rubbish. Anyway, there's always a first time.'

There was always a first time. But I shouldn't have let Ollie talk me into it. And never would have if I hadn't been drunk. The weeks after our finals had been one long party. But this particular party was organised by Ollie's mother, down in Surrey, to show her brilliant son off to the neighbours. The house was mock-Tudor and detached, and the neighbours all seemed to be stockbrokers, or the wives of stockbrokers. I remember sitting on the lawn with Daisy, next to a sundial, watching bats zigzag in the dusk as we got drunk. Everyone got drunk, Ollie too, who made a tearful speech from the top of a flight of stairs saying how sad he was that his father couldn't be there but how happy he was to have met Daisy and how the person he had to thank for that was his best friend Ian. I'd been hiding in the crowd and was embarrassed to hear myself picked out, all the more so since I sensed Ollie's mother didn't much like me. Worse still, he had named me as an associate of Daisy, whom she liked even less. I had become his friend, Ollie went on, keeping the spotlight on me, because he'd never known anyone as competitive: intellectually and in every other way, we were perfectly matched, he said. Our degree results the week before – his a first – made his talk of parity a nonsense. But he described the debates and sporting contests we'd had and insisted on my joining him, at the top of the stairs, to a round of applause. Then he sprang the bet on me. There was no chance of getting out of it. He had me where he wanted me, with witnesses present. I was conned.

'What took you so long?' Em said. 'Your tuna's getting cold.'

She was angry with me, I could tell. I'd hoped the discussion would have moved on while I dawdled in the Gents, but obviously not.

'So this bet,' she said.

'Ollie suggested it,' I said.

'It was you who gave me the idea,' Ollie said.

'I was embarrassed,' I said. 'People were looking. I had no choice.'

'We shook hands on it.'

'Then the dancing started,' Daisy said. 'I remember that bit.'

'And we all got completely pissed and forgot about the bet.'

'Until this year,' Ollie said.

Until this year, when he discovered he had cancer and needed to prove to himself, by beating me, that he had some life in him still – something like that.

I kept my head down as I ate. The main thing was that Ollie was dying. I hadn't the heart to deny him his bet.

'But what exactly *was* the bet?' Em said.

'To compete at different sports and see who wins.'

'Which sports?'

'We left that open. The idea was best of three.'

'A sort of triathlon,' Ollie added.

Em looked at me sternly.

'That's typical of you, Ian,' she said. Her face relaxed as she turned to Ollie and Daisy. 'Ian used to have this squash partner called Chas. They played twice a week for three or four years. And Ian recorded every single result in a notebook.'

'Nonsense,' I said. 'There'd have been no point. He always beat me.'

'You used to pretend that *I* always beat you,' Ollie said, 'but it was pretty even.'

'You were better than me at everything. Just look at our degrees.'

'You spent all your time reading novels instead of law. But you still got a 2:1.'

'Ollie's right,' Daisy said. 'You sailed through without even trying.'

'Ian tries at some things,' Em said, third-personing me crossly. 'He obviously wants to win this bet.'

'We're here to see old friends,' I said. 'The bet's no big deal.'

'A bit of fun, that's all,' Ollie said, seeing how tetchy Em had become.

'The two of you are as bad as each other,' Daisy said.

'It's just strange Ian never told me about it,' Em said.

'I'm sure there's lots he hasn't told you?' Ollie said.

'Really?'

'I expect he hoped Ollie would have more sense than to hold him to it,' Daisy said, saving us all from further embarrassment.

'Of course you were there, too, weren't you?' Em said. 'At the party.'

'I was and I wasn't,' Daisy said.

More was than wasn't. I could remember the dress she wore – light blue with big cream spots and a strap that kept slipping from her shoulder. You couldn't miss her, among the dowdy Surrey snobs.

'I spent half the night throwing up behind the marquee. Ollie's mother was horrified. It's why Ollie and I never married. He was going to announce our engagement that night but when he saw I was drunk he bottled it.'

'The timing was wrong. My mother had only just met you.'

'Long enough to disapprove of me.'

'I did ask you to marry me afterwards. In Cyprus.'

'Rhodes actually.'

'I went down on my knees.'

'It was too late. You missed your chance.'

'You're together, that's what counts,' Em said, mistaking their sparring match for a serious fight and practising her conflict-resolution skills.

'And if you *had* married,' I added, 'you'd probably be divorced by now.'

'So it's not worth people marrying?' Daisy said, setting me up.

'It's not essential.'

On cue, they reached for each other's hands across the table.

'That's our little surprise,' Daisy said.

'We wanted to tell you in person.'

'We're getting married next month.'

I gulped my wine. *Married?* Daisy had always been against marriage. I could remember her saying how she and Ollie didn't need rings to legitimise their love because they had made their vows to each other already, in private. Besides, marriage had unhappy associations for her – long nights kept awake as her parents feuded below.

I'd always respected Daisy for not marrying. Why marry now?

'That's wonderful news,' Em said, her eyes watering. She's sentimental like that.

'Yes, congratulations,' I said, with as much warmth as I could muster.

'None of our friends can believe it,' Daisy said. 'They thought we were married already.'

I had a vision of Ollie and Daisy's friends being summoned

two by two to hear the announcement. How far down the list did we come?

'We've been together for nearly twenty-five years. So it's a wedding and a silver wedding rolled into one.'

'Just a registry office do,' Daisy said.

'With a party afterwards.'

'To which you'll be invited, of course.'

'Sounds lovely,' Em said, chinking her glass with theirs.

'Who'll be best man?' I said, as they chinked mine.

'Search me,' Daisy said. 'Have you chosen someone, Ollie?'

'I doubt I'll bother,' Ollie said. Though I tried not to react, I couldn't help but flinch. 'Unless you're volunteering, Ian.'

'You know I can't make speeches,' I said, making light of the snub.

Before they'd time to protest that I would be excellent, the perfect man for the job in fact, the waitress came to clear the plates.

'We're thinking mid-November,' Ollie said, when she'd gone again. 'We don't want to leave it too long.'

I realised then what the wedding was about. He had proposed because he was dying. Daisy didn't know as much, but he would have explained that there were legal and financial implications in the unlikely event of a spouse's decease. And though in principle she was against marriage, he had talked her round.

None of us had room for crème caramel or apple crumble. When Daisy and Em disappeared to the Ladies, Ollie ordered a dessert wine instead. I examined the label curiously. It dated only from last year.

'It's the nearest I could get,' he explained. 'This year being the other momentous year in my life.'

'Because of the wedding.'

'If you like.'

I didn't like but nor was there time to discuss it and anyway the subject had been ruled off-limits.

'Not more drink,' Daisy said, returning, but she didn't refuse when Ollie filled her glass.

'It'll help you sleep,' he said.

'I need all the help I can get. I swear I heard chains clanking last night.'

'That's just Archie's body jewellery,' Ollie said, quickly adding, before discussion could switch to Archie, 'or Mrs Banks trying to scare us off. My guess is that she and her brood have secretly been living there. That's why she was so hostile when we arrived.'

'I wish someone had been living there,' Daisy said. 'Did Ollie tell you that we found a newspaper lining the wardrobe that dates back to 1976? I don't think the place has been occupied since.'

'If the owner rents it out on the Internet, it must have been,' I said.

'When Ollie looked the other day he couldn't find the website, could you, love?'

'I expect it's being updated,' he said.

'They should update the house while they're at it,' Daisy said. 'It's still 1976 in there. Or 1876. Even 1776. It's freaky.'

The maître d' and the waitress stood to attention by the till. It was past midnight by now, and the restaurant completely empty but for us.

'Time we returned to our ghost,' Ollie said. 'I'll get the bill.'

Despite my efforts, he refused to let me contribute. Which was typically generous, and a massive relief, but which also, as always, put me in his debt.

It seemed only fair for Em to sit in the front while I squashed up with Daisy. With the hood up to keep us warm, Daisy fell asleep almost at once. And with her head resting chastely on my shoulder, I too slept through most of the journey. The one time I did wake – after Ollie had braked to avoid a muntjac deer – he and Em were arguing about professionalism: how close to clients should one get? Did you serve them better by keeping a distance? Was detachment a virtue or a sign of burnout? I often forget Ollie and Em have something in common: they work with people – mostly young men – who've fallen foul of the law.

'I've learned to switch off,' Ollie was saying. 'I'll be given a case, some terrible crime, a rape or murder, and spend weeks getting to know the victim or the accused. In court I give my heart and soul to them. But once the trial's over, I'm gone, job done, I never think about them again. It's the only way to survive without going mad. The same for you, Em. You can't afford to get emotionally involved.'

Typical Ollie, I thought: Mr Stiff Upper Lip. It was only later, as we reached the farmhouse, that I realised what had prompted his monologue: Em must have told him of her encounter with the Lithuanian girl, Magda. I wondered if she had also mentioned the mad plan to take in Magda's baby and the situation as regards us having a child of our own. Em was by nature discreet and knew that to talk freely would be to betray us – and humiliate me. But I'd seen Ollie work his magic on women before. And he had obviously cast a spell on Em, who just a few hours earlier had claimed to be furious with him but was now disclosing matters close to her heart. She always pretended to find Ollie 'difficult'. But it's well known that women find difficult men attractive. And Em *was* attracted to Ollie, earnestly though she denied it. Not that there had ever been any funny business between them, so far as I could tell. But Ollie had the power to make any woman false, even one as loyal as Em.

He and I were old friends. But if he was dying, he wouldn't hesitate to worm confidences from a friend's wife. He would probably not scruple to seduce her, either – had he not told me, just a few hours ago, that he had lost all sense of morality? 'I'm evil,' he'd joked. But what if he was serious? Could a man with nothing to lose be trusted? I don't consider myself a jealous person. But there was something about Ollie that made me feel ugly. And though it was restful to sit there with Daisy's head on my shoulder and the darkness flying by, I knew I had to watch him closely.

'Nightcap?' he said, back at the house.

'Not for me,' Em said, before heading upstairs.

'Nor me,' Daisy said. 'I'll clear the table then get to bed. Trust Archie to leave a mess.'

'Ian?'

'A quick one while I let Rufus out would be grand,' I said.

I swung the French windows open and off he went, nosing over the grass towards the orchard. The sky was a navy ceiling, springing silver leaks. Ollie fetched two basket-weave chairs and we sat on the terrace in the cooling air.

'So,' Ollie said, clinking whisky glasses. 'One–nil to you.'

'What?'

'Our bet. You're ahead.'

'If you say so.'

'But tomorrow's Round Two.'

'What's that consist of?'

'Not sure yet. But I'm losing, so I get to choose.'

An owl hooted, like a fog warning. I felt exposed sitting there, at the edge of the unfrontiered night. Never the bravest of dogs, Rufus seemed nervous too, slinking back from the darkness to lick my hand.

We drank some more. It had been a long day and I felt

woozy. To be honest, I can't recall which of us spoke next. But I could swear it was Ollie who took the initiative.

'Of course a bet is pointless unless it's for money.'

'I wouldn't say pointless.'

'We always agreed it would be for money.'

'Did we?'

'We just didn't stipulate the amount.'

'What do you have in mind?'

'Fifty quid?'

'Don't be daft.'

'A hundred?'

'You're winding me up.'

'What do you suggest, then?'

'Let's say five.'

'Five sounds fine.'

We clinked glasses.

'Grand,' I said.

He paused, taken aback. I couldn't see why.

'Are you serious?' he said. 'I know you like to gamble, but can you afford it?'

'I'm not that poor, Ollie.'

'No, of course, I wasn't meaning to suggest . . .'

'Besides, I'm winning. You're the one taking the risk.'

'Fine. Agreed. Five grand, then,' he said.

Of course I could have said I hadn't intended . . . that the use of the word . . . that he'd twisted my meaning . . . But he had me in a corner.

'If you're sure it won't kill you,' he said.

It wouldn't kill me. But Em would. *Five grand?* It was more than two months' salary, after tax. More than we'd spent buying the car. More than our wedding and honeymoon had cost. More, in effect, than the house, which we'd paid for with a 95 per cent mortgage.

'Five thousand pounds,' I said. 'Wow.'

This was madness – the late hour, the strange house, the heavy drinking, the dateless night. But I knew my reputation was at stake. The bet was less a sporting contest than a test of courage: was I willing to take a risk? Say no and I'd lose anyway – would sink in Ollie's estimation. He was my friend, my dying friend, and this bet his last request. Reject it and I'd be rejecting him.

'We don't have to if you don't want to,' he said, knowing he'd trapped me.

'We've agreed now. Let's shake on it.'

'Five thousand pounds I beat you.'

'Five thousand pounds *I* beat *you*,' I said, giving him my hand.

Saturday

The night sizzled and fried, even with the window wide, the low eaves trapping the heat. I slept fitfully and woke early, detaching myself from Em to lie apart, clammy but cooling, on the sheet. Dust hung in the light beam from the curtain crack. From the height of the sun – a yellow circle behind the gingham squares – I put the time at six. Unknown birds called across the fields and I imagined them as species redeemed from extinction: the corncrake, little bustard or red-backed shrike.

Till recently, I had a gift for putting my problems to sleep when I went to bed. Then something changed and I began to wake at unknown hours and to worry away in the dark; even alcohol, my usual prologue to sleep, was no help. When I saw 'my' GP – the possessive seems misplaced, since I'd never previously seen her – she tried the word depression on me, which was something else to fret about. We agreed that I try some over-the-counter herbal sedative called Somaduce (Comatose as Em christened it), which carried no risk of addiction. Its only effect was to make me listless by day, and, after a month of insomnia (the nights made worse by my indignation at wasting good money), I abandoned it. If I couldn't sleep for worry, that was natural. Why worry about being worried? I was right to be worried. The worrying thing was that I'd taken so long to see it.

That's how I sold my insomnia to myself, jokily, which was a step forward, or rather back to the ironist I used to be. But what had been waking me early for several weeks before Badingley wasn't a generalised midlife crisis but something quite specific. I lay brooding about it that morning, after dreaming of it half the night. Ollie's tumour and the reckless bet I'd made were bad enough. But it was school, and an episode just before the summer holidays, that had me sweating under the eaves.

Few teachers enjoy playground duty. And my mood was not the best that Tuesday lunchtime because Mrs Wilkinson, our dyslexia specialist, had spent so long discussing one of my pupils with me it left no time even for a sandwich. Outside the kids divided in the usual gendered fashion, the girls colluding in quiet clumps close to the building, the boys running wildly at the fringes. As I stood unnoticed by the boiler room, I heard some girls from Year Three singing and clapping hands. I recognised the tune from childhood. But the words and gestures were new.

We are the Derby girls (*clap hands*)
We wear our hair in curls (*pat hair*)
We don't wear dungarees (*rub thighs*)
We show our sexy knees (*touch knees*)
The cocky boy next door (*pat crotch*)
He got me on the floor (*touch ground*)
I gave him 50p (*slap hands*)
To give it all to me (*thrust crotch*)
And now I've got this brat (*rock arms*)
In a high-rise council flat (*reach up*)
We drink and smoke and shag (*wiggle hips*)
We are the Derby slags (*clap hands*)

My first impulse was to intervene and discipline them. But did the girls – seven- and eight-year-olds – understand what they were singing? I'm not used to younger kids; it's the tough nuts, the ten- and eleven-year-olds, I specialise in. And these girls could have learned the song by rote, just as I used to learn carols ('Lo he abhors not the virgin's womb'), uncomprehendingly. Best let it go. If I raised it with our head teacher, Mrs Baynes, she would take no action. I left them to it and walked away.

Even if I'd not been bad-tempered, I would have dealt with Campbell Foster in the same way. I've never taught Campbell – normally I would have had him in Year Five but that year I'd been switched to Year Six as an experiment before switching back again. I'd been aware of him, though. You couldn't not be. You only had to attend Assembly, for which he'd be late or in which he'd be noisy or from which he'd be escorted and made to stand in the corridor. Some kids are trouble for just a term or two. Campbell had been trouble since nursery school – trouble enough for any normal head to have excluded him by now. But Mrs Baynes believed in sticking with kids and 'building their self-esteem'. From what I knew of Campbell, his self-esteem didn't need building up but stamping down. Perhaps if I'd had him, I could have knocked him into shape – not because I'm a better teacher than my colleagues but because I'm a man, and kids like Campbell lack positive male role models.

The thought struck me again that lunchtime, when I spotted him among a crowd of boys in the basketball cage. 'Among' is misleading: he was the ringleader, having purloined a coat from the back of a boy in Year Two – or so I deduced from the boy's pathetic efforts to snatch it back. Campbell and friends stood in a circle, tossing the coat from hand to hand. Every so often it would be dropped and lie on the ground until the Year Two boy made a grab for it, at which point it would be retrieved. The boy was persistent, I'll give him that. For a moment he was even laughing. But then the coat fell at Campbell's feet. The boy snatched a sleeve with one hand and grabbed Campbell's leg with the other. As he did so, Campbell yanked the coat up and kicked out. The boy fell backwards on the concrete, shrieking and wailing.

'What the hell's going on?' I said, striding across.

Silence.

'Well?'

I helped the boy up from the ground and asked if he was hurting anywhere. He was all right, he said, between sniffs. There was a red zip-mark across his palm, but otherwise he seemed unharmed.

I turned to his persecutors.

'*Well?*'

None of them moved. Most were staring at the ground.

'Kid fell over and hurt hisself, sir,' Campbell said.

I insist on the 'sir', but coming from Campbell the word sounded more disrespectful than if he'd not said it.

'He didn't fall over,' I said, 'you pushed him, Campbell.'

'Me, sir?'

'I saw you do it.'

'Youse always blaming me, sir.'

'You're always the cause of the trouble, Campbell.'

'S'not fair.'

'Let Mrs Baynes decide that. You come with me.'

There was a slight pause before he said: 'I ain't going nowhere.'

He seemed to think that since he was off to secondary school in September, there would be no comeback.

'You're going to see the head this minute,' I said.

'No I ain't.'

I see now that it would have been better for me to send the others inside. Their presence was making Campbell more defiant.

'Last chance, Campbell. Will you go of your own free will or do I have to drag you?'

'You can't touch me.'

You can't touch me. Something in me snapped when he said it.

'Right,' I said, stepping towards him.

You hear of teachers – even primary-school teachers – being slapped, punched or knifed by pupils. But as I clutched at his left arm I felt no fear. His right arm swung round – whether to hit me or, as he later claimed, to protect himself is beside the point. All I know is that we were pushing and pulling, with me trying to pinion his arms while he tried to escape, until I grabbed his left ear between my forefinger and thumb, something a teacher (or was it my father?) once did to me. The move was surprisingly effective. Despite having both his arms and legs free, he immediately wilted.

'Tough guy, eh?' I said, breathing heavily as I led him by the ear across the playground. I say 'led' but my arm was stretched diagonally forward with him half a stride ahead, his left cheek tilted towards the sky.

'Let go, sir,' he said, from the side of his mouth, 'you're hurting.'

Tightening my grip, I said, 'Now you know how it feels, Campbell,' adding, for good measure, dreadful cliché though it was: 'Next time pick on someone your own size.'

By this point he was crying, in part because all the other kids in the playground could see how utterly I'd vanquished him. But my grip didn't slacken till we reached Mrs Baynes's office.

The door was open. Campbell, finally released, walked in ahead of me, wailing and rubbing his ear.

'Dear, dear, what's the matter, Campbell?' Mrs Baynes said.

I gave her a full account of the incident, Campbell punctuating it with sobs and strangled objections ('S'not right, Miss'), till Mrs Baynes nodded at me and said, 'Thank you, Mr Goade. Campbell and I will have a quiet chat about this.'

She had her arm round Campbell's shoulder by then. In her position, I too might have comforted a crying child. But after the report she'd just been given of his rudeness, bullying and defiance, I was offended by her conciliatory gesture.

Conflict upsets me and I felt shaky for the rest of the afternoon. When Mrs Baynes intercepted me on my way out at three thirty ('Do you have a moment?'), I assumed it would be to commend me for having intervened so incisively, or if not commend (teachers don't expect to be thanked) to reassure me I had her full support.

'Campbell alleges that you grabbed his ear,' she began, unreassuringly.

'I held him by the ear,' I said. 'It was the only way to make him cooperate.'

'The only way?'

'When I tried to take his arm, he lashed out. I had no choice.'

'It seems to me you had several. You could have stood your ground till he relented. You could have rung the bell early, so everyone went inside. Or you could have come and fetched me.'

'He'd bullied a smaller boy. And he was challenging my authority. I had to act.'

'Absolutely. But as you know, physical coercion should be used only in extreme cases.'

'In my judgement this was extreme,' I said.

'We have to be so careful, Ian. His ear did look rather sore.' She smiled. 'He can be a trying boy. I'm sure you didn't mean to hurt him. And I don't want to make an issue of this.' I sensed there was a 'but' coming but she staunched it. 'You get off home. With any luck it will all be forgotten by tomorrow.'

Em thinks that Mrs Baynes has it in for me and she said so again that evening. It was humiliating enough when Miss Cooper, ten years my junior, got the deputy headship, a post everyone assumed would go to me. But for Mrs Baynes to have said, by way of consolation, 'I'm sure other schools will have deputy headships you can apply for, Ian,' rubbed salt in the wound. I have applied for seven deputy headships in recent years and all have gone to teachers with less experience. I know I make a lousy interviewee: too nervous, too intense, too eager to prove my worth. But my probity and my record as a teacher speak for themselves.

I saw no sign of Campbell for the rest of that week. I assumed he was either in school, lying low, or truanting again.

The following Monday Mrs Baynes summoned me to her office during the morning break.

'Sit down, Ian,' she said, peering over the rim of her glasses. 'Campbell Foster's mother came to see me last Wednesday, very upset. I hoped that once I spoke to her, she would calm down. But she was back again this morning.' She took the glasses off and dangled them from her right hand. 'Unfortunately, she refuses to let the matter drop.'

'Meaning what?'

'She intends to make an official complaint.'

'What would that achieve?'

'She thinks you should be reprimanded,' she said. 'At the very least.'

I had brought my coffee with me, in a Derby County mug, and smiled at Mrs Baynes before taking a swig – God, some of the parents at this school, what a hassle for us both. She didn't smile back.

'Let me speak to her,' I said. 'I'm sure when she hears what happened –'

'She has heard. From Campbell.'

'Then Campbell's lying.'

'It's not what Campbell *told* her. It's his ear.'

'I barely touched it.'

She continued to dangle her spectacles.

'They showed me a doctor's letter. It speaks of inflammation and temporary loss of hearing.'

'Nothing I did could have caused that. I'll call on her after school and explain.'

'It wouldn't be in your interests, Ian. She's very angry.'

'What *should* I do then?'

'For now, there's nothing you can do. Obviously I'd like to avoid the matter going to the governors, but –'

'The governors?'

'That's the usual procedure, as I'm sure you know: an independent investigation of the incident, followed by a governors' meeting, and where the teacher is found to be at fault an official reprimand, suspension or even . . . But let's not get ahead of ourselves.' She slipped the glasses back on. 'I'll keep you informed of any developments, Ian.'

Em told me not to worry. That the parents of problem kids always sided with them as a matter of principle. But that with all the officialdom involved in lodging a complaint, few of them saw it through and fewer still succeeded. Em is a fount of good sense and I believed her.

Like Mrs Baynes, she strongly advised me against seeing Campbell's mother in person. So when I knocked at 44

Wythern Road one night the following week, having prised the address from the school secretary, I knew I was acting rashly. But I have dealt with difficult parents before. What was there to lose?

'Yeah?' said a male voice. The face was pale, the body sprouting from the vest also. It threw me for a second. As did the tattoo on his shoulder and the shorts. There'd been no mention of a Mr Foster. Was this the father or stepfather? My confusion must have showed. 'Yeah?' he said again, more aggressively.

'It's Ian Goade from the school.'

His eyes stared at me through a fog. Then the sun came up. For a moment I thought he was going to hit me.

'Petal!' he called over his shoulder, then folded his arms and leaned against the door frame. I'd more sense than to ask could I step inside.

'I was just passing,' I said, to break the silence.

'You wait there,' he said.

Mrs Foster appeared, tall, attractive, unexpectedly straight-haired. Was Petal her name or an endearment? She seemed more friendly than her partner till he said: 'It's that teacher what done Campbell.'

'Ian Goade, pleased to meet you,' I said.

'You've a nerve,' she said.

'I think if you heard what actually happened –'

'We know what happened.'

'– and let me describe the sequence of events.'

'There's only one event here,' she said. 'You hurt my boy. You, a grown man, and him an eleven-year-old. Think yourself lucky I stopped my husband settling the score.' Whether her husband was the man standing there wasn't clear – nor at that moment particularly relevant.

'Campbell was misbehaving in the playground.'

'We're not stupid,' she said, which she clearly wasn't, though I was less sure about the partner. 'We know Campbell can be a handful. But if you can't control kids without hitting them, you're not fit to be a teacher.'

'I didn't hit him.'

'There were witnesses.'

'I'm sorry you've been misled.'

'You've only come here to save your skin.'

'That's not the reason.'

'I've nothing more to say, mister. We'll see you in court.'

I wanted to tell her that a disciplinary hearing isn't like court. That she was wasting her time. That it would be better to settle this between us. But she'd already disappeared inside.

'You heard,' said the man in the vest, closing the door. 'Fuck off.'

Em, exasperated, said I'd made things worse for myself. Campbell's mother would proceed now whatever. I might even be accused of harassing her. I had better start preparing my defence. 'If you have one,' she added.

In bed, later, she apologised ('I'm sure you didn't intend to be rough with him. You hardly ever lose your temper these days'). But I couldn't sleep, and went online with my anxieties, and found references to outer-ear trauma, auricular cartilage damage, and the risk that lobular tears and excessive swelling could cause permanent damage to a person's hearing.

Ridiculous, when all I'd done was hold him firmly.

My colleagues at school were vaguely sympathetic, because they know what Campbell is like. But none had been present at the time and I was too proud to approach the teachers' union for advice. I knew we were allowed to use 'reasonable force' in restraining pupils. But when I consulted the relevant paragraph of the Education Act online, I discovered the following: 'Deliberate use of physical contact to punish a pupil, cause pain or injury or humiliation is unlawful, regardless of the severity of the pupil's behaviour or the degree of provocation.' I could see myself losing everything – my job, the respect of my colleagues, my reputation.

Though half resigned to the hearing going ahead, I did make two more attempts to prevent it. First I tried to catch a word with Campbell in the playground, not to apologise to the little bastard but to show concern for his welfare. 'Not talking to you, sir,' he said, rushing past. I also went to see Mrs Baynes: could we not come up with a compromise that would avoid the case being referred to the governors?

'It's good of you to offer,' she said, 'but even if you *do* resign the hearing will have to go ahead.'

'I wasn't offering to resign.'

'Oh – what are you offering?'

'I'm thinking of the good name of the school,' I said.

'So are the governors,' Mrs Baynes said. 'A disciplinary hearing will reassure the parents that physical abuse of children is not tolerated here.'

'But I didn't abuse Campbell. All I did was hold his ear.'

'That's for the governors to decide. I'm sure they'll deal with it fairly.'

'When the only witnesses were kids? Who're all too afraid of Campbell to tell the truth?'

'In a situation like this, children are essentially truthful. Anyway, there *was* one adult witness. Me. I saw the state Campbell was in when you brought him to my room.'

'You know there was nothing much wrong with him then.'

'I'll report the truth as I saw it, Ian.'

That's where the case stood when we broke up for summer. Had the incident taken place a week or two earlier, there might have been time to settle it before the end of term. But the governors' next meeting, of which the disciplinary hearing would form part, was scheduled for early September, the day before school resumed.

Now September had almost arrived. The hearing was next Wednesday.

No wonder I couldn't sleep. And yet I must have slept, because when I opened my eyes again – sprung them from my dream's dark loop – the yellow circle had risen behind the gingham and the beam through the curtain crack was brighter. I felt rested, and calmer than I had for weeks, as if the dancing dust motes were celebrating my release. Ollie's news had put my problems in perspective: I had my health at least. Even the bet we'd made last night seemed less than threatening.

I threw some clothes on and slipped from the room without disturbing Em. The stairs were steeply raked and carpetless, but I negotiated them noiselessly, conscious that Daisy was sleeping just along the landing. Ollie, I assumed, would be fussing round the kitchen, kettle boiled, draining board cleared and radio tuned to the morning news – he'd always been an early riser. But the door was on its latch and when I entered there was only Rufus, paddling his tail with pleasure to see me. I let him out, made myself tea and sat on the terrace. The tea tasted odd – I'm used to tea bags, not the real thing – but I was grateful for the moisture. I closed my eyes and let the sun flood them. Ollie's absence was surprising but a relief.

He had said that the nearest shop was the garage on the main road, and that's where Rufus and I headed, left at the end of the drive and down through the village. The air was dry and the day already parched: no dew, no sap, no pollen, only seedless pods and flowers withering on their stalks. Even the rooks above the churchyard sounded hoarse. EVERYTHING MUST GO said the empty window of the general stores, and everything had. But two other shops seemed to be in business: Auntie's Antiques, which claimed to open daily from 11 to 4, and Two Wheels Good, which had old-fashioned bikes in the window, shiny and ready for hire. The pub, the Old Swan, didn't look closed, either: out in front, a standing wooden sign – double-sided and held together with a rope, like the letter A – boasted a range of beers and snacks. I walked on, looking for life, but saw no one. Predictably, as we passed the best-kept verge in the village, in front of an Edwardian villa, Rufus hunkered down, arse just above the ground, in that hunched, embarrassed posture dogs adopt when they're shitting. I'd not brought a pooper-scooper or a plastic bag. But nobody was around to see, so I pretended I hadn't seen, either.

Beyond the primary school with its metal railings, we passed a cul-de-sac of pebble-dash semis from the fifties. A few cars were dotted about, Ford Escorts and Minis, but again there was no sign of life. Perhaps rural inhabitants are always like this, I thought, slow to rise and lackadaisical. Or perhaps the inertia was peculiar to Badingley. It seemed a little creepy, either way – as if the village were a ghost village, lost in the heat haze of its past.

At the junction with the main road, we reached the modern world. Cream caravans raced by, and Euro-juggernauts. I grabbed Rufus and put him on his lead. He's normally obedient – I'm strict about punishing him if he misbehaves – but today he strained ahead, excited by the new habitat. 'Heel,' I said, reining him in until the road dipped before the garage (I could see the ESSO sign ahead), where he tugged so hard towards a blackthorn hedge that I let myself be taken, assuming he needed another dump. A couple of bluebottles were circling the source. Under clumps of cow parsley, an owl lay in a bed of its own feathers, freshly dead.

'Sit, sit, sit, SIT,' I urged Rufus, to stop him acting like the gun dog he was. Though the owl's face was smashed in, and a trickle of blood tinged the flat beak, the feathers – pearl brown and lacy white – were unblemished. Male or female? If male owls are large, then male, but the whiteness seemed female, the shade of a wedding dress. If Rod had been there, he'd have dissected the owl with his penknife. Even I couldn't resist slipping my hand into the feathers. The body wasn't warm but it didn't have the coldness of the grass. Had the owl died only an hour ago then, in the grey dawn mist? Whatever struck must have been moving at speed to hurl it so far. A high-sided van or lorry, perhaps. With the speed, and the weight, the windscreen must have shattered or cracked. Even if it hadn't, the blow must have been terrific. Peering down at the corpse, like a surgeon in theatre, my faithful assistant trembling beside me, I could imagine it all: the huge white bird whirling out of the dawn, no time for evasive action, the driver instinctively ducking as it hit. Did he stop and walk back, or keep going? The heavy grass verge showed no sign of disturbance, nor was the road pitted with broken glass. He must have driven on, then. Well, why not? He would have known the owl was dead. Yet not to check and be sure . . . Owls were rare these days and this one might have young to feed. You couldn't blame the driver for killing it but you could blame him for his indifference. Who can take a life, even by accident, and not feel a touch of remorse?

In the kind of books we give to our more advanced Year Sixes, a dead owl would be an omen of catastrophe. But I felt privileged to see one at such close quarters. Holding Rufus back with one hand, I uprooted a handful of ferns and cow parsley and covered the corpse as best I could.

As I paid for the milk and papers at the garage, I thought

of telling the lad behind the counter. But what would he care? And how to explain my sense of excitement? The English countryside is tarred and feathered with roadkills. To someone who lived there, it wouldn't be news.

BADINGLEY, PLEASE DRIVE CAREFULLY the village sign said as we walked back, then underneath in smaller letters 'Population –'. There'd been a figure once – 10? 100? 1,000? – till someone scratched it out. We passed the school, the village green, the thatched pottery, the church with its gangling spire – and saw no one. It was as though a space had been cleared specially for me. I'd a lot on my mind or should have had. But as I walked up the drive towards the farmhouse – the sun on my bare arms, dog rose in the hedges, Rufus's fur burning gold – I felt sharp, bright, eager, refreshed, euphoric.

There was still no sign of life when I re-entered the house. I'd bought two papers to read, one tabloid, one broadsheet, a habit of Ollie's at university which I thought he might enjoy seeing revived: 'Important to see how the other half lives,' he used to say, and though my chippy inner self objected to him saying it (I *was* that other half, the *Sun* had been my father's daily paper), I kept my trap shut. Had I not gone to uni to better my prospects? And wasn't a requirement of self-betterment learning to sneer at the culture I'd left behind? Nowadays I rarely bother with newspapers. But the prospect of reading snippets aloud to Ollie was oddly enjoyable – a deferral of the day when he would no longer be around.

That he wasn't around even then – nine o'clock and the sun pouring in – confirmed the worst: he must be ill.

Reluctant to believe it, I walked round to the barn: perhaps he was tinkering with his car. My eyes adjusted to the dusty void. It was less a barn than a lean-to extension, which served both as a garage (with an inspection pit covered by wooden planks) and as a workshop. The two halves were divided by a partition made up of horizontal boards; the boards were nailed to upright posts, which rested on a low brick wall. A grey inflatable boat hung from the ceiling, an ancient hosepipe coiled round itself in a corner, and a couple of bikes leaned against the wooden boards. I stepped through a narrow opening into the workshop. According to Ollie, the building had once been a coffin-maker's – easy to believe since all the posts were caked in candlewax (without candles, long working days and night-time vigils would not have been possible). The floor was bare earth and in one corner someone had chalked a downward arrow and the word 'RATS'. The thin cobwebbed window at the end was draped with dead moths and butterflies, like a display of world flags. A wide workbench sat beneath it, and three shelves holding small tools. Larger tools hung from the wall: scythes, picks, shovels, sickles, forks, flails and other museum pieces. Ollie's car was the newest object in the barn by about a century. As I left, I put my hand on the fly-frilled bonnet and radiator grille. Stone cold. The car hadn't moved since last night and nor, it seemed, had Ollie.

Back in the house, I filled a bowl of water for Rufus, boiled the kettle and carried a tray upstairs. Em drinks Earl Grey, I prefer ordinary (English Breakfast as they now call it), but this morning we both had Assam, made in a pot, with real tea leaves.

'Morning, love.'

She was wearing a white nightdress, with lacy frills, and the look and feel of it as I bent over to kiss her, along with her little nose and sleep-hooded eyes, made me think of the owl.

Em's keen on nature but when I told her she reacted with

indifference. It wasn't the owl she wanted to talk about but Ollie.

'However ill he is, it's outrageous of him not to tell Daisy,' she said.

I was beginning to regret having confided in her, especially when Ollie had asked me to tell no one. But Em wasn't no one.

'Maybe he wants to be certain before he does,' I said, pouring the tea.

'He told *you*.'

'We go back a long way.'

'So does Daisy. And they live together.'

I lay on the bed and cuddled up.

'That could be another reason,' I said.

'What?'

'Because I'm less directly affected, he found it easier to tell me. Whereas he's afraid Daisy will go to pieces.'

'What patronising crap. Daisy's tough as nails.'

'Or maybe he was using me as a guinea pig. To see the impact of coming out with it. As a trial run.'

'If ever you get ill, I expect you to tell me at once.'

'Of course. But you know Ollie. He likes to feel he can cope on his own.'

'You can't cope with cancer on your own. It affects the people around you. Sparing them isn't protective, it's disabling. If you don't make him tell Daisy, then *I'll* tell her.'

'That's blackmail.'

'It's one couple helping another couple. That's what friends are for. And in return . . . Let that fly out, will you?'

I went to the window but it was open already. The fly hung there against the glass, swaddled in spider threads, rocking backwards and forwards. No point trying to rescue it.

'In return what?' I said.

'Ollie can advise you how to handle the disciplinary hearing.'

'I told you in the car. I don't want to discuss it. Anyway, he's got enough on his plate.'

'It's the kind of thing Ollie loves to get his head round.'

'It's not my job to provide him with mental stimulation.'

'You're happy enough providing him with physical.'

'I knew you'd be cross about that.'

'What do I care if you want to play silly games? Provided there's no money riding on it.'

'Of course not.'

She sat up and looked me in the eye.

'Sure? You know what you're like with betting.'

'That's all over with,' I said.

She kept her eyes on me a few more seconds then relaxed.

'I wondered why you'd spent the summer getting fit,' she said, ruffling my hair.

'I had to do something while you were working.'

'You went to the gym every day.'

'It's a good place to hang out.'

'And you cycled round half the Midlands.'

'You had the car.'

'Not to mention all the hours at the driving range.'

'Smacking golf balls is good therapy.'

'Don't worry, your secret's safe with me,' she said. 'As long as you promise to talk Ollie into telling Daisy.'

'Why don't you talk to him? The two of you seemed pretty friendly last night.'

'Sorry?'

'Coming home in the car. Anybody would think you fancied him.'

'Don't be ridiculous. What are you on about?'

Her indignation disarmed me. What *was* I on about? I'd been half drunk and they'd only been talking.

'I don't know, I just –'

'Are you feeling unloved, Ian? That's stupid. Would you like to pull those curtains and get into bed.'

When I opened the curtains twenty minutes later, the fly was neatly mummified and bubble-wrapped, ready for ingestion.

Em was exaggerating my fitness regime. It's true I'd been exercising through the summer. But the purpose of it was to be healthier rather than to win a contest that might never take place.

It also took my mind off the business at school. Each day I'd choose a route of thirty to forty miles and set off on my bike as Em left for work. Or I'd go to the driving range and whack balls off the rubber mats – long drives that sang towards the far wire fence or neat little chips into the ring of tyres at fifty metres. Either way, cycling or golf, I'd be at the gym by mid-afternoon. 'Gym's so boring,' people say. But I loved pushing myself while the television screens stacked above brought news of far-off catastrophes. And I loved watching the metres clock up, whether I rowed, pedalled or ran them. The calorie counter, too, and the knowledge (or illusion) of pounds falling off. I tried every variation on the cross-trainer: Random, Quick Start, Hill Climb, Sprint, Endurance. The black metal weights rose higher in their stacks. Not a day passed without some new personal best, on whichever apparatus. I pumped iron, straddled bars, balanced on medicine balls, saw off rival boat crews, powered over 1-in-3 hills, vibrated on the power-plate till my teeth chattered. My skin glowed. My muscles hardened. A different man stared back from the mirror, sweat seeping like blood from his prickly scalp. I felt reborn, godlike.

By the time we arrived in Badingley, I was fitter than I'd

been for years. But that's not saying much. And you can take my word for it that I'm not particularly competitive. All I wanted was to keep my end up with Ollie – to lose with dignity rather than be trounced.

From the moment he arrived, I could see that Daisy's interest in Milo was more than professional. Most men are like me: we resent women finding other men attractive. But with Milo the attractiveness couldn't be denied. He had sandy curls, a pink boyish face, broad shoulders and oversized feet. His trousers (cut off just below the knee) and his light blue polo shirt made him look like a model from the fashion pages promoting smart-but-casual summer wear. And he was tall, with a leanness that (unlike Ollie's) suggested purposeful languor, not angst. Above all, there was his gentleness with his daughters, who – shy at having to meet a bunch of strangers – each took refuge in an upper thigh, Bethany bagging his left and Natalie his right. Milo stroked their hair and (between greetings to us) whispered reassurances until they gradually unclasped. I can't imagine anyone making a better first impression. I hated him on sight.

I'm sure that Ollie felt exactly the same. As Daisy's partner, he was used to meeting artists and designers. And as Milo's host, it was his duty to be polite. But I knew what he was thinking: you charlatan, you sycophant, you pseud.

'You poor darlings, you look exhausted,' Daisy said, in her worst, affected manner, as if Milo had just driven from the Outer Hebrides, not London.

'It wasn't too bad,' he said, to his credit. With two children in the car, the journey couldn't have been fun. But Em and I had come twice as far.

'Let's get you all a drink,' Daisy said, like a Sister of Mercy.

She had been presenting Milo as a pitiful victim ever since

the previous lunchtime – that is, from the moment she admitted that she had not been able to change his dates and that, if his daughters' recent bout of flu didn't prohibit it, he would probably turn up for Saturday lunch and even possibly stay over on Saturday night, after which he'd doubtless push off early on the Sunday, though there was always an outside chance that he would stay over that night too. I soon inferred that Milo would be staying the whole damn weekend. Why Daisy bothered to disguise it I don't know. It was her right to invite Milo whenever (and for however long) she liked. Why should we care? But I could tell she felt awkward from the way she emphasised his deservingness: his wife Bianca had gone to America for a whole month and the poor guy was struggling to cope. Having seen through Daisy's other stratagem, I made the mistake of falling for this one. I'd expected a deadbeat not a Greek god.

We sat on the terrace drinking coffee in the baking heat while Daisy and Em got lunch ready and Milo's girls did the kind of inconsequential things that little girls do. Ollie made conversation as best he could but I knew he was exasperated. The plan had been for the two of us to play tennis from eleven till one. But, having been barred from doing so by Daisy, on the grounds that Milo was due at midday and that our absence would seem rude, we'd hung around after breakfast reading the papers – not a problem as far as I was concerned (in the stifling heat I'd no appetite for Round Two of our contest), but frustrating for Ollie, especially when Milo didn't arrive till after one.

All of which made lunch predictably tense, though the day might still have passed off without incident, but for Archie.

None of us had seen him since the previous evening, and Daisy and Ollie seemed content for it to stay that way: the lunch table was laid for seven, not eight, and nothing was said about him joining us. But while drinks were served in the garden (much the same ritual as the previous day but with kids present to spoil it), Em slipped back inside to find him. 'Where's Em got to?' Daisy asked more than once, before turning back to Milo, who was explaining to us that though his post as a creative director for one of the corporates left him less and less time to pursue his own work, his first love was the project he'd been working on in private since leaving art school. I couldn't get my head round the thing but it seemed he had used a scalpel to scrape skin from different parts of his body, with a video camera trained on his face to record his physical reactions, and electrodes plugged to his head to record the effects on his brain. From this he'd created a work called *Body Pain/Ecstasy*, with magnified images of his veins and blood cells, and a soundtrack created by converting his brain movements into musical notes. Over the past few years, he told us, he'd created a dozen or more multimedia 'Body Narratives' but he didn't yet feel ready to exhibit them. Thank God for that, I thought – may your sick, narcissistic shite remain unseen for ever. But Daisy kept saying how *wonderful* the project was (she'd evidently been to his studio) and how *terribly important* he chisel out time to complete it (even if, so it seemed to me, he'd then be diddling the company she had found him a well-paid job with). Daisy's gushing made me want to puke and I was on the verge of disappearing into the house when Em reappeared with a sly little smile on her face.

Two minutes later Archie followed, wearing long shorts and a vest, and looking marginally less pallid than he had the day before. Daisy and Ollie both seemed apprehensive, as though he was bound to do something shameful or barbaric. And when Archie made straight for the champagne, knocking back a first glass in one swig before pouring himself a second, they became jumpier still. But Archie, smiling, seemed genuinely pleased to meet the new guests (all three of whom were closer in age to him than the rest of us were) and listened patiently as Milo went on about his gruesome artwork. Lunch was on the table but when Natalie and Bethany asked could they go into the field beyond the orchard to look at the straw bales, Daisy said that lunch could wait, and Archie delegated himself to escort them, along with Rufus.

'Nice lad,' Milo said.

'Lad' came patronisingly from someone who looked about twenty. But Archie was supposed to be my godson, and he *was* nice, and I was heartened to see him coming out of himself.

I forget what we talked about over lunch, except that at one point I told the girls to stop feeding Rufus under the table and that Em overruled me ('Just don't give him chicken bones'). The atmosphere was strained throughout. But the real trouble began only afterwards, with the treasure hunt, which Archie intended as a distraction while the rest of us helped Daisy clear the table. Natalie and Bethany closed their eyes while he hid sweets for them round the garden. We heard his 'Cold . . . Warmer . . . Very hot now' as they searched, and their shrieks of pleasure as they found the coloured wrappers. Then they all went into the barn, from which, after some minutes, they emerged dragging the large inflatable boat I'd seen hanging from the rafters. Archie had already pumped it up and it looked in good order, despite the dust-black cobwebs clinging to its side.

'See what we found, Daddy.'

'Can we sail it on the sea, Daddy?'

'You said there was a beach, Daddy.'

'Oh, Daddy, don't be mean.'

Picking up on the general adult reluctance to move (we were sitting in deckchairs by then, boozed out, with Ollie and Em both asleep), Archie suggested they forget the beach till later and meanwhile fill the inflatable with water 'to make a swimming pool'. Smart boy, I thought, watching him unroll the hosepipe, hook the nozzle over the side and turn the tap on. The inflatable was slow to fill, since the sides were surprisingly deep, and the girls – now in their swimsuits – took turns spraying each other. But finally water was lapping over the side. That's the last thing I remember. A bee-heavy torpor had descended on the day, and, despite the shrieks of excitement from the boat-cum-pool, I soon dropped off in my deckchair.

I dreamt a barber turned up at my school carrying two cutlasses, one in each hand. He'd come to cut the children's hair for them, but insisted on cutting mine first. I sat in an infant chair, with a graduation robe around my neck, while a class of eight-year-olds sang 'Penny Lane'. Snippets of hair fell and became snakes. Then the barber turned into Mrs Baynes, who lifted a cutlass high above her head and brought it down with a scream.

The scream was Daisy's, as she ran across the grass to where Milo was dragging Bethany from the pool. He laid her face down on the grass, pushing down on her shoulders and turning her head to one side so he could expel the water from her lungs. Or that's how it seemed to me, as I leapt up and hurried over. But my view was obscured by Ollie and Em running ahead of me, and it occurs to me now that it can't have happened like that – surely the proper method would have been to lay her on her back. The question's academic, anyway, since she was coughing and very much alive by the time I got there. And despite Daisy's melodramatics as we stood round – 'God, she could have died' – Milo said she'd simply swallowed too much water (he'd pulled her out just to be on the safe side) and Bethany, coughing and sobbing, said she was all right.

'Where's Archie?' Ollie said. 'He's meant to be in charge.'

On cue, Archie appeared through the French windows, with Natalie grasping his hand.

'Where've you been?' Ollie said.

'Inside,' he said, unaware of the drama, 'obviously.'

'I went to do pee-pees,' Natalie said. 'Archie was helping.'

'How were you helping, Archie?' Ollie said, suspiciously.

'How do you think, Dad? I showed her where the bog was and got some lemonade.'

'With a straw, see, Daddy,' Natalie said, brandishing a glass.

It was then that Archie noticed Bethany, tearful by the pool.

'You were meant to be looking after both of them, you idiot,' Ollie said.

'Bethany's only little, Archie,' Daisy said.

'You weren't to know she can't swim,' Milo said, hushing them both. 'And she only swallowed a mouthful, didn't you, precious? No harm done, Archie. Let's forget it.'

'That's sweet of you,' Daisy said, laying a hand on Milo's arm.

In his daze, Archie didn't realise what had momentarily been alleged against him – wilful neglect of one child, paedophiliac preoccupation with the other. Perhaps over the next hour or so, he did come to realise, and that explained his subsequent behaviour. All he did, in the meantime, when Milo took the two girls inside to change out of their swimsuits, was walk over to the inflatable, heave it up by the rope handle on one side, and tip it over, letting the water flood across the lawn.

For myself, I think the blame lay with Milo. If Bethany couldn't swim, why wasn't she wearing armbands? When kids from our school are taken to the swimming baths, we follow strict rules. You can't afford to take risks as Milo had done, chatting inanely to Daisy then dozing off while his daughter's life was at risk. And yet he'd managed to emerge as a hero, at least in Daisy's eyes. Arsehole.

Representing the likes of Milo makes Daisy's a busy job. I've heard her talk about it so often I know what's involved: the employers who call her up, hungry for good designers and art directors; the illustrators fresh out of art college who plague her with their portfolios; the talented all-female team she has assembled. It's frothy media stuff, not work of the kind that Em and I do. But when Daisy places someone with a company, 20 per cent of their first year's salary goes to her, and there are people on her books she has placed four or five times. I wouldn't be surprised if she earns as much as Ollie does.

Once, on impulse, I went to her office. The entrance lobby had a high ceiling and bare brick wall, with a red leather sofa for visitors. Through the opaque glass door I could see figures drifting like ghosts. Daisy and her team, just feet away.

The girl on reception – who really *was* a girl, about sixteen at a guess, doing work experience – asked what my business was.

'I'm here to see Daisy Brabant,' I said.

'Do you have an appointment?'

'No, but she's an old friend.'

'Sorry, Ms Brabant's fully booked today.'

Where do girls that age get to be so confident? It's not just a middle-class London thing. We've had girls leave our primary school and before you know it they're waiting on tables in Sydney, playing gigs in New York, or getting their kit off in men's magazines. This girl looked as if she'd done all that already. She wore a headset, with a microphone under her chin.

'I'm sure Daisy will want to see me,' I said.

The girl examined what I was wearing. Especially the shoes, which I'd shoved on in a hurry as I left home. They were black leather, scuffed from hours spent monitoring school playgrounds. Not artist shoes. Not CEO shoes. Not ethical design company shoes.

'She's out at the moment,' the girl said.

If that was the case, why not say it in the first place? Till then Daisy hadn't been absent, not in so many words.

'I don't mind waiting.'

She punched some keys and looked at the screen, tilting it away from me as she did.

'She's busy with appointments till after six.'

'I'm a friend. She'll squeeze me in.'

'They're out-of-the-office appointments. She won't be back.'

It would have been easy to bully the girl into submission. But I had my pride.

'Just tell her Ian called,' I said.

'Is there a surname?'

Is there a surname? The cheek of it. Was it likely I'd been born without one?

'Just tell her Ian – she'll know who.'

She looked interested at last, sizing me up as an ex-boyfriend or lover. Perhaps if I'd waited she would have found a gap in Daisy's diary. But I was gone, slamming the door behind me. The poor girl would be in trouble when Daisy found out.

It briefly occurred to me that Daisy was hiding out back. That she'd seen me enter the building. That the girl was being given instructions from her headset or on the computer screen. But that way lay paranoia.

In a cafe down the street, with a clear view of the entrance, I waited till six thirty. Daisy neither arrived nor departed during that time. The girl must have been telling the truth.

It was raining when I left the cafe and the streets near the Tube were crowded. At one point, my umbrella knocked into someone's coming the other way. 'Sorry,' I said, but whoever it was had already disappeared into the crowd. A click of spokes, a boff of fabric, then nothing – two passing strangers who'd briefly collided then moved on.

I was surprised when Daisy didn't call me next day. Apparently she never got the message, because when I told her, some months later, she was mortified. You must come another time, she said, I'm in the office every day except Friday, when I work from home. Ollie raised his eyebrows: get real, why would Ian make a special trip just to see your office? We were in the living room of their house in Primrose Hill at the time; I'd come down for Archie's second birthday – he was playing with Lego on the floor. Daisy had cut her hair, which, disappointingly, fell only to her shoulders. By then I'd moved in with Em but wasn't ready to introduce her to them. We'd been a trio. How would they feel about becoming a quartet?

I never did get to see Daisy's office – unlike Milo, who must have been there many times. That was natural enough. He was on her books. Keeping up with his work was important to her. But as we sat in the garden at Badingley, with Daisy fussing over him, I imagined them in her office late at night, her colleagues having long departed. There he sits, playing his new artwork on a laptop, an eleven-minute video of bodily fluids (blood, sweat, semen) as seen under a microscope, a homage to the light shows once associated with sixties rock groups, but technologically far in advance of them, more sensuous too, and with gentler music. Daisy, watching, is a consummate professional well aware that Milo is married. But with artists, of course, that never counts for much. And she can't help but be aroused by the intimacy – Milo is sitting right next to her, his thigh touching hers, the hairs on the back of his wrist catching late gold sunlight as he rotates the mouse and the video climaxes with a fountain of fluid.

Sometimes I get carried away, or my mind does, in spite of me. But without some basis in reality, where would such images have come from? I'm an ordinary bloke, a teacher, with a meagre fantasy life. So when something starts up in me like that, unwilled, I have to trust it.

Think the best of folk, my dad says, and they let you down. Think the worst and they can't hurt you. Even my dad sometimes gets things right.

'Forty–love,' Ollie called as my mis-hit backhand landed six feet long. Three set points. I hadn't intended the first set to be surrendered so quickly. Still, I can't pretend I was giving the game my all. Any displeasure in losing was offset by the sight of Ollie finally enjoying himself. I'd been worried whether he could play at all. But here he was, destroying me.

He hit the next serve down the middle, on the line – an ace. First set, 6–1. What was that nonsense yesterday on the golf course about the tumour wrecking his powers of concentration? His game this afternoon was faultless.

'Best of three sets?' he said, walking towards the net.

'That's what we agreed,' I said.

He had arrived in a strop, annoyed at having our contest postponed, and his bad mood continued through the opening games. But now, a set up after only twenty minutes, he allowed himself a smile.

'You don't want to change sides?' he said.

'I don't think so,' I said.

'To make it fairer.'

'What do you think, Milo?' I said.

'I vote we stay as we are. I'm just warming up.'

'Hear that, Ollie?' I said. 'Don't write us off just yet.'

'What's it fucking matter who wins anyway?' Archie said.

'Less of the language,' Ollie said.

'Piss off, Dad. You're not my keeper.'

If I'd been quicker-witted, I would have accepted Ollie's offer – or seen the unwisdom of lining up as Milo had suggested: 'The visitors versus the Moores.' Most tennis players fall out with their opponents, but when a father is playing with a son, or a husband with a wife, odds are that any falling-out will be between partners. So far the only hint of trouble had been Ollie's reluctance to acknowledge Archie and vice versa. I hadn't expected the hand-slapping-after-every-point camaraderie you see in doubles at Wimbledon, but their mutual avoidance strategies were eerie. If they were this glum with each other when ahead, what would happen should they start to lose?

For now there was no danger of that. It was my turn to serve again. Last time I'd hit six serves in succession into the net then left a lob from Ollie which landed in.

I didn't make the same mistakes this time. My first two serves landed in the tramlines. Love–fifteen.

Though they weren't here to watch, it was Daisy and Em who had got us playing doubles. When Ollie announced, after the pool mishap, that he and I were off to play tennis in Frissingfold, Daisy insisted we take Milo with us, since she knew he enjoyed a game of tennis, too. That she knew this added to my suspicions: surely hobbies weren't something they'd have discussed if their relationship was strictly business. Perhaps the same thought had occurred to Ollie, but what really irritated him was having Round Two of our contest further delayed. Milo looked embarrassed – he must have seen that Ollie was unhappy at the proposal – and said he would stay with the girls. Oh, Em and I will look after the girls, Daisy said. That's kind, Milo said, but three's an awkward number and I mustn't intrude. For a moment there was stalemate. Then Em intervened: How about Archie making up a four? You used to play a lot of tennis, didn't you, Archie? Neither Daisy nor Ollie seemed interested in this suggestion; it was as if Em hadn't spoken. But Em kept pushing and Archie – for whom his parents' opposition was probably a spur – said sure, cool, he'd not played tennis in a while.

So it was that the four of us headed off in Ollie's MGB, with Archie and me crammed in the back. The only cars we passed were vintage cars (there must have been some rally going on) and the countryside lay stunned in the heat: meadows, hedgerows, moated farms with dung-brown outbuildings, all sleeping the sleep of an earlier century. But once we reached the main road, the landscape changed. Sprayed acres of agri-glut sweated under plastic. And despite the blue sky, a pesticidal gloom seemed to infect everything, even the shoppers on Frissingfold's busy main street.

Archie's return was too pacy for me. Love–thirty. Then Ollie caught the net tape and the ball dropped on our side.

The courts were in the Municipal Country Park, behind high walls, in what had once been Frissingfold Hall. There were three of them, laid end to end, but no one was playing on the other two.

Archie sliced a backhand down the middle. Milo politely left it for me and I left it for Milo. Game to them.

Ollie had had the foresight to bring water and we stood swigging it at the edge of the court.

'Shall I take the forehand side this set?' Milo said.

'Sure,' I said.

My backhand is no better than my forehand, but I didn't like losing so comprehensively and anything was worth a try.

The switch had an immediate effect. Milo passed Ollie with a forehand return from Archie's serve, Ollie netted my lob, and though we missed the first break point at 15–40, a wayward volley from Ollie gave us the game. Encouraged, I went up to the net on Milo's serve and put away a couple of smashes – we won that game too. Ollie had seemed to welcome us drawing level but he was cross at falling behind. His mood darkened on his own service game, which he lost to love, with Milo punishing two weak serves and Archie wildly misjudging two topspin drives. Father and son exchanged looks at that point. In truth Archie wasn't playing badly, especially for someone who looked as if he'd spent the past year in bed, and Milo kept shouting 'Well done' in encouragement. But that wasn't the same as his father saying it. If nothing else, a bit of praise beforehand might have made Archie readier to ignore Ollie's reaction when his attempted lob sailed high over the fence into the next court and put them 3–1 down. It was only a look, a rolling of the eye, but still.

'What did you say?' Archie said.

'I didn't say anything,' Ollie said.

'Yeah, well, piss off, you're not so fucking brilliant yourself.'

'Go and fetch the ball, will you?' Ollie said.

'No one's going to steal it, Dad. We've plenty more.'

It was my turn to serve, and I used the moment to defuse the situation, pretending I hadn't heard the exchange.

'Ready?' I shouted from the baseline. 'Or do you want to concede now?'

Like me, Ollie had doubtless assumed that Milo would be a hopeless tennis player, on the grounds that no artist can be good at sport. But now his eye was in, Milo hit some decent shots. Might he and I have gone on to win the set? Probably not – my own contribution was erratic, and all it needed was for Ollie and Archie to regain their composure. But in the event we didn't find out.

It happened with the score at 15–30. My serve fell short, asking to be hit, and Archie, moving in, drove a topspin deep to my backhand. I did well to reach it, stumbling as I made contact and scraping my knees and left palm on the ground as I fell. If the high lob I clawed back was more luck than judgement, I enjoyed the sight of our opponents – both up at the net, waiting for the kill – coming to terms with the fact that the ball would land behind them. They dithered a moment, unsure whose task it was to retrieve it, till Ollie, with an impatient huff, turned back and ran to mid-court, where the ball was coming down. I'd hoisted it so high that he still had time to get behind it, let it drop, wait, steady himself and hammer it back. But he was thrown by having to play it at all and, rushing, tried to smash it at the height of its bounce. It wasn't that he failed to connect – no shot that afternoon was hit with more venom. But instead of hitting it short to Milo's left, where I was marooned behind the baseline, on my bum, and effectively out of the game, he belted it to Milo's right. Which would have been fine, and have made a spectacular winner, but for the fact that Archie was standing at the net. He turned to see where the ball had got to (its flight and bounce having taken an eternity) and discovered the answer as it slammed into his temple just above the right eye.

His shock on impact made me think of the dead tree at Badingley, limbs and tendrils arrested in all directions. Then he went down like a giant redwood, and lay there on the asphalt, felled and concussed. Ollie had smacked the ball with pace, but I did wonder, even in that instant, whether Archie would have collapsed quite so dramatically if the ball had been hit by anyone but his father. Milo, up at the net, was first to reach him. And despite my own little injury, slivers of blood seeping up through my shredded palm, I was soon there, too. Only Ollie was slow to react: he stood, mid-court, in bewilderment, as though still following the line of the ball and calculating where it would land (a perfect winner just inside the baseline had his son not interrupted its flight).

'Are you OK?' Milo asked, leaning down.

Archie was prostrate but breathing.

'My fucking head hurts,' he said.

'Where?' I said.

He was rubbing the side of his head but when he took his hand away I could see no sign of swelling. His iris and pupil looked OK.

Milo fetched some water, sloshed it in Archie's face and made him drink. He was shaky and in pain but – with Milo taking one arm and me the other – strong enough to stand up. Ollie had been keeping his distance but now he bent to retrieve Archie's racket from the court.

'All right?' he said.

'No thanks to you,' Archie said.

'I've told you before – when your partner's behind you, you have to be ready to duck.'

'So it's my fault, Dad?'

'I'm not saying that.'

'You've not said sorry, either.'

'You were in the wrong position. The shot was on target.'

'The shot hit me in the face. Apologise, Dad.'

'People apologise when they've done something wrong. I'm sorry if you were hurt –'

'*If*. Do you think I'm putting it on?'

'Of course not. But you're over the worst. And we've a match to finish. Thirty–all and 3–1. It's getting interesting.'

He put the racket in Archie's hand.

'Is that all you care about,' Archie said, 'finishing the match?'

Archie wasn't so much holding the racket as balancing it in his palm, as if the way it tipped would tell him what to do next.

'Let's sit down and rest a while,' Milo said. 'We could all do with a break.'

'Resting's not allowed when Dad plays,' Archie said, 'even when someone's nearly been killed.'

For a moment it seemed that might be enough for Archie – that his tantrum had passed and he would resume. But then he gripped the racket, took a step back and hurled it across the court.

'Fuck your match.' As he moved away, he turned to Milo and me. 'No disrespect to you two, but Dad's a prick.'

Milo made a grab for him but he was too fast.

'Leave him,' Ollie said, a superfluous command since Archie was already through the gate in the corner of the court and striding away. A teenager in high dudgeon – what could we do? 'Don't worry,' Ollie added, 'he'll be back.'

'I hate to see him upset,' Milo said.

'Of course. But it wasn't so bad an injury, was it, Ian?'

'No,' I said.

I too hated seeing Archie upset. But I suspected him of exaggerating his injuries in order to get at his father. And though Ollie's parenting left much to be desired, he was right not to be soft. Toughness and discipline are essential with kids. If Archie had been my son, I'd have drilled that into him earlier, when he was small.

I can't say I enjoyed the knock-up that followed, two onto one, with Milo and me (playing to a singles court) against Ollie (playing to the doubles). Eventually I sat it out and let the two of them play a match. If Milo's tennis style was annoying (all fancy dinks and poofy drop shots), his brown-nosing was worse. I lost count of how many times he cried, 'Cracking shot, Ollie.' Not that the contest was uneven. And not that Ollie seemed to notice how desperate Milo was to ingratiate himself. On the contrary, Ollie was enjoying the match and said as much, loudly, when, with the score 4–3 in his favour, they changed ends. 'An impressive opponent, eh, Ian?' I did my best to smile. Tennis isn't my strong suit, but he didn't need to stick the knife in like that. And there was no call for him to be so fulsome when Milo levelled the set at 4–4. 'Well played.'

At 5–4 Ollie had a break point but his topspin drive landed out. Just.

The next two games went to deuce and could have gone either way.

At 6–6, I suggested they call it quits. Ollie was geared up for a tiebreak, naturally enough. But it was now past six, we'd had the court for over two hours, and Archie hadn't returned.

'Ian's right,' Milo said. 'We ought to look for Archie.'

'Good on you, Milo,' I said. 'Thank God one of you can see sense.'

As Milo wandered off to gather up the balls, I raised my eyebrows at Ollie and mouthed, 'Wuss.' It was fine for me, as a spectator, to urge them to quit. But for Milo to capitulate was pathetic.

We did our best to find Archie, trawling Frissingfold's main street, bus station and cafes. We also looked in all five pubs, resisting a drink till we got to the last of them. By that point Milo was fretting about returning and putting his daughters to bed – if we were staying he would find a taxi, he said. To me that seemed a sensible suggestion: why should Ollie and I be made to rush our beers? But Ollie wouldn't hear of it and crammed us back in the MGB. I half expected that we'd come across Archie, thumb out in search of a lift. But there was no sign.

There were no road signs, either. Once off the main road they disappeared, as if the only people who travelled this way, on the B-nought-nought-something-or-other, were people who lived locally and didn't need to be reminded of their bearings.

'They removed all road signs during the war and never put them back,' Ollie said. Luckily he knew the way. I wondered if Archie did.

'He's gone off like this before,' Ollie said. 'He always turns up.'

I didn't feel as sanguine as Ollie. Nor as sanguine as Daisy, who, when the three of us walked into the living room, failed to ask why Archie wasn't with us. Strangely Em didn't question his absence, either. It was only when Ollie finally admitted we'd mislaid him that the truth emerged.

'Archie didn't mention a row,' Daisy said.

'He's here?'

'He was here.'

'Where is he now?'

'On his way to some music festival at Snipham. He said he'd stopped playing tennis because he was tired. Then while he was walking round Frissingfold he ran into some people he knew from school, who were off to this gig. You just missed him: he stopped off to get his sleeping bag. He won't be back till morning.'

'Did he seem all right?' Milo said.

'Perfectly.'

In the general relief that Archie was all right I hardly noticed the implausibility of the story. Surely the odds of him coming across school friends in Frissingfold were remote.

Who'd be a father? Over the next hour I realised why I had chosen not to have children. Perhaps 'chosen' is too strong: officially it's still open to us to have them. But lately there's been something half-hearted about our efforts, the reluctant half, the heartless half, being me. I might have children for Em's sake; I might have them for my own sake, insofar as their absence has begun to affect our marriage. But children per se, for themselves, I can do without. My colleagues at school make envious remarks around four o'clock as they head home to theirs: 'It's all right for you, Ian: you can forget about kids till tomorrow morning.' It's true I don't have to deal with their mess, their demands, their unreason and self-absorption. But forgetting is another matter, since at home I still have Em: an evening when she doesn't get onto the subject is rare. There are compensations. You can't have kids without sex, so we have an active sex life. Actually you can have kids without sex, thanks to fertility clinics. But masturbation into a sample jar isn't my idea of fun. I once asked Em: do you see me as a breeding machine? Of course not, she said, children will be the expression of our love for each other. But suppose the children don't happen, I said, where will that leave the love? She didn't reply. My fear is that if we can't have kids, Em won't want sex any more, since it doesn't do the job. And that if we do have kids, she won't want sex either, since the job will have been done.

It's a tricky area. And a subject I don't like to discuss. All I'm saying is that I hated having Natalie and Bethany around that evening.

At first they were upstairs, having a bath, which wasn't so bad. Indeed, with Milo supervising, Em assisting and Daisy busy in the kitchen, it gave me the opportunity for a tête-à-tête with Ollie. We had not been alone all day. And I had promised Em that I would tackle him.

We sat on the terrace watching the sun descend.

'What do you make of Milo?' I said, approaching the subject in a roundabout way.

'Yes, nice chap,' he said.

'Nice-ish anyway.'

'Why the ish?'

'Ignore it. I'm a cynic.'

'Come on, Ian, spit it out.'

'When people are nice, I always wonder how deep it goes.'

'He seems honest enough.'

'Yes. Apart from that dodgy call.'

'Was there a dodgy call?'

'At 5–4, remember. You had match point. And he called your shot out.'

'I thought it was out.'

'I thought it clipped the line. If it had been me, I'd have given you the point or played it again.'

'Doesn't matter – we had a good knock.'

'Of course. And I dare say he genuinely thought it long even if it wasn't. Let's give him the benefit of the doubt.'

I was on the brink of changing tack, the words ready in my head: *You have to tell Daisy about the tumour*. But then Bethany and Natalie ran past in their pyjamas, and the moment was gone. Milo soon caught them, and carried them in, one under each arm, their squeals of protest and pleasure piercing the dusk. But he didn't succeed in removing them upstairs. I could hear them in the kitchen, demanding that Milo make them a snack, though they'd been fed only an hour ago. Some snack: butterfly pasta, garlic-free bolognese sauce, grated mild Cheddar, longways-sliced cucumber and organic baby plum tomatoes with two-thirds diluted apple juice to drink – nothing less specific would do, though most of the meal was left untouched, needless to say. Then they claimed they'd been promised a game before bed, and having quickly tired of playing tennis with each other (using two ancient wooden rackets they'd found in the barn), they rowdily played snap with Milo and Em. Finally, under duress, they went upstairs. That might have been the moment to tackle Ollie but the noise from above – the trampolining on mattresses and squabbling over who had which bed – was too distracting. I blame Milo as much as the girls: he'd shown what a soft touch he was earlier, on the tennis court with Archie, and the girls exploited it to the full. But Em also played a part in hyping them up. Why they needed to come down again to have stories read to them, and why she succumbed to this demand, I couldn't see. 'Time for sleepies,' Milo said at last and, after gentle persuasion failed to work, carried them screaming to bed. Naturally they demanded another story, as a penalty. And naturally they crept downstairs again when Milo attempted to rejoin us. *Whenever* he attempted to rejoin us, that is, since they crept down several more times, giggling at first but later complaining that they found their bedroom 'scary'. Finally Em offered to go up and sit with them. Some half an hour later, *she* came down, and peace prevailed above. It was ten o'clock by then, and we were all starving.

Boys are more of a handful than girls, people say (I've said it myself), and a screaming baby is harder to deal with than a screaming toddler. But I can't imagine being more irritated than Natalie and Bethany made me that evening. If I'd not been so anaesthetised by drink, I would have slapped them.

My memory's pretty good on the whole. My first polio injection, Uncle Jimmy's brown-stained fingers, the fish on its side in the canal, the rickety school desk with my initials (carved by penknife) on its lid, black ants gutting a pop-eyed frog, the yellow stain on page 412 of the library copy of *Sons and Lovers*, the rib of beef we ate for Sunday dinner the week my dad won two hundred quid on the pools: it's all there, indelibly. And yet Badingley, which ought to be etched on my soul, slips away at times – or refuses to come into focus, like something wrapped in tissue and shut away in a drawer. Did Ollie really say this or Daisy that? I remember a mass of things but nothing distinctly.

Still, I don't forget the source of my being there at all – a certain day at university.

Late October in my second year, and I'm walking to the library one morning when I see a girl coming towards me, with a beret at a jaunty angle, and a denim skirt, a waist-hugging jacket and brown knee-length boots. Though on the small side, she's otherwise so perfect that I do what I always do at the approach of a beautiful woman, avert my eyes in case the sight of me should cause her to frown, weep, vomit or in some other way express revulsion and thereby (because of me) make herself look less lovely than she is. But I also sneak a look as we pass each other, and this time, instead of discovering a contemptuous stare or a silent mocking laugh or a scornful toss of the hair, I see the girl is smiling at me. I hesitate, thinking she wants to speak, but she's already walking away, hair falling down her back and a bell going off (a fire alarm in the Science Block) where her voice might have been.

I tell myself she mistook me for someone else, yet I'm so uplifted by the experience that after leaving the library that evening I return to the student bar for the first time since Ollie cold-shouldered me there with his rugby team, and who do I see the moment I walk in? It seems such an unlikely co-incidence that I look away, fearing a mirage, but when I turn back she is still there, in a red dress this time, and strappy shoes, and with a black-bead necklace, but unmistakably the same person with the same long hair and, incredibly, smiling at me again.

Daisy. Though I don't know that yet.

She is sitting with another girl. Lacking the bottle to go

over to them, I stand at the bar, knocking pints back and nerving myself to make a move. I dare say I would still have been there past closing time had she not come up to the bar.

'Hey there . . .'

'Hey.'

'Can I squeeze through?'

'No problem,' I say, and prepare to step aside, but then add, in the voice of someone more confident than I am: 'Better still, let me buy you a drink.'

Daisy has always denied that she noticed me that morning or recognised me that night. She says she was simply going to the bar and that I happened to be standing in her way. (I don't believe her: I think women like Daisy hate to acknowledge taking the initiative.) She also claims that when I offered to buy her a drink, she refused, pointing out that she had a friend with her, but that I wouldn't take no for an answer. All I remember is walking back to the table, sitting down and trying to make conversation, notionally with both of them but really with Daisy. Which may be why, after ten minutes or so, the friend got up, apologising for being a party-pooper, and said goodnight. 'She was bored,' Daisy said later, 'and you'd been drinking a lot.' That may be true but it doesn't explain why Daisy failed to leave with her. ('You insisted on buying me a last drink,' she claims, but that doesn't quite hang together, either: she could have said no.) Whatever the case, the fact is that she let me walk her home to her hall of residence. She didn't ask me in. Nor did I have the gall to attempt to kiss her goodnight. ('Liar,' she said later, 'you lunged at me but I pushed you away.') But I asked if I could see her again, and she said yes, and that's something even she doesn't now dispute.

(When I say now, I don't mean ten o'clock on a late-August night in Badingley but the last time we talked about this. I can't remember when exactly that was. But over the years a received – or disputed – version of events has evolved between us.)

So, to recap: on a late-October night in my second year at uni I meet Daisy and ask her out. But she's probably right about me being slightly tipsy on that occasion because I fail to write down her telephone or room number and realise that I don't know her surname. And it takes a week of increasingly desperate hanging about in the vicinity of her hall before I 'accidentally' bump into her one morning as she is leaving for a lecture – an art history lecture in the Humanities Block, which I pretend is en route to my own destination, the Law Block, despite them lying on opposite sides of the campus (a fact she would know if she weren't a fresher in her first weeks).

'So are you doing anything tomorrow night?' I ask.

'Mmm, not sure yet.'

'How about a film? *Platoon* is on.'

'I don't like violence.'

'The Pogues are playing in town.'

'It's sold out.'

'Or we could go for a Chinese.'

'I hate Chinese.'

'Or Indian. Or Thai. Or Greek. Or . . .'

A clock is striking the hour behind us.

'I'm late,' she says, looking flustered under her beret. ('I'm late,' she would say, for different reasons, six months later.)

'Pick you up at eight?' I say, in a last-ditch move.

'OK,' she says, rushing off with a bag over her right shoulder and her left hand holding the beret on as she runs.

('You were like a terrier with a stoat,' she said later. 'And I was afraid of being locked out of the lecture. So I said yes.')

I buy a denim shirt for the occasion, and some deodorant,

and (just in case, though I've never used one before and know there's no chance really) a packet of condoms.

The meal is an Italian: she has gnocchi with salad and me pizza and chips. Conversation is awkward – until the Chianti kicks in and we find some common ground. She's Leeds and I'm Manchester. Different cities, true, but we're both from working-class families, we're both only children, and we've both come straight to uni from inner-city comprehensives. Daisy confesses she feels ill at ease among the other first years in her hall, with their tales of backpacking in South-East Asia. I reciprocate with a parody of these Vietnam vets – middle-class kids who parade their gap years like battle scars. Daisy laughs. We talk about our parents, and how narrow their lives seem, and Daisy says that her parents' marriage is so grim that she knows she'll never marry, and I'm already so infatuated that hearing her say it comes as a disappointment. We describe our bedrooms at home, and name the books we've read and the bands we've seen, and recall the teachers who wrote us off as university material because of where we came from. A sense of alienation draws us together. We are a pair of ducks among geese.

('Excuse me. I'm no duck. All you're saying is we found a couple of things we had in common.')

This time, back at her hall, Daisy does ask me up (not up, strictly speaking, but inside and along, since her room lies on the ground floor). She goes off to make coffee in the communal kitchen, while I dither in her room between the only two places to sit, the plastic chair under her built-in desk or the edge of the bed. I'm worried the former position will look wimpish and the latter presumptuous, but finally settle on the bed – if I just perch on the edge she won't take offence, I decide. And really the bed is *all* edge: its narrowness prohibits more than one (slender) person from lying on it at one time. It's the right choice: when she returns carrying two mugs with lurid pink elephants on them, she plonks herself down next to me, and we chat while drinking the coffee until, mug drained, she switches position, sitting with her knees bent and her back against the bedhead, a switch that leaves her left foot close to my left hand, and though my first touch is involuntary (as I twist round to talk to her my index finger brushes her red-painted big toe) she doesn't take fright, and presently I touch her again, resting my hand casually on her left arch, and then stroking it, and then, less surreptitiously, running the hand from her toes to her ankle, in a gentle massage which she seems to like and which gives me the courage, when she closes her eyes, to stretch across (no easy manoeuvre, so contorted is my posture) and kiss her on the lips.

She kisses me back. ('No, I didn't. I just let you kiss me.' 'Rubbish, you were enjoying it.' 'I'm not saying I didn't enjoy it but I stayed passive.' 'Not the next time you didn't.')

The next time is a week later, after the cinema (not *Platoon* but *Manon des Sources*), and the venue is her room again, and this time we succeed – God knows how – in lying alongside each other, hip to hip, or rather (since she's so small) hip to stomach, in which position our mouths are level and our lips can't help but meet. Far from not kissing me, she puts her tongue in my mouth, which no girl has ever done to me before, apart from Tracey Shindler, as an experiment, when we were thirteen.

Kissing and being kissed by Daisy is amazing. We're in love. ('You were in love. I was weak.')

Love demands that I see her every day but she says she wants to take things slowly. I don't doubt her sincerity but I know that taking things slowly will work against me – that as time passes, and the disorientation and loneliness of being a fresher pass with it, she may decide our relationship is a mistake, just as joining the Archaeology Society and the Mountaineering Club were mistakes, and that if she's going to make the most of university, and meet new people, she needs to drop me, like a dog dropping a slobbery old tennis ball, and instead, as Ollie would put it, play the field. I also know she has underestimated her attractiveness – I've seen other men looking at her when we go out, and though I've tried to stop *her* seeing *them* the day will come when I'm not there and someone moves in on her. And since that somebody will be richer and better-looking than I am, odds are she will welcome his attentions. If she were committed to me, such problems wouldn't arise. But she refuses to accept me as her 'boyfriend', though I describe myself as such to anyone who asks and several who don't.

('You were so possessive. It got on my tits.' 'Whereas I got nowhere near your tits.' 'Come on, you're exaggerating – I wasn't *that* mean.')

True enough, she isn't that mean. Though the drawback of her narrow bed is that we have to lie on our sides, with no movement except hand and mouth movement, the advantage is that our bodies touch at all points (if they didn't one of us would fall out). And sometimes, instead of lying face to face, we lie with our backs to the wall, me hard up against it with Daisy cradled in front of me. She says she feels safe like that, with her back pressed against my chest and my right arm wrapped round her waist – so safe she usually falls asleep, which can be uncomfortable (my left arm, squashed, gets pins and needles), but is also in some ways a relief: asleep, she's perhaps not aware of my hard-on. I sometimes think how nice it would be to lie on top of her. But that's more than she will allow. And in effect we're equally intimate sideways, whether spooned or lip to lip. Though we keep our clothes on, both of us get very excited. It's chaste but extremely hot.

('Hot because the central heating was on, maybe. But I don't remember getting excited. If I had been, I'd have had sex with you. It's not as if I was a virgin.' 'I thought you were.' 'I tried telling you but you were so jealous you wouldn't listen.' 'Me, jealous?' 'Yes, you, Ian. Very jealous indeed.')

One night, after a month or so of this, we go to my place for the first time. I'd have asked her earlier but for a fear she'd be put off – with five men as tenants, the house is fairly squalid. (Don't imagine the Japanese postgrads are any more domesticated than we are: they leave their empty beer cans everywhere.) From coffee in the living room, we proceed to my bedroom. On the bed, which though a single is eighteen inches wider than Daisy's bed, we do our usual immobile, sidelong thing, front-to-back followed by mouth-to-mouth. In between the kissing, she asks me to tell her what I've been reading or watching on television, another routine of ours and one which always turns her on. ('I liked hearing you talk, that's all – you made me laugh.') Then she rolls over and lies flat, allowing me to perch between her thighs and rub my hands over her body, as I've never been able to before. Midway through this, my circling hand movements now focusing on her breasts and a second button already undone, I hear the front door slam, and footsteps clump upstairs, then Ollie's voice call out 'Ian?' For a horrible moment I think he's going to walk in, but I keep silent and after a pause the footsteps continue, and the door to his bedroom opens and closes, and then music – U2 – starts up on the other side of the wall. 'Who's that?' Daisy asks. 'Just Ollie,' I say. 'I like his taste in music,' she says, and laughs, and kisses me, and sits up and unclips her bra at the back, and I finally get to feel her naked breasts, and to kiss her nipples, and all the time U2 are streaming through the wall and desire is streaming through Daisy, and though she won't allow me inside her jeans, grabbing my hand as I try to unzip them and whispering, 'Not today, chuck,' I'm far from discouraged, since 'Not today' isn't a refusal so much as a 'Maybe next time', when she isn't having a period.

('I wasn't having a period. I just didn't feel ready. I don't think I'd ever have felt ready. But I had to say *something*.')

Though she won't take her blouse off, I'm excited enough anyway and feel amazed that we're together when a girl like Daisy could have her pick of men. I even feel grateful to Ollie, but for whose re-immersion in sport and estrangement from me I might never have met Daisy – and whose arrival and choice of music tonight have undoubtedly played a part in advancing our sex life, even if it hasn't advanced to sex itself.

The sense of gratitude lasts as long as the time it takes for Daisy to kiss me, say she must get back, straighten her clothes, open the bedroom door and step out onto the landing. Had I opened it, the door would have made less noise, because I know how to turn the knob so it doesn't rattle. Even so, I'm surprised Ollie could hear it above the music, which he must have done, because before we've reached the stairs, there he is standing in the door frame of his room, bollock-naked.

I doubt Daisy's giggle is meant to be flirtatious. But that's what she does, giggle. And though Ollie looks embarrassed, and mumbles, 'Sorry, just wondered what was going on,' he's not as quick to go back inside his room as he might be. How much time Daisy has to clock his genitalia is beside the point: since she'd not seen *me* naked, she can't have been making comparisons. What is important is that Ollie had time to clock her. Granted, he would have seen her eventually; I couldn't expect to keep her a secret for ever. But that he saw her then, in the semi-darkness, with her cheeks glowing and her eyes burning and (frankly) sex coming off her in waves, made all the difference.

('Sex wasn't coming off me in waves. We were just having fun.' 'Fun?' 'Yeah, Ian, fun – remember fun? It was never serious between us, but you were fun to be with back then.')

When I return from walking Daisy to her hall, Ollie's waiting for me, on the landing, not naked now but in a silk dressing gown with a tasselled belt. And his words are pretty much the same as Daisy's were earlier, bar a change of tense and the insertion of enraptured italics: 'Who was *that*?'

As I say, my memory sometimes lets me down. But I'll never forget those first few weeks with Daisy.

'Global warming?' Ollie said. 'Give us a break.'

'Come on, what else could it be? Look at the weather we've had. Floods, droughts, hurricanes, earthquakes.'

'Next thing you'll be on about the ozone layer.'

'Absolutely, because –'

'And the melting of the polar ice caps.'

'Yes, they're becoming a major –'

'And rising sea levels.'

'The experts say –'

'A bunch of hippies working for Greenpeace aren't experts. The real scientists take a different line.'

'Which scientists are those?'

'The ones you lot don't bother to read.'

Ollie cast his eyes around the table and grinned, implicating us all. It was four against one – a relay team against a solitary athlete – and he was enjoying himself. At university, he'd had only me to steamroll. Since then he'd swung whole juries. Four against one was easy.

We were outside, on the terrace, at the metal table, with candles and tapers brightening the muggy dark. Daisy had told us that the meal would be simple, and perhaps by her standards it was: red mullet soup with saffron followed by saddle of lamb with couscous (cheese soufflé was the veggie alternative). Preparing the meal had taken her all evening. But Daisy prided herself on looking after friends. More than once she nervously asked whether 'everyone' – meaning one person in particular – was enjoying the meal. Ollie twice chided her for 'fussing' and, though he showed no signs of resenting her special guest, I certainly did.

An owl tooted its horn from the fields. It was good to know, after this morning, that there were still owls.

'Global warming is a fact,' Milo said, taking the baton. 'Only the oil companies and their stooges deny it.'

'I deny it too,' Ollie said.

'Bumblebees in January can't be right,' Em said.

'Nature changes. It's called evolution.'

'What do you know?' Daisy said, not-so-gently mocking him.

'More than you think.'

I strained to catch an undertone. But if he suspected Daisy's relationship with Milo, he wasn't letting on. They were next to each other, close enough to paddle hands or play footsie. But Ollie's only concern was to win the argument.

'One hot summer and everyone says the planet's fucked,' he said. 'There were hot summers when I was a kid. When we came here in '76, it didn't rain once.'

'Rainfall's not the issue,' Milo said, prompting a vigorous my-word-no nod from Daisy. 'We're talking about rising temperatures and the long-term effect of greenhouse gases.'

'Read the research and you'll find there's no consensus. Anyone heard of tropospheric cooling?'

We all shook our heads. Ollie paused to savour this triumph – ignoramuses! – before going on.

'The troposphere is the lower level of the atmosphere – the

first twelve miles or so, below the stratosphere, where all the weather comes from. Anyway, these two guys have done some research and they've found the troposphere isn't hotting up, it's getting cooler. Which blows the global-warming theory out of the water. Meanwhile, another scientist has found the glaciers aren't receding, they're advancing. And others even argue that carbon dioxide emission has had a beneficial effect – it's made the planet more lush for plants.'

'So you think we should sit back and do nothing?' Em said, looking to me for support – in her view, to deny global warming is as bad as denying the Holocaust. I sipped my wine and turned away. It would have been easy for me to rebut Ollie. But why give a cancer victim a hard time? Besides, I was enjoying seeing him get the better of Milo.

'Man shouldn't play God with the climate,' he said. 'I think we should know our place.'

'Know our place and wait for Armageddon,' Milo said. 'Deny my girls the chance of a future. Deny your Archie a future. Deny yourself a future. That's a great solution.'

No one should resort to sarcasm in a debate. I can remember Ollie wiping the floor with me on the few occasions I made that mistake. But with Milo he simply smiled and said: 'If you've a better solution, I'd like to hear it.'

The monologue that followed was predictable: wind farms, solar energy, carbon management, blah-blah – we didn't need some crappy artist to regurgitate it all. Yet Ollie listened respectfully. It took me a while to work out why: that phrase about being denied a future had sent a chill through him.

Finally Milo wound up. Darkness brushed against the windows. An awkward silence fell.

'Dessert anyone?' Daisy said, breaking the spell.

As Em joined Milo in condemning the wickedness of plastic bags and cheap air travel, Daisy and I carried the plates inside.

The washing-up bowl was full of hot water, and though she said she would do it later, I insisted. We took our places at the sink, me with a dishcloth, her with a tea towel, like a couple from the 1950s.

I saw no point beating about the bush.

'Archie told me about not going to school,' I said.

'We should have told you long ago,' she said. 'It upsets Ollie to talk about it, that's all.'

'I noticed the tensions between them.'

'Ollie finds it hard. Archie can be horrible – to me as well. He's all anger and hormones.'

'I was the same at his age.'

'Me too. But my parents were crap. We've tried not to be.'

'You're wonderful parents,' I said, though they hadn't been: children need time and attention, and Ollie and Daisy were too absorbed in their careers to set consistent standards. With a different partner and lifestyle, Daisy would have been a good mother. But I could hardly say that, so I tried to be positive instead.

'Coming on holiday is bound to help,' I said.

'We had to drag him here. He wanted to stay in London.'

'I'm sure he'll sort himself out,' I said. 'He used to be such a sweet kid.'

'I'm surprised you remember.'

'Of course I remember. When he first started walking, for instance, and . . .'

Back and forth we went over the sink: I'd pass her a sudsy plate and she'd dry it, and we'd recall the happier times when Archie was little.

'We make a good team,' I said, passing her a bowl with cherries painted round the rim.

'We do,' she laughed, before lowering her voice. 'By the way, what do you think of Milo?'

'Oh, you know,' I said, trying my hardest, 'who could fail to like him?'

'I'm sorry Bianca's not here. She's a textile artist. She dotes on him. They're a lovely couple.'

'I'm sure they are,' I said, though I wondered how exclusive Milo's coupling was.

'He's so great with his kids, too,' she said.

Too? What else did she think he was so great at? Not wanting to know, I dumped the last few knife blades on the draining board, shook the froth from my hands and headed for the bathroom.

Daisy and Ollie met that night outside my bedroom, then. Need I go on? Still, what looks inevitable in hindsight did not appear so at the time. For instance, how am I to know, when I meet Daisy for a drink in a bland off-campus pub that I've specifically chosen because of its lack of appeal to students, that Ollie will be waiting for us, alone at the bar, a 'coincidence' he has planned after sneaking a look in my diary, in which I foolishly set down the time and venue alongside Daisy's name? And should I see through Daisy's deceit when she turns up at the house the following week not at seven, as arranged, but at six, with Ollie not yet out for the evening and me not yet in, a 'mistake' that allows them an hour alone together? Because I'm in love with her, and he's my friend, I want to think the best of them. But the best, as far as they're concerned, is to be with each other, with me nowhere in sight. I don't think they actually do it until the Saturday night, four weeks later, when they break it to me that they've been 'seeing' each other; doing it is their reward to themselves for being honest with me, never mind that they've been dishonest for the previous month. I'm even willing to acknowledge their 'sensitivity' in not doing it in

Ollie's bedroom, where I would have heard them. Still, they betrayed me: what other word will do?

What they fail to foresee is how expert I will become at sleuthing. It begins the night they break it to me in the kitchen and stroll back to her hall of residence, not anticipating that I will follow at a safe distance, watch them go in and position myself in a clump of bushes with a clear view of her bedroom, and later (in the small hours and the bitter cold) creep up to the window and attempt to peer through the curtains. Irrespective of what I see (nothing), in my mind there's no doubt that they've overcome the drawbacks of her narrow bed and have been fucking for hours. My one hope is that Ollie is (in his own words) playing the field and, once sated with her body, will grow bored and whistle her off. Indignant though I feel on Daisy's behalf, I trust she will learn a useful lesson from this and recognise her rightful lover, the one who truly has her interests at heart.

I go on punishing myself – straining to keep a corner in the thing I love – not just that Saturday but for weeks afterwards. Every night I'm waiting in shadows when they arrive, arm in arm, at her hall of residence, Ollie having more or less moved in. Once the entrance door has swung shut behind them I head for my clump of bushes, reaching it in time to see the light come on in her room and one of them, usually Ollie, walk across to draw the curtains, the two wrinkled blue drapes meeting with disappointing efficiency in the middle. Any hope of catching them in flagrante is denied me, though I sometimes sneak up to the window ledge in the hope of hearing something, and on one occasion disturb the female student in the next room, who opens the window, leans out and seems less than convinced when I explain that I only stopped to tie my shoelaces. Thereafter, I stick to my clump of bushes, compelled to lodge there every night, even though my feet are freezing, my heart is breaking, and my espionage affords no view of its targets.

I remember Daisy lying with her back to me and my arm curving round her body and how secure that made her feel. So secure that she took up with someone else.

My academic work suffers. But I've no interest in law anyway. And I'm not so eaten up with jealousy as to give up books: while I sit there in the bushes I read *Crime and Punishment* several times with the aid of a pencil torch purchased in Woolworths (my only sleuthing tool apart from the sleeping bag and brandy flask that get me through colder nights). Carousing students sometimes pass close by in the darkness and more than once I think I've been spotted, but no one comes to investigate. Campus security barely exists: I could store several tons of gelignite in the bushes and no one would notice. Indeed, had my two stalkees not been alerted to my presence, the vigil might have lasted indefinitely. (Is it the torch that gives me away? The print of my nose on the window-pane? Or have I become the subject of campus gossip?) Once again, though I hate to admit it, they go about their task with sensitivity, doubling back from the swing doors one night to intercept me on my way into the bushes, inviting me to Daisy's room, setting aside their anger at being spied on, and explaining that – hurt though I must feel and sorry though they are to be the cause – it is time I accepted their relationship, because it's deep, the real thing, love, and were it not for Daisy's aversion to marriage (which Ollie, winking as he says this, hopes to cure one day) they would probably be engaged by now, for they know, as surely as anyone knows anything, that they're in this together for life.

The word 'marriage' almost does the trick. I've been tortured by images of them fucking. By telling me their relationship is more than sexual, they remove the carnal sting.

The other thing that consoles me is Daisy saying, when Ollie wanders off to the kitchen to make us all coffee, 'I'm late. My period, that is. Don't tell Ollie I told you. God knows what we'll do. I'm not ready to have a baby, can't face an abortion and don't believe in marriage – what a mess.' To confide in me like that Daisy must genuinely be fond of me, I realise. And though I feel bitter that she rejected me, she helps me get over that, too, when we meet (unbeknown to Ollie) one day the following week, and discuss our relationship, and she puts me right about my various misapprehensions: 'Ollie's my lover, but you're my friend. And that means – well, I don't have to tell you. My period came, by the way. Phew.'

I don't have to tell you. What she means, I grasp at once, is that though she's infatuated with Ollie it's me to whom she feels closer and finds it easier to talk. Knowing that helps heal my torment.

Ollie also helps, in more practical ways: one, by passing me his lecture notes, so I can catch up; two, by insisting we play golf or squash at least once a week; three, by telling me, over a drink, that if ever he breaks down Daisy's resistance he wants me to be his best man.

I don't become his best man because the pregnancy scare passes and Daisy rejects his proposals. But the significance of the invitation never leaves me. Best man, closest friend, deadliest rival.

One Sunday in the summer term the three of us hire bikes and explore the countryside as a threesome. Cycling along, Ollie recounts some of his adventures at Sandhurst, a series of hair's-breadth escapes, miracles of endurance and disasters turned triumphs. Daisy, captivated, loves him for the risks he took and he loves her for being so girlishly, pliably impressed by them. Impatient and irritated (if he was such a fucking military hero at Sandhurst, why did he quit?), I pedal away from their cosy little peloton and speed ahead, only to find Ollie coming after me. We race each other to the next village, where we stop at a pub, Daisy rolling in ten minutes behind us. Despite the difficulties, the outing's adjudged a success, and we make plans for several more.

Under Ollie's wing, Daisy becomes a swan. It's her destiny. They're a couple. I have to let go.

By the end of that summer, during which I work in a pub in Prestatyn and have sex with two women (one of whom likes to be roughed up), I reckon to be cured.

And I was cured, until Badingley.

'Looks lovely,' Em said. 'What is it?'

'Blueberry sorbet with rosemary oil and meringue grissini,' Daisy said.

'I don't know how you do it.'

'There are peaches or plums if you prefer.'

'I'm fine with the sorbet.'

'With or without the meringues?'

Em hesitated and I threw her a look. I didn't mean to imply that meringues were a bad idea for someone who was or *ought to be* watching her weight, but I fear that's how she took it, because her 'With' was spoken with defiance and she glared at me as she took the dish, as if to say, 'Fuck you, I'll eat what I like, what's it matter if I'm half a stone heavier than the diet freaks recommend, surely enjoying myself is more important, we only have the one life, and being thin isn't the same as being healthy, look at you, Ian, you're down the gym half the week but when it comes to being virile . . .' – *as if* to say all that but instead turning to Ollie and saying: 'Has Ian told you about his disciplinary hearing?'

I hadn't, of course. Nor did I intend to, what with Milo

present, a virtual stranger, and a sultry night in the middle of nowhere being the wrong time and place. Em only brought it up to get her own back for the look I'd given her. Or to punish me for not persuading Ollie to tell Daisy about his tumour (which she knew from my shiftiness I hadn't). Or for ducking out of the global-warming argument. Or because she'd hardly seen me all day. Or for failing to give her a child. Whichever, it was malicious.

'Sounds intriguing, Ian,' Ollie said. 'Do tell.'

I told, sensing the lightness drain from the evening as I did: Campbell Foster, his long record of misbehaviour, the bullying episode, my intervention, his defiance, my escorting of him to see Mrs Baynes, her lack of support, his mother's complaint, the failure of the school governors to have the matter sorted before the end of term, which meant the case had been hanging over me for two months.

'The governors meet on Wednesday,' I said.

'Ian's last free day before term begins,' Em added.

'Unless they suspend me,' I said, 'in which case I'll be free for some time.'

'Poor Ian,' Daisy said, 'what an ordeal.'

'Sounds like you need a good lawyer,' Ollie said.

'When you say you "escorted" him,' Milo said, 'how exactly?'

Bastard for asking. Pale moths flew at the flames and fell away. I'd a feeling of being spied on from the darkness, by some loony with binoculars and a gun.

I explained that I'd taken Campbell by the ear: not grabbed, squeezed, pinched, pulled, yanked or any of the words since used by others, but – as was the case – taken.

'You didn't belt the little bleeder?' Ollie said.

'Of course not.'

'You do have quite a temper sometimes.'

'I don't know what you're talking about,' I said. I did know what he was talking about but to connect the two events was absurd.

The candles blazed around us like a theatre set, with me in the spotlight, centre-stage.

'With a name like that, Campbell's black I take it?' Ollie said.

'We're a multi-ethnic school. It's of no relevance.'

'You aren't being accused of racism?'

'Not exactly,' I said.

'Not *exactly*?'

'There are no grounds. But it could come up.'

'That's outrageous,' Daisy said. 'If there are no grounds, how can it come up?'

'That's what local authorities are like these days,' Ollie said, with weary familiarity. 'Political correctness, et cetera.'

'It's not the local authority,' Em said, taking it personally because she works for one. 'There's been some previous history with the boy.'

'Ian told us that,' Daisy said, on my side. 'He's obviously a troublemaker.'

'I mean some previous history between him and Ian,' Em said, dragging me deeper in.

I avoided looking at Em. She should have kept her mouth shut. But I didn't want to seem ruffled.

'Long story,' I said, and told it.

For the past few years I've run the football team at school – which is ironic when you consider that ball smacking me in the face when I was five, but in a school with only one male member of staff, who else was there? It took me ages to get permission to start a team. Even then I met resistance. The only games allowed at school were non-competitive games – 'cooperative games' as they were called by Mrs Baynes, to whom individualism was taboo. I won her round with talk of teamwork, mutual encouragement, morale-building, an equal role for boys and girls, everything short of doing without goal-posts. And because the kids themselves were strongly in favour, along with their parents (the boys and dads anyway), football was installed on a trial basis. My role as coach was to develop 'standards of excellence', while pretending every kid was equally good – the great fear being that someone might be emotionally 'injured'. At first I stuck to training (heading, passing, keepie-uppie), but the kids grew bored without a game so for the last ten minutes it would be Reds against Blues, with even sides and debatable refereeing decisions to ensure a draw – a 'joint win', as Mrs Baynes called it. She once came along to watch and told the kids to think of themselves as ants, prospering by working together. To teach humans to emulate ants struck me as unhelpful. But I played along, so the kids could play football.

'Team football' flourished, until it came to picking a football team. The non-competitive ethos had all but obliterated school teams from the area, but a few remained and I arranged half a dozen fixtures. Mrs Baynes was anxious: how would the children feel were they to lose? How would they feel if they weren't selected in the first place? Every child who wanted to play must be included, she said. In a school of 160 pupils that wasn't practical, so we compromised by keeping the team to Years Five and Six, with the rest of the school assured their time would come. By Year Six, most girls have outgrown football, and most boys without talent realise it and opt out. So in the end, for our first fixture, we had a team of eighteen, which with a flexible use of substitutes worked fine.

In my experience black kids are better footballers than white kids: stronger, faster, more agile, more adept with the ball. And one of the best footballers to come through our school was Campbell Foster, who would have been good enough to play for the school at seven had we allowed it. Unfortunately, he was also horribly selfish with the ball. And when things weren't going his way, he would lose interest, sulk, walk off, abuse his teammates, and (literally) score own goals. At the start of his final year last autumn, I had great hopes of him nonetheless and made him captain for the first game. (We have a rota system for captaincy, as you might expect, but I meant it as a vote of confidence and he knew it.) If we had won that game, he might have prospered, but we lost by the odd goal, largely because at crucial moments Campbell refused to pass, as I made a point of explaining to him afterwards. For the next game I was referee as well as coach, a not unusual case of doubling up, and substituted Campbell early on for dangling from our opponents' goalposts and refusing to come down (we were losing three–nil at the time). I gave him a talking-to after that and it seemed to help: thanks to his goals, our next two games were victories (a word I tried to avoid with Mrs Baynes, who preferred to speak of 'advantageous score margins'). But in the next game, I sent him off when he punched an opponent. Campbell claimed the other boy had hit him first. But even if he did, that was no cause for retaliation, and as a punishment, I didn't pick him for the sixth and last game of the season – back in March, three months before the incident in the playground.

'That's the history between us,' I said, nodding assent as Ollie held the bottle over my glass.

'Sounds like you dealt with him perfectly fairly,' Ollie said.

'But you shouldn't have said what you did,' Em said.

'I meant it affectionately,' I said. 'My mum used to say it to me.'

'What?' Everyone was looking in expectation.

'Ian called him a little monkey,' Em said.

'As a mild rebuke, not in anger. He'd just run the length of the pitch, hogging the ball, and scored. "Very good, Campbell, but next time pass to someone, you little monkey." What's racist about that?'

'*I* know you didn't intend to be racist,' Em said. 'But did he know?'

'He was fine. He took it in good heart.'

'It came out later. After the ear business he told his mum you'd called him bad names.'

Everyone fell silent.

'I feel like you're cross-examining me,' I said to Em.

'I'm playing devil's advocate. I know what tribunals are like.'

'She's right, Ian,' Ollie said. 'It pays to have your defence ready.'

'I don't need a defence. I can handle this. I'm innocent.'

'Sorry, mate, but that's where you're wrong.'

At that point Daisy stood up and offered herb tea and coffee, so I never discovered which of my assertions Ollie was refuting. I forget what else was said: doubtless Milo in his smarmy way expressed sympathy and hoped the tribunal would clear my name. Remorseful, Em reached for my hand but I pulled it away. I knew her motives had been benign – to stop me 'bottling things up' and get Ollie to advise me. But to drag up every last detail was painful.

We sat on for an hour, with the smoky tapers in a square around us and Cheddar and blue Stilton on the table. I can't remember much of what was said once we retreated indoors, except for Daisy apologising for the accommodation again and saying how she wouldn't blame us if we never spent another weekend with them. Don't be daft, Em said, but I was thinking, no, we won't spend any more weekends with you because I'm not going to be humiliated like that again and anyway Ollie will soon be dead.

'I think I'll hit the hay,' Em said, shortly afterwards. It was late, and she often gets tired. More surprising was to hear Ollie saying 'Me, too': he's usually the last to go. Perhaps the cancer was affecting him, though in his place I'd certainly have stayed up longer, to be on guard, since Milo and Daisy were no longer engaging with the rest of us but in cahoots prattling about art on the sofa.

'And I need to take the dog for a walk,' I said, embarrassed by their intimacy.

'At this hour?' Em said. 'Take his lead in case he runs off.'

'It's OK. I won't go far.'

Rufus's ears had pricked up when I said 'walk', and he hauled himself from under the table and padded behind me down the corridor to the front door. Em was just ahead and, eager to make up, paused to kiss me at the foot of the stairs. She raised her eyebrows as she did. Putting our row to bed, I raised mine back, in sign language. *Long day; yes, too long. Sorry about earlier; no worries. Be quick, I want you in bed; you bet.* Before I'd got the lead on Rufus, she was already over my head, creaking across the landing to our room.

There's nothing like the cosmos to put things in perspective. And the million chaste stars overhead stopped me thinking about Daisy and Milo for at least ten minutes, the time it took to walk Rufus up and down the drive. A sliver of moon grew from the shade of its dying double. I'd rarely seen so clear a night and felt in no rush to re-enter the house. When I'd noticed the ancient picnic table in the orchard the previous day, I'd wondered what it was for – surely no one would sit down to eat at so ramshackle a structure. Now, as I lay prostrate on it, four wooden planks beneath my back, I embraced it as an observatory or planetarium: unhampered by trees and hedges, I could see to the horizon in all directions. And what a sky, so bright it seemed to be uplit from earth, or reflected back, as if the planets were our own lives glittering down at us. Off his lead, nose to the grass, Rufus snuffled for hedgehogs and field mice, then darted back, bemused by my horizontality, to lick my hands. I had folded them beneath my head so that I lay at a slight tilt, with the Plough straight ahead of me, the one constellation I could still confidently identify, though as a child I knew them all by heart. Every minute or so, there'd be a sudden swish at the edge of vision, like a silver zip being pulled down. But by the time I looked, it would be gone. I couldn't remember seeing shooting stars during the weeks I'd sat outside Daisy's hall of residence. But I remembered the sensation of being shut out, and of life behind a lamplit window going on without me. Here it was happening again.

There was a difference, though – not my being older, or married, or knowing it was Milo rather than Ollie in there, but the fact that the downstairs windows were tall and uncurtained. If I turned sideways, I could see them, two heads together on the sofa, not together-together, kissing, but close enough to make an innocent observer assume they must be a couple – and close enough to make me peel myself from the picnic table and move in for a better view. From what I could make out, they were perched at opposite ends of the sofa, facing each other – too far apart to be holding hands, but with their legs up and (I guessed) their feet touching in the middle. Whatever it was they were discussing had made them animated, with Milo waving his arms about and Daisy shaking her head. I felt sick, as sick as Ollie, but to stand there and watch, knowing they couldn't see me, was irresistible. It was only when Rufus appeared, jumping up to lick my face, that I withdrew into the darkness, afraid his movements would catch their attention. I took up residence on the table again. Next time I turned to peer in, the two figures had gone. To separate beds? Or to embrace in a quiet corner somewhere? Anything seemed possible.

A gust stirred in the blackness, polishing the stars. Despite the warmth of the night, the wood of the picnic table felt damp beneath my back and after a while I pulled myself up and sat cross-legged, staring out across the fields and imagining I could hear the roar of breakers beyond them. What had cured me all those years ago was Daisy telling me that she loved Ollie as she could never love anyone else. The inevitability of it was her story, and had gone on being her story, and I believed it, as I also believed, paradoxically, that she felt more comfortable with me than with him. I remember a night back at the house in my third year – them on the sofa, me in a chair. We were talking about the kind of lives we wanted after graduating: where we'd live, what kind of work we'd do, how many children we'd have, the usual hopes and dreams. Suddenly Daisy slid down from her seat and knelt at Ollie's feet, or rather between his feet, laying her head on his left thigh and reaching towards his face with her right hand, which he took and held, before putting her fingers in his mouth one after the other. I've since wondered if they meant it as a taunt. But I'm sure they didn't notice my hard-on. And at the time I took it as a spontaneous declaration of desire: she was in thrall to his body and so was he.

Now she was in thrall to Milo.

I felt disorientated, under the stars. Did it matter that Ollie was dying and his relationship with Daisy falling apart? We weren't as close as we used to be. I only saw them every few years. And yet it did matter, not for nostalgic reasons but because the life I'd led, and the choices I'd made, rested on Ollie and Daisy staying together.

I was surprised by how angry I felt, not just with Milo and

Daisy, but with Ollie too. Why wasn't he fighting the tumour? Why wasn't he fighting Milo? He was too accepting, too resigned.

I was angry with him for another reason: that reference to my having a temper – as if he suspected me of being violent with Campbell Foster because I'd a record of violence in the past. The accusation was deeply unfair and concerned an episode from years before which Ollie had misunderstood.

It happened one Sunday, shortly after he and Daisy got together. The previous weekend – lonely, miserable, and with time to kill – I'd gone shopping in town and returned with a tea mug I liked both for its design (a big looping handle and an ace of diamonds motif) and its rich turquoise colour. That morning I couldn't find it. I searched my bedroom and the kitchen, without success. It seemed plain the offender was Ollie, at that moment in bed with Daisy in her hall of residence. A furtive search of his room didn't unearth the mug. But he had seen me with it. And there'd been a rare exchange between us earlier that week, when I might even have mentioned buying it. Had he broken it and chucked it in the bin? Hidden it to taunt me? Stolen it as a dare to amuse his rugby friends? Or to amuse Daisy, another of his thefts from me? As I sat there drinking coffee from one of the landlord's ugly, chipped mugs I seethed with rage and thought about trashing Ollie's room. At that very moment the smallest of the three Japanese students, Yukio, walked in. He was carrying two mugs, one of them mine. I didn't wait for explanations, just snatched the mug and, leaving it on the worktop for safety, launched myself at him, yelling oaths he couldn't understand. He fell backwards on the brick floor, banging his head. I continued to shout as he lay there concussed. Not for one moment did I think of kicking him. On the contrary, once I'd worked out my aggression, I bent down to help him to his feet. He misunderstood, though, cowering as I leaned over him. Just then the front door banged and Ollie walked in. Misreading the situation, he rushed to restrain me. I explained about the mug, omitting to mention that my surge of anger had been caused by him. Helped upright, Yukio said he'd found the mug in the living room (where I'd watched television the night before) and was intending to wash it up. I apologised and shook his hand, saying the mug had enormous sentimental value, which wasn't altogether a lie. There were no repercussions – except that Yukio moved out not long afterwards and Ollie stored the episode away to use against me.

It's true I occasionally lose my temper. But I don't get into fights with men, and apart from obliging that slag in Prestatyn I've never been rough with women. For Ollie to bring up the Yukio incident, when I was facing charges of professional misconduct, was vicious and underhand.

But he's ill, I muttered to myself. He's lashing out against everyone and everything. The tumour is to blame, not him.

Below me, on the grass, Rufus began to whine: his master was acting strangely and he wanted to go in. I'd no idea of the time, or how long I'd been sitting there, but the air was chilly and the stars had lost their sheen. 'Come on, then,' I said, climbing down from the picnic table. As we moved towards the lit cube of the house, the only sound was the swoosh of grass wetting our feet, like an incoming tide.

'Is that you, Milo?' Daisy said, as I crept into the living room.

'No, it's me, Ian,' I said.

She was lying curled on the sofa where she'd been sitting with Milo. Her back was towards me and her dress had ridden up, exposing her thighs. As I stared, she rolled over, pulled the dress down and sat up.

'Sorry, I must have fallen asleep,' she said, and perhaps she had. But there was a wine bottle on the floor and her eyes weren't blotchy with tiredness but from crying.

'People went to bed,' she said, 'and I sat here talking to Milo, then he went to bed, too. I'd forgotten you were still up.'

'It's just as well I am. You'd have been here till morning.'

'It's comfortable enough.'

'You don't look comfortable,' I said. 'You look unhappy.'

'No, really, I'm . . .'

She wanted to deny it but the word 'unhappy' broke her defences and her chin trembled before she could say that she was fine. She turned her face away, and for a time I just stood there in the hope she'd cry herself out. But when the crying got louder, loud enough to wake people, I moved across to sit next to her – and as the cushions sagged with my weight, she turned towards me, arms theatrically held out and eyes tightly closed. I didn't know where to put myself but Daisy's arms locked around me, and my chest became a sponge for her tears. To stroke her and murmur 'There, there' seemed inadequate. But when she whispered 'That feels good' I stopped worrying and hugged her tighter.

We must have sat there like that – her head on my chest, my arms round her, both of us gently rocking – for ten minutes or more.

'Could you bear to get me some tissues?' she said, into my chest.

I grabbed a handful from the bathroom. While she sniffled into them, I lingered in the kitchen, pretending to hunt for a glass, so she'd have time to recompose herself.

'Poor Ian,' she said, accepting the water. 'You drive all this way for a jolly weekend and what do you get?'

'Never mind me,' I said.

'Your socks are all wet, look. How did that happen?'

She was right. My snooping in the grass had soaked them.

'Take them off – you'll catch a chill.'

'OK,' I said, reaching down, 'but it's you we should be worrying about. What's the matter?'

'I had too much wine at dinner. I always get tearful when I drink.'

'But there must be a reason. Tearful about what?'

'About Milo.'

Though the answer was no surprise, I couldn't hide my dismay.

'Oh.'

'It's finished. The marriage, our relationship, the lot. I'd no idea. I assumed everything was OK. Don't look at me like that, Ian.'

I wasn't conscious of looking like anything.

'I thought he was your client.'

'He is. Was. That's all over with.'

'He just ended things between you?'

'Yes. He's off to New York.'

'I'm sure you'll find someone else to take his place,' I said, as unsarcastically as I could.

'Of course. There are dozens of good art directors in London. But it's upsetting. I'll miss him terribly.'

'So what does he do for you that Ollie can't?'

'Don't be silly – Ollie isn't an artist.'

'Oh, so it's because Milo's an artist that you've been sleeping with him.'

'*Sleeping* with him? Where did you get that idea?'

'He just ended your relationship. You said so.'

'Our *business* relationship. It's he and Bianca who have broken up.'

'What?'

'She was only meant to be going home to the States for a

month. But things have been difficult for some time apparently and now she's announced she's staying. She's found a flat in Brooklyn, and a school for the girls. Milo says he's going to find a job and move nearby, so they can share childcare.'

'It makes sense. So why the tears?'

'I know it's silly. But he's a good friend. Bianca too. It always upsets me when friends break up.'

I took her hand to hide my impatience. To cry over someone like Milo would have been indulgent at any time but it was especially so now, with Ollie terminally ill. But she didn't know about the tumour, of course, and Ollie had sworn me not to tell.

'Those poor little girls,' she said.

'Kids are resilient,' I said, stroking her arm.

'It's sad all the same.'

If Daisy was so worried about kids being fucked up by their parents, she should look closer to home. But rather than say this, I kept stroking her arm.

'Let me get you a drink,' I said eventually.

'I've drunk too much already.'

'I'll take that as a yes.'

I fetched two clean wine glasses from the kitchen.

'Turn the lights off, will you?' she said.

I sat at the opposite end on the sofa, with my back to the armrest, just like her. Our knees were bent and our feet were touching. The only light in the room was moonlight.

'I can't believe you thought I was sleeping with Milo,' she said, more teasing than indignant.

'He's obviously attracted to you.'

'Is he?'

'Any man would be.'

'Ah, now you're being *gallant*.'

'I mean it,' I said. 'You know that.'

'Yes. You're very loyal. To me as well as Em.'

I wasn't used to her flirting with me. Nor to her slurring her words. But I would not have said she was drunk.

'I'm pleased you and Em are happy together,' she said.

'We are.' I wasn't going to mention the children issue. Or money problems. Or my occasional visits to websites.

'I used to worry about you,' she said. 'But things have turned out all right. Come and give me a hug.'

Or perhaps I was the one who suggested the hug. It doesn't matter either way. We'd been friends for over twenty years, and the hug was simply to celebrate that. But because Daisy was lying against the armrest, finding a position to hug her from was tricky. She seemed ready to sit up to make it easier, but instead I gently slid her towards me, and shoved her bottom towards the sofa back, and lay down next to her, so that we were together on our sides, just as we used to be on her narrow student bed, with each of us looking over the other's shoulder: a cheerful, tender, horizontal embrace. She was the one facing out and, firmly though I pressed into her, I felt in danger of falling backwards onto the floor, and for some reason – all that wine probably – I found this funny. My laughter wasn't out-loud but she registered the tremor through my body.

'What's the joke?' she said.

'I'm about to fall off.'

'We'd better sit up, then.'

'No, if you just shift and . . .'

The only shifting possible was for her to slide outwards and down, and me clamber inwards and up, and though the manoeuvre wasn't complex I found it awkward to effect, in part because I knew how we would end up, with me lying on top and her legs parted to accommodate me, a posture which would have shocked the other people in the house if they had seen us. Still, she didn't seem especially embarrassed by my shuffling movements, and even managed to tilt her head forward and drink from the glass which, despite lying flat, she'd hung on to and kept from spilling – further evidence, to me, that she couldn't be drunk.

'Oh, I do love you,' I said, speaking a truth but also parodying what people in our position traditionally say as a prelude to sex.

'Dear Ian,' she said, 'you're a good friend.'

Encouraged, I kissed her, chastely, on the brow, then no less chastely on each cheek, and nibbled her ears, which she refused to reciprocate, but she did grab my nose and waggle it, saying 'Nice big nose', and at that point I thought she must be drunk, because her eyes were closed, with a dreamy expression across her face, but I did also wonder if in saying 'Nice big nose' she meant to acknowledge she could feel what was happening in my groin, and as I kissed her on the chin (the last safe place I could think of) I decided she must have meant it, or couldn't not now be aware. Her eyes were still closed, happily, trustingly, almost as if she'd dropped off, and this gave me the courage to do the next thing, which was to kiss her lips, actually only one corner of her upper lip, but her eyes stayed shut so I kissed the opposite corner, and then each corner of the lower lip, at which point, feeling her stiffen, I thought about stopping – perhaps the friendly hugs had gone far enough. Except that she then seemed to relax again, so I kissed her some more, not lightly, either, and after that, or after my next kiss full on her lips, or the one after that, with my tongue in her mouth, or without a shadow of doubt after the kiss on her stomach when I'd pulled up her dress, there was no possibility of our stopping, not me anyway, not her either I'm sure, though she did say no, sharply, and push my chest as if to force me upward, but that no, and the subsequent noes, three or four of them, were reflex rather than genuine (belated attempts to prevent what she wanted to happen from happening) and I found them easy to stifle, and if her final noisy guilt-struck no, accompanied by a bite to my shoulder while her nails raked down my back, was certainly not lacking conviction, I sensed its purpose was to excite us both further, to add to our passion rather than offer resistance. I kept on going to the end, feeling her body quake beneath me in the aftermath, not because she was crying but because – I assumed – she too had come. The thought of Em, sleeping alone in all innocence upstairs, might normally – normally! – have taken the edge off my pleasure. But I felt triumphant, heroic, physically renewed, a shimmery gym-mirror version of myself, and, rather than recoiling, I gripped her tighter and kissed her some more, as if to resuscitate her. She had gone limp now, sad and rag-doll-like, defeated by her own desire. Once or twice she tried to push me off, not I think because she disliked the weight of me on her but from embarrassment. When I couldn't be budged she lay still again. At some point she reached for a tissue, and threaded it between her thighs, a gesture that made me kiss her on the cheek, the flow between us still strong as we lay there in the knowledge of what we had done, our hearts beating together and our legs intertwined, a position we'd not have altered for some time had we not heard footsteps on the gravel beyond the house, and immediately afterwards a key turning in the door along the corridor.

It's strange what spurts into your head when you're having sex. All the stranger in this case, since the memory, though an episode from university, did not involve Daisy.

One weekend during our second year, a friend of Ollie's from boarding school – Toby I think he was called – came up to stay. They left me out of their various outings but I was fine with that: we all compartmentalise, and if one of my old school friends had come to visit me I would have done the same. Still, as it happened, I did run into Toby. On the Saturday night, the sound of voices in the kitchen drew me down from the bedroom, and there, next to Ollie, on a high stool, was a stocky, red-haired young man drinking coffee out of my turquoise mug. Though Ollie looked far from pleased to see me, Toby insisted I join them, which I did, helping myself to coffee in another mug, which was old and cracked, but carefully controlling my temper. (It's typical of Ollie that, despite the earlier episode with Yukio, he'd simply not noticed Toby using my mug.) I'd been expecting some wealthy curled darling but was pleasantly surprised by Toby's geniality; he seemed almost relieved to see me, as if a weekend spent with Ollie was proving a strain. I must have stayed talking for an hour, and would have stayed longer but for an awkwardness that arose when we discussed their boarding school. I forget what led up to it, but having confirmed that Toby had been a prefect – or 'monitor' as they called them – I made some joke about the likes of him and me not being 'head boy material', with a meaningful nod at Ollie. Toby looked bemused for a second then flushed brick-red. Ollie quickly changed the subject. I made my excuses soon afterwards, aware I'd made some gaffe or spoken out of turn. Ollie didn't allude to the episode afterwards, except to comment that Toby was a good bloke, but like all gingers (a word he pronounced with two hard 'g's) quick-tempered and jealous. I inferred that Toby had been desperate to become head boy himself – and that my remark had annoyed him by rubbing it in. Perhaps he even thought that Ollie had been sneering at him behind his back, and that my comment was a pre-planned joke at his expense. You can never underestimate people's paranoia. I began to see why Ollie valued his friendship with me.

Later, as I came to know Ollie better, I saw the episode could be interpreted differently. What if Toby had flushed red from embarrassment at seeing his friend caught out? That's to say, what if Ollie had lied to me about being head boy? Parts of his past didn't quite hang together. Hearing him boast of his military adventures to Daisy, who rather than mock (just as we had mocked the gap-year vets) hung on his every word, I sometimes wondered if his time at Sandhurst had been quite so colourful, supposing he'd been there at all. His claim to have bought the very MG his father had once owned seemed a story in the same mould – more wishful thinking than reality.

Perhaps that's why the memory of Toby came back to me in Badingley. And Daisy wasn't quite as peripheral to the story as I implied. In fact, the reason Ollie was entertaining Toby that weekend was that Daisy had gone home to see her parents in Leeds. And the reason she'd gone home was to placate them, after a terrible scene a couple of weekends before. As Daisy tells it, Mr and Mrs Brabant turned up unannounced at her hall of residence at ten o'clock on a Sunday morning. Normally at that time Mrs Brabant would have been in church, confessing her sins, but Daisy's were the sins preoccupying her that day, specifically the sin of premarital sex. She and Ollie weren't caught in the act, but when he emerged from where he was hiding in the bathroom Daisy couldn't deny that he'd spent the night there. Her mother called her a lewd minx who'd be damned in Hell. Her father called Ollie a rutting goat who'd ruined his daughter. According to Daisy, what shut them up was Ollie saying how deeply he loved her and that he hoped to marry her if she'd only consent. According to Ollie, what did it was his public-school accent: a lordly sentence or two and the Brabants were tugging their forelocks. Within the hour, they scurried back to Leeds, where Daisy went to visit them two weeks later, to show that, whatever her sins, she was still a dutiful daughter.

She was of course mystified as to what had brought them in the first place. Intuition was my suggestion. But Ollie thought an anonymous letter or phone call more likely, and Daisy wondered whether someone had it in for them both, perhaps the next-door neighbour in her hall of residence who sometimes banged on the wall during their lovemaking. Whatever the reality, the stunt backfired. Rather than being driven apart, Ollie and Daisy drew closer, and have remained together – utterly loyal to each other – ever since.

Utterly loyal as far as I know. (You never do know, do you?)

Loyal until Badingley, when Daisy gave her body to me and these memories came surging back.

Snapped on, the chandelier hit us like a spotlight.

'Archie! What are you doing?'

'I could ask you the same question, Mum.'

'I'm sitting here with Ian, as you can see.'

'Hi, Ian.'

I would have preferred an 'Uncle Ian', but perhaps he was getting too old for that.

'Hi, Archie.'

'It's three in the morning, Mum. You never stay up this late.'

'I didn't feel sleepy.'

'Yeah, right.'

'What else would I be doing?'

'It's obvious what you've been doing. Drinking. There's an empty bottle on the floor and a whole load more on the table.'

Next to the bottle lay the tissue, which had fallen when Daisy adjusted her dress. But Archie didn't notice it and would have attached no significance to it even if he had.

'Give me a hug,' Daisy said, standing up and throwing her arms round him. 'I've been worried about you.'

She hung there with her hands round his neck, eyes closed, legs shaky, face against his chest. He put his right arm round her shoulders but kept his left hand in the pocket of his jeans, unsure what to do with it and embarrassed by the role reversal – a child forced to parent his parent. I too was embarrassed. Daisy seemed all over the place. Carry on like this and she'd give us away.

'What's up, Mum? You're being really weird.'

'You went off in such a rush,' she said, finally detaching herself and smoothing down her dress. 'All I knew was you were at a sleepover.'

'I've not been to a sleepover since I was nine.'

'You know what I mean – going to a pop festival and staying overnight.'

'Yeah, well, the gig was awesome but the campsite was crap. No room in anyone's tent and too cold to sleep outside. Some guys there were driving this way, so I got a lift to the top of the road.'

'You made some new friends, then?'

'*Ooh, goody, some new little friends for Archie*,' he sneered. Now her arms were no longer round him, normal hostilities could be resumed. 'Christ, Mum. Yeah, I met some people and chilled with them, and I'm probably going back tomorrow. Anyway, I'm off to bed.'

As he trooped upstairs, he made sure to clump on each wooden step. I began to see what Ollie and Daisy had to put up with.

'That was close,' I said, reaching for Daisy. 'You don't think he saw us?'

She lifted her hands to keep me at bay.

'It was dark in here,' she said. 'Probably not.'

'It's lucky you asked me to turn the light off.'

She wasn't listening so I didn't mention the rest of the luck. That he hadn't come in by the French windows. That we'd had time to straighten our clothes. That he'd failed to recognise the smell of sweat and sex.

'I'm going to bed,' she said.

'Me too,' I said. 'Pity it's not the same one.'

The semen-soaked tissue was still lying on the floor. I picked it up and dropped it in the waste-paper basket on my way to the kitchen.

Daisy was standing by the sink.

'Bad head,' she said, running the tap. 'I drank way too much.'

'You seem fine,' I said, not ready for excuses.

'This house is so weird,' she said. More denial: in a weird house, she was implying, people did weird things.

I grabbed her arm as she walked past, desperate to hold her again. She whirled round, as if I'd burned her.

'Don't you *dare*.'

Her anger would have upset me if I'd known her less well. But I shrugged and let her go. To come to terms with what we'd done would take time – till tomorrow morning at least.

Archie was right about the evidence of our debauchery. On the dining table, there were five empty bottles (one champagne, two reds and two whites), as well as two more in the living room. I found a cardboard box in the cupboard under the stairs and filled it as quietly as I could, adding an empty gin bottle (Ollie and I had been drinking G & Ts before supper) to fill the last space. I would have sworn I was sober but when I unlatched the door to the utility room, with the intention of depositing the box, I stumbled down the single step and pitched forwards onto the hairy blanket where Rufus had his bed. He had gone there on returning from our midnight excursion but it was pure chance I'd shut the door. Had he wandered through, might the spell have been broken and Daisy and I, embarrassed, drawn back from making love? Who knows. But finding myself on the hairy rug I hugged him in gratitude and, suddenly weary, lay down beside him, with a mixture of guilt and euphoria. The guilt was twofold: I'd betrayed both my wife and my best friend. But the euphoria was stronger: I'd finally fucked the first woman I loved.

Sunday

In the dream, Milo and I were digging holes while Daisy watched – whoever finished first would marry her. Milo's hole went down six feet and he was standing shoulder-deep in it, about to win, when his ribs flew apart like broken laths and the heart inside them became a brain – then a tumour. As the tumour wriggled on the ground, I heaped rocks on it. 'Ian,' it cried, turning into Ollie's face, 'Ian . . .'

The knock on the door was a gentle knock, as if intended for only one of us, and it came with a whispered 'Ian'. I slid from the sheets, appalled to be awake. After two hours on the rug with Rufus, I'd only just gone to bed.

'Ian!' I heard again.

'Coming!' I whispered back, trying not to wake Em.

I was coming but taking my time about it since the voice outside the door was Ollie's – the real Ollie, not the Ollie in my dream. My first thought was that Daisy had confessed to him. And though I realised before I turned the handle that a cuckolded husband, out for revenge, would be hammering and screaming at the door, not whispering through it, my hand on the knob was shaking, and not only from the alcohol of the night before.

'*There* you are,' Ollie whispered, though I was barely there at all.

He was wearing black nylon leggings and a black nylon top,

as if slicked in oil. I felt like the slithery one but it was he who looked the part.

'Come on,' he hissed, 'it's time.'

'What?'

'It's time for the race.'

'Which race?'

'The bike race. We talked about it last night, remember.'

I didn't.

'Let's get cracking before the others are up.'

Hung-over and half naked, I didn't have the energy to argue. I didn't have the energy to race, either, but that was beside the point. Even sober and dressed, I would have found it hard to resist Ollie, his hands tensing in readiness, the nerves twitching in his cheek. I grabbed a T-shirt, shorts and trainers as softly as I could, desperate that Em should sleep on. Despite my nausea, relief flooded through me. Ollie didn't know about last night. Nor – full of life as he was – did he appear to be dying.

How I dressed and got downstairs I've no idea. My body must have done it for me.

The double wooden doors to the garage were wide open, with two bikes propped against them. Crouched beside the spokes, Ollie was angrily pumping tyres.

The bikes were lean, with handlebars like rams' horns.

'Where did these come from?' I said.

'I rented them. There's a shop in the village.'

'They look pretty old.'

'They *are* old. They stopped making bikes like these in the 1970s. Take the red one. You'll need to raise the saddle. Daisy used it last.'

My bike at home is a mountain bike: thick frame, broad saddle, high handles, fat tyres. This bike had drop handlebars coiled in black tape, and the frame and wheels looked so thin I feared they'd buckle under me. Worst of all was the saddle, short in length, narrow in width, and viciously tapered at the front: even Daisy, with her little bum, must have struggled to perch on it, but at least she didn't have testicles to worry about. I wondered which would be worse, the injuries I'd get from staying in the saddle or those I'd suffer from falling off.

Though Daisy's legs are much shorter than mine, I raised the saddle only half an inch. I would ride with my bum in the air, as jockeys do.

'Helmet?' Ollie said, proffering a yellow plastic vented dome.

'Do we have to?' I said. A helmet would be horrendous in the heat.

'Up to you, mate.'

'Are you wearing yours?'

A matching yellow helmet sat high on his head. But he hadn't yet fastened the strap.

'Not if you're not,' he said.

It didn't seem reckless to do without.

We rode in parallel down the drive, Ollie to the left of the grass seam, me – wobbling – to the right. Reaching down to grip the drop handlebars felt precarious, so I rode with my hands on top of the fork.

At the end of the drive, we turned right into the lane. The blue sky had gone brown towards the horizon, as though scorched by the heat of the earth.

'We'll stick together to the coast,' Ollie said, 'so you get to know the route. Then turn round and race back. It's only twenty miles. It won't kill us.'

'Speak for yourself,' I said.

Of course it occurred to me that Ollie's energy level was abnormal – that the brain tumour could be making him manic.

I even worried about the effects a vigorous bike ride might have: under stress, mightn't a tumour swell and burst? But there was no resisting his enthusiasm.

As we rode, he rattled on about bikes. Raleigh now imported them from Taiwan, he said. And did I know that tubular tyres, like wine, improve with age? Oh, and by the way, when Reg Harris came out of retirement to become British sprint champion at the age of fifty-four, he was riding a Raleigh just like ours. Some of the talk was too technical for me: the relative virtues of derailleur gears and Sturmey-Archers, of cutaway lugs, light alloy forks and ring-brazed frames. He said he'd learned it not from cycling magazines but from his father, who when they came on holiday here had rented bikes from the same shop.

Ollie aside, the day was silent, just the whirr of spokes. The narrow lane ran through high arching hedgerows with wheat (not yet harvested) massing behind them and the two of us between, thus:

-(..)-

In his funereal nylon, Ollie set a gentle pace at first, cruising the three miles to the next village before forking left at a duck pond. After that, as we entered a pine forest, he pushed on. The day was too hot already and the shade between the firs brought no relief. My breath was heavier than Ollie's, my T-shirt wetter. I hung back, saving myself for the return. Not that I cared as much as he did about winning. But I didn't want to lose by a mile.

'This is the easy bit,' he said, slowing down so I could catch up. 'There are two big hills before the coast.'

'Oh good,' I said.

He looked at me in mock suspicion.

'You weren't up to any naughty business last night?'

'What?'

'Marital nooky – it dilutes the testosterone. You seem a bit sluggish. Real athletes never have sex before a race.'

'It's not a race, Ollie. It's a Sunday fun run.'

'Fun, yes. But also Round Two of the bet.'

It wasn't that I had forgotten but I needed to hear him confirm it.

'With five thousand quid riding on it.'

'Unless you want to double that. Feeling lucky?'

Did I say that or did he? I can't remember now. My palms were sticky and my head hurt from the night before.

I'd got lucky with Daisy. Or had I? Nothing felt real.

'Tempted?'

'No.'

'Where's your steel, man? Don't be a pussy.'

Silence hung heavy in the pines. The only breeze was our own momentum.

'OK, we'll double it.'

'Done.'

It was weak of me to get into it – but also logical. I was one–nil up already. And though I wouldn't call myself fit, I do ride to school every day, and had stepped up my mileage in the holidays, not (as Em alleged) to prepare for the contest but for the pleasure. Ollie, meanwhile, was ill.

For the next few miles the route was flat and I didn't touch my gears. But as we left the forest and reached the first hill – a short but steep ascent near a pig farm – I changed down. Whether too jerkily or in the wrong direction I don't know, but something jammed and clunked and the chain came off.

Ollie was off his bike and seeing to mine almost before I'd dismounted. The chain had caught between the sprocket and the frame. I thought he would need a lever to free it but a minute of writhing and it came clear. He fed the chain back on the teeth then held the rear wheel in the air and ran through the gears.

Behind him pigs were nosing through dry mud. The hedge swarmed with brambles and late-summer flies.

'I meant to warn you that the gears are sensitive,' he said, handing the bike back, his fingers as oil-black as his clothes. 'You should be fine now.'

I didn't doubt he'd taken the better bike but I trusted him to put mine in order.

'I'll wheel it to the top,' I said. We weren't yet racing, after all.

He pushed off, calling back over his shoulder: 'Daisy did the same thing. She hasn't a clue about gears, either. You're a right pair.'

I took it slowly up the hill, unable to suppress the memory, silently climbing to the summit with her, sweating, panting, soaked to the skin. I had always loved her. And last night she had loved me back.

Ollie was hovering on the ridge like a vulture.

'Suffering?' he said.

'A little.'

'You stayed up talking, then?'

'Yes.'

I remounted, ready to roll. Though the pig farm lay behind us, the smell lingered in my nostrils.

Once we were back, I'd catch her in private, to discuss the next step.

'How was Daisy?' he said.

'Sorry?'

'How did she seem?'

'Why ask me? She's *your* wife.'

'Doesn't mean I understand her. Do you understand Em?'

Did I? Not an unkind bone in her body, people said of her.

But bones are neither kind nor unkind. Bones are just bones. And Em was just Em, affectionate when I deserved affection but angry when I didn't, which seemed to be increasingly the case.

'Daisy's been distracted lately,' he said. 'I don't know why.'

It couldn't be the tumour, if he'd not told her. Was it Milo then? But she had assured me they were just friends.

'She seemed fine,' I said.

The descent wasn't steep but it was long and my neck hurt from reaching down to squeeze the brakes. In the flat along the bottom, the fields were being watered and where the spray fell across the road, mixing with dirt, the surface was muddy. Ollie, just ahead of me, had no mudguards and I laughed to myself as a stripe appeared up the middle of his back – a tyre-wide line of mud, brown on black, like the mark of Cain.

Em was my rock. But rocks aren't amenable, rocks offer no comfort, rocks can crush and kill – and lately she had hardened against me. Perhaps it would be better if we parted. Someone else could give her a child, while – with Ollie dead and Milo off the scene – I made a life with Daisy.

Mens sana in corpore sano, they say. But sometimes, when I'm exercising, wild thoughts invade me and I'm not what I am.

As we climbed the second hill, Ollie pressed ahead. It was another mile before I caught him up at a T-junction.

'It's straight across here,' he said, 'then down to the sea. OK?'

Though we rode alongside, he seemed to have run out of conversation. 'How was Daisy?' he had asked, clearly worried. Had he intuited that he might lose her, even before he died?

As we neared the coast, the landscape changed from grassland to bracken, a whiff of brine mixed in with sage and thyme. Bank holiday Sunday was the highpoint of the summer season, but it was early morning, and the beach we were heading for remote – the last half-mile an unmade road – and when we finally hit the shingle (a hit it was, the small smooth stones subsiding under our tyres and stopping us in a flurry and a smack), there were only a few sad fishermen to see, their angled green umbrellas serving as parasols. We dismounted and wheeled our bikes over the shingle, stopping at the tideline and sitting down, each of us with a drinks bottle unclipped from the frame, the water tepid and tasting of plastic but refreshing for all that. Our bikes sat upended behind us, like two pairs of giant spectacles, no breeze to stir the wheels, the sea a putrid turquoise. With our shoes and socks off, we sat throwing pebbles at a wooden stick (one point for hitting, three for knocking it over, first to twenty), a game that might have become serious and which I suggested, only half joking, might replace the bike race, but which Ollie, 17–16 behind, abruptly terminated. Time was short, he said, and we ought to go. I cooled my toes before we did. The waves were too languid to call breakers, flopping pathetically at my feet.

'Ready?' Ollie said.

'Ready.'

'First one to the house makes tea.'

'Do you want Assam or Earl Grey?'

'Fuck you.'

Up the unmade road, a fisherman was arriving with his gear and stared as we panted by. With those long legs of his, Ollie had all the advantages, and I was tempted to let him go. His morale would suffer terribly if I beat him again, and by losing I could atone for last night. Yet I owed it to him to compete. He would expect no less of me.

At the T-junction he was ahead by fifty yards or so, a gap

I could easily narrow if I chose, though he, for his part, could surely open it up again, since – terminally ill or not – he seemed to have plenty in reserve.

It was a cat-and-mouse game. Competitive, certainly, but not life-and-death. I wanted to win but there would be benefits in losing. So I told myself till we reached the second hill.

In retrospect, I may have misread what happened. I'd seen how quickly Ollie could negotiate hills, but he made no move on the first one and I'd little difficulty keeping him in my sights. On the plateau, I closed right up, into his slipstream. We were hunched low for maximum speed, our bodies flat against the frame, our heads beneath our shoulders. Glancing round, he seemed surprised to see me, then smiled. There are friendly smiles, and sarcastic smiles, and because I couldn't believe Ollie was feeling friendly – with me up his backside, not shaken off – I decided he was taunting me: *Wimp, sneak, get alongside, come on you puny whipster, overtake me and set the pace for a while, why should I do all the work here?* Provoked, I pedalled harder, my heart revving and my breath coming in clumps. As I crept up by his rear wheel, I was so focused on passing him I didn't see what happened, just felt the jolt, the judder of something striking my front wheel, an object large enough to tilt the bike to one side and make me career off left, braking, wrestling, struggling to stay upright, with the grass verge rushing at me and a metal fence which I knew would smash my skull and be the death of me because I wasn't wearing a helmet, an omission which was surely Ollie's fault for having offered me one so half-heartedly. All this in an instant before I skidded to a halt.

I stood there trembling but unharmed. The bike was upright, and whatever struck the wheel hadn't broken the spokes. I looked ahead to where Ollie was streaming up the hill. I looked behind to where the offending object lay in the road: a wooden branch rather than a metal rod, but there were no trees around and I hadn't seen it lying in the road. To examine it would take time and Ollie was already way ahead.

I felt shaky, like someone in a road crash too shocked to recall what led up to it. But I did remember Ollie's face, and that smile – sinister, even malevolent – and then the bang to the wheel which, were I not an experienced cyclist, would surely have sent me headlong.

Ruthless though he was, I couldn't believe my old friend had thrown a heavy branch or swung an iron bar with the intention of wrecking my spokes or, worse, of knocking me off. I couldn't believe it and yet I did. That he'd not looked round, even once, only clinched it.

I set off in pursuit, thinking back to the night before – Daisy's dreamy face, the flow of her body, her nails raking my back in excitement. She must have been waiting for me, unmarried, all these years. To Ollie – a cheat and liar – I owed nothing, not even guilt. I'd already taken Daisy off him. Now I would take ten grand off him, too.

Propelled by rage and self-righteousness, I caught him on the far side of the hill. For a moment, his manner disarmed me. He was ambling, barely pedalling at all in fact, and as I drew alongside he smiled – with no hint of malice – and said: 'You all right? I was beginning to worry.'

'I'm fine,' I said, 'no thanks to you.'

'Fighting talk, eh? Good.'

'You bet I'm fighting.'

'Great.'

I couldn't be sure Ollie had tried to make me crash. But a sense of outrage fired me up. Twenty years back, he'd stolen Daisy from me. He'd not scruple to steal Em from me, either. He deserved to be beaten.

And I think I could have beaten him. There were only four miles left, along the flat, and I was pumped up, adrenalin coursing through me, the shock of my near catastrophe sending a chill to combat the heat. For two miles or so I set the pace, with Ollie in my slipstream biding his time. When he finally made his move, I pretended I'd no energy left and tucked in behind, calculating how long to wait before accelerating past again. Whether I took him half a mile out or outsprinted him up the farmhouse drive seemed an irrelevance, since I felt in control. Even when he upped the pace and – as I responded – my foot slipped off the pedal (which painfully shinned me and left a cross-hatch of scratches up my leg), the slip was over in an instant, and I felt confident about clawing him back. Why I didn't – why Ollie drew steadily away – still baffles me. I suppose that I hit the wall marathon runners talk about. Or that I was suffering from sunstroke, dehydration and lack of sleep. Or lacked the sadism to humiliate him a second time. He was in my sights and I didn't give up till the last two hundred yards. But when he turned into the drive, I knew it was over: at that point he could have fallen off and still got home ahead of me. Easing off, I leaned down to examine my wheel again. The spokes were intact, the tyres fully pumped up. Hardest of all to admit, the object that struck my hub had probably not been thrown by Ollie. He had beaten me fair and square.

I no longer felt guilty about Daisy. Fucking her was due punishment for all the times Ollie had fucked with me. We were even.

I skidded to a halt then flopped forward on the bike frame, like a rower collapsing on his oars at the end of a boat race.

'One–all,' he said. 'When's the decider?'

* * *

As a rule I don't like discussing money; few Englishmen do. Perhaps if I earned more I'd be less inhibited. But teachers are paid badly, as everyone knows, and primary-school teachers – especially those, like me, unfairly denied promotion – do worst of all. All I've ever wanted is for Em and me to have what other middle-class professionals take for granted – a decent house, foreign holidays, a new car now and then. Our salaries alone could never buy those. To live as we do, I've had to raise our income by other means.

I'm not a big-time gambler compared to some I know. But my father instilled the habit when he used me as his runner. And it persisted at university and beyond. Betting shops, poker games, fruit and slot machines are in the genes. And more recently, there have been websites, so various and alluring and easy to use. I began with just the one, but playing on several makes more sense, just as spreading your bets does – safety in numbers. It's the sites that have run me into debt, I don't mind admitting. I had hoped to wean myself off them during the summer. All that cycling, golf and going to the gym was meant to distract me. It didn't work. Every afternoon I stopped off somewhere for a flutter or roll. And at home in the evening there was the Internet. It needn't have been like that. I could have cooked supper, taken Em to the pub, sat watching television. But most nights she either fell asleep on the sofa or went to her room to work, and that's when temptation came back in. Marooned, I'd turn on the PC for something to do, and before I knew it, three hours later, I'd be down a few hundred quid, or occasionally, gloriously, up a few hundred, my finances radically altered without my even having to leave the house.

It's not a sickness. I'm no addict. I could stop tomorrow. But if I stopped I'd no longer experience the moments of triumph. 'You're afraid of happiness,' Em once said. She has a point. I think happiness is overrated. A man should experience the full range of emotions, bad as well as good. But I'm not *afraid* of happiness. I've known happiness on slots and fruits, and I've known it on sites. And once you've tasted it, life's never the same. When you're on a roll, flush with dosh from an ace and king. Or when you're skint and an inch from quitting, but there's a horse at 50–1 you put your last tenner on and it comes in. Those are moments stronger than love.

When Em first discovered my habit she was upset, naturally – not so much because she had to bail me out (with a couple of thousand she had been saving for a holiday) but because I'd kept the truth from her. She felt betrayed, she said, as if she'd been living with a stranger. I promised to give up, and I did, for nearly a year. The second time I was down less than a thousand, a piddling sum. But before Em agreed to clear the debt she made me promise to contact Gamblers Anonymous. I did look at their site – a site for people addicted to sites – but having read the stuff on the noticeboard I knew it wasn't for me. I'm a middle-class professional in a responsible job, not a loser. The common refrain from the partners of addicts goes: *He doesn't know when to stop*. I'm not like that. I know my limits. If I go further than seems rational, it's not from weakness but from strength – because I know my luck's about to turn, with a 27 on the wheel, say, or a 9 of diamonds.

Most punters are like my dad. They tell you they've studied the form on the racing pages. But for all the good it does them, they might as well close their eyes and use a pin. The same with poker: when my dad played with his cronies, he used to reckon he knew which cards they were holding from their expressions – yet he'd finish out of pocket every time. I'm not like that. I have a system. One of my tricks is to use variants on 1729, which (as all mathematicians know) is a special number. On a roulette wheel 7 sits next to 29. And whenever I've won with four of a kind in stud poker, it's been with aces, twos, sevens or nines. It's a matter of keeping your head and sticking to the laws of probability. Did you realise that with two dice there are six ways of throwing seven but only five ways of throwing six? Knowledge like that can change your life.

If I lost my way in the weeks before Badingley, Campbell Foster and the tribunal were to blame. I had been looking forward to a weekend away because temptation would be removed: out in the sticks there would be no betting shops or Internet, and even if there were I'd be too proud to frequent them with Daisy and Ollie around.

Yes, Badingley would be a break, I thought – till Ollie conned me into making the biggest bet of my life.

There was a surprise when we entered the living room. Though it wasn't yet ten, Em and Daisy were sitting there fully dressed. And opposite them, on the sofa (the sofa where I'd lain with Daisy a few hours earlier, and which I imagined might still be damp with our exertions), sat a stranger. He was a man of about sixty, small in build and with the kind of face usually seen only on toby jugs: bulging eyes, slobbery lips, bulbous nose and raw-red cheeks. A local tradesman, I thought, come here to flog us fish or firewood, until I took in his suit, with its cheap city sheen. He looked awkward in it, not as a farm worker might, wearing it as Sunday best, nor because the day was too hot for ties, but because the boldness of the stripes and double-breasted collar over-whelmed him.

'Darling,' Daisy said, addressing Ollie not me, 'Mr Charles is here about the house.'

'It's Quarles, in fact, with a Q,' the toby-jug man said,

standing to shake hands. 'Albert Quarles.' His left heel was built up, I noticed – three or four times as thick as the right.

'Ah, our landlord,' Ollie said. 'We didn't know you were in Badingley.'

'I'm not, as a rule,' Mr Quarles said. 'But I felt it imperative to pay a visit.'

'Imperative' sounded curious, coming from him. But it worked on Ollie.

'Do please sit down,' he said. 'I trust the girls have offered you coffee.'

'Yes, indeed,' Mr Quarles said, nodding at the cafetière on the table. 'And excellent it is too.'

'Right then. How can we help?'

I could tell from his excessive politeness that Ollie was pissed off. He was hot, he was hungry and he wanted a shower.

'I had two reasons for calling. First, to check that you were happy with the accommodation.'

'Perfectly,' Ollie said, not looking at Daisy.

'Because I understood from Mrs Banks you had some complaints.'

I remembered Daisy describing Mrs Banks as a battleaxe.

'Whatever gave her that idea?'

'She said you said that the house looked damp and unlived in.'

'Me? Really?'

'And that the owner should be strung up.'

'Not at all.'

'She was adamant.'

Ollie shook his head, and the two of them sat in silence, not sure where to go next, until Daisy spoke.

'That must have been me, Mr Quarles.' I looked forward to her giving him what for but all she said was: 'When we arrived it was raining heavily and there were a couple of leaks.'

'Leaks? I'm not aware of any leaks.'

'Well, they sounded like leaks. The point is it was late, and dark, and I was tired after the journey, and not at my best, and I may have said something I didn't really mean.'

'I don't often rent the place out,' Mr Quarles said, ready to be placated, 'and I pride myself on satisfying clients.'

'We're very happy here,' Ollie said.

'And we're sorry for upsetting Mrs Banks.'

Daisy isn't usually deferential. Was she afraid of a scene? Desperate to get shot of Mr Quarles? Or out of sorts from the previous night?

'That's all right,' Mr Quarles said. 'Between ourselves, Mrs Banks can be oversensitive.'

'You mean she dragged you all the way here to throw us out?' Ollie said.

'No. I had a second reason for calling. I was intrigued by what you said when you booked, Mr Moore.'

'I'll get more coffee,' Daisy said, now the discussion had moved on. Her face looked pale, her hair lacking its usual sheen. Had last night been too intense for her? Doubtless she'd lain awake, guilty and fretful, then been forced downstairs by Mr Quarles's arrival. Em's presence must have been difficult too: there she was, full of goodwill, helping to cope with the strange intruder, unaware that Daisy had seduced me.

'In your email you said you'd stayed here before,' Mr Quarles said.

'That's right, as a teenager.'

'Under the name Moore?'

'Yes. My father's name.'

'It's odd. My father used the place as a holiday home and only let it out three or four times a year at most. I'm the same.'

'We were lucky then.'

'He kept a visitors' book. When I looked through I couldn't find the name Moore.'

'I recognise the house, the barn, everything. We were here in 1976.'

'I remember that summer,' Mr Quarles said. 'My wife and I came with the children.'

'Not in late August. That's when we were here.'

'I suppose it's possible. Bit of a mystery, though.'

'Not to me,' Ollie said.

Embarrassed by the impasse, Em began asking Mr Quarles about his family and I got up and left the room. My plan was to snatch a word with Daisy – even a kiss. But as I entered the kitchen, she swept past with the coffee. To return would have looked odd, so I walked out onto the terrace. No sign of Milo. It was too much to hope he had returned to London; maybe he'd gone out for the day.

I felt embarrassed for Ollie. The story of finding the house had seemed fishy from the start and now Mr Quarles had made it look even less plausible. Perhaps the tumour was disrupting Ollie's normal brain functions or had skewed his memory. The need to devise fantastic stories was disturbing nonetheless.

Rufus trotted past as I stood brooding, and I followed him as far as the orchard fence, through which he squeezed in search of rabbit scents in the field. Shorn of its wheat cover, the scorched earth had split open, like crazy paving or shattered glass. I called Rufus back before the stubble could lacerate his pads. Leaving the orchard, we ambled to the end of the drive. Most of the blackberries in the hedge had shrivelled to ash but those lower down looked more promising – until I touched them and they imploded, black corpse blood staining my palms. I knelt and wiped my fingers in the grass, like a killer removing the evidence. When I looked up again, there was Mr Quarles, tottering towards us on his raised heel. It seemed to take for ever, as if the house had him in its force field and wouldn't let go.

'Long walk back to Belgium,' I joked when he finally arrived.

Rufus doesn't usually bark at people but I had to shush him.

'Sorry?'

'I understand you live in Belgium.'

'No, I'm in London these days. Though I did . . .'

Rufus barked again so I missed the rest. It was irrelevant anyway. Clearly Belgium was another of Ollie's fantasies.

'Did you sort out the confusion?' I said.

'Sorry?'

'About my friend staying here in 1976.'

'It's a puzzle,' Mr Quarles said, reluctant to make Ollie look any more foolish. 'But I'm happy to take Mr Moore's word for it.'

When I reconstruct the events of that weekend, I find it hard to be sure what I was thinking or feeling at particular points. But perhaps you'll believe me when I say that it was then, on the drive, next to the rotting blackberries, with Mr Quarles, that I understood for the first time what a liar Ollie was. I should have seen it years ago. The man was false as water. He lied as easily as he breathed.

I felt sad but vindicated. If he couldn't be trusted to tell the truth, I owed him nothing.

'Well, I'd better not keep you,' I said.

'It's all right,' Mr Quarles said, 'I'm waiting for Mr Moore.'

'Really?'

'We're going to church together.'

'Church?' I said. 'Since when did Ollie go to church?'

'He went last week, apparently.'

'With Daisy?'

'On his own.'

'Christ. Has he had a religious conversion?'

'He said he found it restful there. He wasn't planning to go today but then he felt sorry for Mr Quarles.'

I'd gone up to our room to undress for a shower and Em had followed. It felt awkward being alone with her after last night, but the bathroom was occupied – by Milo or one of the girls, I presumed – so for now I had no choice.

'Why sorry?'

'Weren't you there when he told us? It's an awful story. Mr Quarles lost his whole family in an accident. His wife and two boys. It happened up here somewhere.'

'Recently?'

'Twenty or thirty years ago. All the same.'

'A car crash no doubt. That's what the locals are famous for – bad driving and incest.'

'They were drowned. Mr Quarles should have been with them but some problem came up so his wife took the boat out without him. She was an experienced sailor, he said. But a storm got up and they capsized.'

Em sat down and rootled in her handbag.

'Now do you understand why he might want to go to church?' she said, peering at her mobile phone. 'Ollie too, given . . . you know.'

That would explain it, of course: Ollie seeking solace in his hour of need. The thought made me angry, nonetheless. I didn't like to think of him as weak.

'Church isn't going to cure him,' I said. 'Or bring back Mr Quarles's family.'

'No, but it might help them cope.'

Typical Em. So calm and understanding. Sometimes her halo infuriates me.

'If God gave me a terminal illness or killed my family,' I said, 'I wouldn't pray to Him, I'd burn His fucking church down.'

'What's wrong with you this morning?' she said, looking up from her phone. 'Did you lose your little race?'

'That's nothing to do with it. I hate people using faith as a comfort blanket.'

'Why shouldn't they? Faith's empowering. You could do with more of it yourself, Ian.'

'What's that supposed to mean?'

'Faith in yourself, faith in your friends. You're too suspicious.'

'There's a lot to be suspicious of. Trust people and they betray you.'

'Have I betrayed you?'

'You're an exception.'

To my relief, she went back to playing with her mobile. Betrayal was too near the bone.

'Still no damn signal.' She held the face of her mobile up. 'Magda could have been trying to get hold of me.'

My socks were sweaty and hard to roll off. I sat on the edge of the bed to make it easier.

'Forget Magda,' I said. 'Give yourself a break.'

'If you'd seen the state she was in –'

'So what? You're not on duty. You're supposed to be relaxing.'

'How can I relax, with all these cobwebs and creaky floorboards and weapons on the wall? It's spooky here. Don't you find it spooky?'

'It's too hot to be spooky.'

'Well, it gives me the creeps.'

My socks were finally off. I stood up and dropped my boxer shorts, turning away from Em as I did, in case my nakedness gave me away.

'*You* were late to bed last night,' she said, more teasing than reproachful.

'I know,' I said, wrapping a towel round my waist.

'What time was it?'

'Dunno. I lost track. Milo was there. We were talking. Then Archie came in.'

'And Daisy?'

'Yes, Daisy was up, too.' I heard the bolt slide across the hall, just in time. 'That's someone coming out of the bathroom.'

'Are we staying tonight?' she said, before I could make it out the door.

'That's the arrangement.'

'They'd understand if we left,' she said. 'I've work to do. Your hearing's on Wednesday.' She stood up and put her arms round me. 'We could beat the traffic and have tomorrow to ourselves.'

'It would look rude,' I said, pulling away.

'No one would miss us. We could drop in on your parents and have tea. I know they'd like it.'

'On a bank holiday weekend? They'll be in Blackpool with all the other morons.'

'When did your parents ever go to Blackpool? You always make out they're working class, when they're not. Your dad had that job at –'

'I don't want to see them. Anyway, I promised Ollie we'd stay.'

'Ach, you boys and your stupid bet.'

I opened the door. She let me go. I'd got away with it.

Under the thin, hot spray, I took my punishment. Let me be pricked to death with burning needles. Let me be irradiated. Let me be washed in gulfs of liquid fire.

* * *

It was Em who suggested a swim – anything to escape the house. Breakfast had been perfunctory (cereal and fruit) and lunch just sandwiches, the heat killing all appetite. We lolled under the parasol, only Milo's girls – sealed in factor 80 sunscreen – stirring from the shade. Even Ollie was relaxed for once, as if church had purged his nervous energy. Beyond the orchard, a heat haze trembled over the stubble. It was a day to make you dream of freezer shelves, blizzards, the down draught from helicopters, the spangled fur of huskies.

Archie was asleep or had gone off to his gig. No one seemed to know. We were all far too hot to care.

'Walk anyone?' Em said.

Silence.

'Game of boules?'

Silence.

'How about a dip?'

'Now you're talking.'

It was the prospect of cold that drew us – even the sun at its hottest couldn't warm the North Sea. Ollie, taking charge, consulted his map to find a beach that ought to be quiet. Milo swept the girls off to get their swimsuits. Em gently berated me in the bedroom, whispering that she'd rather we were driving home. I kissed her on the cheek, like Judas. For me the point of the excursion was to get some time alone with Daisy.

We went in two cars, Milo driving his hosts while Bethany and Natalie came with us. They'd taken a shine to Em, who kept them going with nursery rhymes, riddles, I-spy games and silly jokes. Not knowing the way, I followed Milo, my eyes on Daisy in the back seat. Once or twice she turned and waved but there was no special affection, nothing for me. I was still brooding about her performance at lunch, when Milo said he feared he'd outstayed his welcome and was wondering about heading back. Good idea, I thought. But Daisy would have none of it, seizing his hand and begging Ollie to 'make sweet Milo and his lovely girls *please, please* stay another night'. I ought to have been feeling happy – it was me, not Milo, she'd slept with last night – but I needed some flag or token of her love.

The lanes were narrow and deep, and it was half an hour before we saw the sea.

My idea of a beach comes from childhood holidays in Bridlington: donkeys, ice creams, yellow sand, silent yachts out in the bay. I didn't expect to find a beach like that near Badingley. But nor was I ready for the bleakness. It's true that I arrived full of bad feeling, angry at Daisy, irritated with Em, jealous of Milo and dismayed by Ollie. But the melancholy of the coastline owed nothing to my mood.

We drew up near a ruined church, the girls leaping out before I'd killed the engine, frustrated, as we all were, by how long it had taken to arrive. The sea lay straight ahead, beyond the church, like a flat grey mirror, but Ollie said the sand cliffs were too steep at that point and led us off diagonally, round the edge of an open field. From there a path bent seaward through gorse and bracken. The girls ran excitedly ahead, Ollie – self-appointed leader – struggling to keep up. Em took my hand and smiled, grateful for the hint of breeze. Daisy and Milo were lagging behind; after his announcement last night, they had business to discuss. I mustn't be impatient. Our moment would come.

The sea took its colour from the blue above, but a murky brown showed through, like old paint beneath a new coat.

At a stile, we entered a bird sanctuary or nature reserve, I'm not sure which – all I noticed was the sign: EXTREME FIRE DANGER – NO BARBECUES OR CAMPFIRES. The bracken was tinder under our feet, and I could imagine the whole lot going up in flames. Two sticks rubbed together would be enough. Or a metal heel striking flint. Or a dropped cigarette stub. The known world had turned flimsy and combustible.

Up ahead Ollie and the girls drew to a halt. When we reached them, we saw why. The path petered out in air; from the sheared-off sand cliff, it was a twenty-foot drop to the beach below. Ollie and I were for jumping, but the others overruled us, so back we tracked, curving inland again, till freshly trodden bracken showed a path off right and we descended gently to the shore. We took off our trainers and flip-flops, digging our toes into the pebbly sand and hearing the sea's repeated slap-and-swish.

'Great,' we all said, 'really great,' but it was not.

Plastic bottles had washed up on the shoreline. Jellyfish drifted in the shallows like polythene bags. But the real killer was the wooden sign: NO SWIMMING: DANGEROUS CURRENTS. Ollie, shame-faced, was apologetic – he'd been here thirty years ago and ought to have remembered the rip tide. I wandered in up to my knees but no further, the current tugging at my feet. Despite my fear, it was tempting to give in, let go, be carried out past the breakers to the immense, cathartic cold. From the shallows, I threw stones for Rufus, careful not to land them too far out.

Offshore, two white buoys held steadfast against the wash. What was their purpose? I wondered. To provide moorings? Or serve as a warning? And if the latter, a warning of what? I could remember, as a boy, being given a little paperback called *I-Spy at the Seaside*, which included a description of buoys marking the place of wrecks ('always painted green, with the word WRECK in white letters'). They carried a score of 20 if you spied one, as much as for spotting a lighthouse or a seal. The *I-Spy* books were hard to get hold of by the time I was born but my mother picked them up at jumble sales and I became a collector, frustrated only by my failure to acquire numbers 29 (*People in Uniform*) and 35 (*Everyday Machines*). I carried them round with me constantly, eager to acquire fresh points. I-Spy became my nickname at school – I-Spy Ian, watcher and sleuth.

Getting into the spirit, I invented an I-spy game for Natalie and Bethany: three points for spotting a crab, two for a cuttle-fish, one for a minnow. For thirty seconds they were interested, then boredom set in.

'Hold my hands, girls,' Em said, taking over. Beyond them, Milo and Ollie stood in the shallows, knee-deep in divorce law by the sound of it; if Ollie resented the intrusion – divorce wasn't his field – he was too polite to show it. Daisy, meanwhile, had wandered off, beachcombing along the shingle.

With the others distracted, I sidled after her. Beyond the horizon lay Denmark and beyond Denmark the Arctic, its icebergs shrinking in the global stew.

'Oh, it's you,' she said, feigning surprise when I caught her up – she couldn't have failed to hear me scrunching over the shingle.

A bra strap had fallen from her shoulder and she absent-mindedly pulled it back. Her other hand was full of gleanings.

'What have you got?' I said.

'Amber. Driftwood. Gulls' feathers. Flotsam and jetsam. What *is* flotsam and jetsam? You're the teacher.'

'Flotsam's washed-up cargo or wreckage. Jetsam's stuff the crew throw overboard to lighten the load.'

'So flotsam's accidentally lost and jetsam's deliberately discarded.'

'Exactly,' I said.

'Well, you learn something every day.'

I glanced behind. No one had moved.

'What else have you learned?' I said.

'Dunno,' she said, not with me.

'What did you learn last night?' I said.

'Last night?' she said, thinking it a game. 'Last night I learned . . . that my husband can be extremely argumentative.'

'You knew that already,' I said. 'You also learned about Milo going to New York.'

'I did. Worse luck.'

'And later?'

'Later?'

'You know what I mean by later.'

Three waves broke in the silence.

'I don't want to talk about it,' she said, looking nervously towards the others. 'I was drunk.'

'You were wonderful.'

'You were rough.'

'I wanted you so badly.'

'We lost our heads.'

'I didn't lose mine,' I said.

'Don't say that. It makes it worse.'

'It's what I've always wanted.'

'That doesn't make it forgivable.'

'Don't go all moral on me.'

She flinched, as though I'd implied she'd been a slut on the sofa. I mumbled and mammered, trying to explain, but she turned away and bent to gather some bladderwrack.

'It's like bubble wrap,' she said, popping a black polyp.

'I'm being serious,' I said.

'And I'm being practical, Ian. We're with other people. End of story.'

'It's not the end, it's the beginning. We made love.'

'That wasn't love.'

'It was for me.'

'We'd been drinking. It wasn't real.'

'It's more real than anything I've ever done.'

I reached for her hand but she pulled away, spilling stones and feathers.

'Don't,' she said, kneeling on the shingle to gather them up, 'the others will see.'

I turned to look. High in the thinning cliffs, martins swooped out of their hatches. Below them – leafless, broken, eerily naked – salt-worn tree trunks lay like corpses in the sand. No one was near. Milo's girls were coming our way but still fifty yards off.

'I know you feel bad towards Ollie,' I said, kneeling to help her.

'Not just Ollie, Em.'

'What people don't know can't hurt them.'

'I don't believe that. Anyway, it's no excuse.'

'I've stopped wanting Em. There's no desire any more. You came before her. You still do.'

'That's silly, Ian. You two have a life together.'

'Not after last night.'

'Stop going on about last night. It didn't mean anything. Get that in your thick skull, will you?'

As Milo's girls ran up, she brandished a stone, holding it to the sun. The stone had a hole in it. Lemmel stones we call them in the Pennines.

'Look,' she said, performing for them, 'a stone with no heart.'

I wandered off, down to the tide, letting the surf wash the grit from my toes. Which was worse: to be called thick, or to be told our lovemaking had no meaning? Mr Nobody, that was me – a nothing man who'd had nothing sex with a woman who felt nothing for him. I'd been used then chucked away.

'You all right?' Ollie said, catching up.

'I'm ready to head back,' I said, wishing we'd never come – not to the coast, not to Badingley, not at all.

'The quickest route's along the beach. Daisy's leading the way, look.'

And so she was, her golden legs striding off, with Milo, Em and the girls close behind.

We headed after them, through the shingle below the sand cliffs. According to Ollie, several feet of land fell in the sea each year. He could remember a house standing on the cliffs when he was last here. Erosion was a natural process.

'No bollocks about global warming, please.'

'Certainly not,' I said. 'I'll leave that to Milo.'

Clouds lined the horizon, the first we'd seen in days. Wafts of sage came from the clifftop and ozone from the sea. But the heat felt oppressive, runnels of sweat seeping down my back. Natalie and Bethany had stopped to paddle again. Two stick figures stood beyond them, fuzzy in sea fret – Milo and Daisy it must be. She'd surely not tell him what had happened last night, but I imagined her mocking me, the nerd from Ilkeston, with his clumsy credulity. Or perhaps, since I meant nothing to her, she would tell him, and they'd laugh together at my crassness. Perhaps she'd done it with him, too, and that *had* meant something. She might have fucked me purely to spite him, after he'd told her he was going to New York. Whatever the truth, they were close now. The mist half obscured them but I could see that they were walking arm in arm.

I stopped to pick up a chunk of driftwood.

'Has Daisy known Milo long?' I said, handing it to Ollie.

'A couple of years maybe. Why?'

'No reason. I'd have guessed longer.'

'She's done a lot for his career.'

'That figures.'

'Sorry?'

'I'm just surprised she invited him up here when you're on holiday.'

'You know Daisy,' he said, tossing the driftwood in the sea, 'she loves company.'

'And he loves hers, that's obvious,' I said.

'Is it?'

'He admires her. I wasn't implying there's anything more.'

I picked up a flat stone and weighed it in my hand, then walked to the edge of the tide and skimmed it: o-o-o-o-o it went, before disappearing.

Ollie followed suit, as I knew he would: o-o-o-o-o-o-o his went, beating mine by two skips.

We skimmed stones out into the blue-brown sea, while dark clouds heaped up on the horizon. Ollie's record was eleven bounces.

'You don't mean Milo's – you know?' he said, stepping deeper in the current.

'What?'

'He seems too involved in his kids to be leching after Daisy. And too married. Doesn't he? What do you think?'

'What do *I* think?'

'Stop parroting me, Ian. I asked you a question.'

'Hang on, I'm up to my knees here,' I said. We waded back through the breakers. 'You can't expect me to tell you every thought I have.'

'It's a simple question.'

'I should have kept my mouth shut. There's no need to be jealous.'

'What's jealousy got to do with it?'

'Nothing. That's my point. Those clouds are getting darker, you know.'

I said it to distract him but it was true. They were building from the horizon and shaded with diagonal streaks of black. Another of the *I-Spy* books I'd had as a child was on clouds and I could still remember some of the terms – cirrostratus and castellatus and cumulonimbus. For a time I'd been a collector of clouds: clouds rippled like sand when the tide has gone out; clouds tagging along after a storm, like slow runners late to the finish line; clouds like dust covers in an empty room; clouds like galleons, battleships, barrage balloons, pillowcases, mares' tails, dandelion clocks, shoals of mackerel; clouds like milk spills, snowdrifts, ink stains, snot streams; clouds the colour of school blackboards; clouds that turn cloudier as they approach, like a glass of anise with water added; clouds stacking up like planes over Heathrow. I pointed out the gathering storm. But Ollie gave it barely a glance. Once set on something, he wasn't distractable.

'They *have* been spending a lot of time together,' he said.

'That's her job. Or was her job. It won't be much longer.'

'Sorry?'

'Didn't she tell you? I assumed she would have.'

'Tell me what?'

'Milo's moving to New York. His marriage has broken up.'

'She might have mentioned it,' he said, though I knew from his look that she hadn't. Despite all the lies he'd told, I felt a surge of pity for him.

'He's a single man again. You can tell. He has that look. The look of a man who's –'

An Arctic tern swooped low above us, cutting me off.

'What, on the prowl?' Ollie said.

'Lonely, that's all I meant. Anyway, when he goes to New York, Daisy will soon be over him.'

'*Over* him?'

'I'm not saying there's anything dodgy going on, just that she finds it hard to be detached.'

'You think she's too fond of him?'

'I expect she has to be fond of him to represent him properly. She's also fond of his wife – his ex, I mean. Sorry, I don't know why I brought it up. You've nothing to worry about.'

I hadn't intended to set Ollie on the rack – not till my suspicions had more substance. But sometimes things spill out before you know it.

As we walked on I babbled away, to take his mind off Milo and Daisy. Had he booked tennis for tomorrow morning? Would we be playing just the one set or best of three? The cliffs were lower by now and darkly textured, more clay-and-shale than shingle-and-sand. Out at sea it was raining. A large black cloud stretched down to the waves, like God unclenching His hand to let the water through.

We strode on to where the others were waiting.

'I haven't upset you?' I said, before they could hear.

'Not a jot, not a jot.'

'Just forget everything I said, OK.'

'OK,' he said, though I knew he wouldn't forget a word.

As well as the time in London when I didn't see Daisy, there was another occasion, shortly afterwards, when I did. I'd been sent on a two-day training course near Paddington and the first day was so dull I bunked off for the second. I called Daisy from the B & B shortly after nine. It was a Friday and Archie was at nursery. I'll come to the house, I said, but Daisy suggested a cafe in Hampstead, a couple of Tube stops away from her home. I arrived early, chose a coffee I'd never heard of, and waited in the window, under the A and F of CAFE, so I could see her coming down the street. I told myself that if she was late – as she proved to be, by twenty-two minutes

– it wasn't indifference but the opposite. The same with her reluctance to see me at the house: what she feared was her desire for me – with no one around to restrain us, anything might happen. I'd never understood what had gone wrong between us. Fruits and slots had helped distract me but I still thought about her constantly. Before I committed to Em, I needed to lay Daisy to rest.

I was perfectly positioned for her arrival but she was almost through the door before I recognised her.

'You've cut your hair,' I said, more accusing than I meant. She was wearing black trousers, a jacket buttoned up to her neck and hair cut tight against her scalp.

'Do you like it?'

'It's different.'

'You prefer it long.'

'I'll get used to it,' I said.

I offered her coffee but she said she couldn't stay long and that a glass of water would be fine. She chattered on, tense, high-pitched, like a dentist's drill. Ollie was spending more and more time on the provincial trial circuit. They were having a new kitchen put in. Her closest colleague at the recruitment agency was leaving to have a baby. It was Daisy talking, and me listening, and though I wished she'd relax and undo her coat and say 'bath' and 'grass', or 'love' and 'chuck', as she used to do, I was happy just to be with her again. Only the hair distressed me. *Dis-tress*, I thought, as her words flowed over me. To have one's tresses cut off. And to be unhappy. Either or both.

She talked on, running the clock down. I didn't have long.

'So are you happy?' I said.

She laughed, taken aback.

'Why wouldn't I be?'

'That's not an answer.'

'Don't I sound happy?'

That wasn't an answer, either, but I let it pass.

'I'm amazed you cope, living down south.'

'I love it in London.'

'With a small child to look after.'

'He's a delight.'

'And Ollie away such a lot.'

'I'm glad of it. I'd hate having him under my feet.'

Her tone was jokey. But humour can be a defence.

'It must get lonely.'

'I've lots of friends,' she said, looking at her watch. However unhappy, she couldn't admit it.

'I just wanted to say,' I said, knowing I'd not have another chance, 'that if things are going badly, if you need someone to turn to, if you feel you've made a mistake, if . . . well, I don't have to tell you.'

'And I don't have to tell *you*,' she said, reclaiming her catchphrase.

It could have meant many things. But from her lips, I understood at once: *It's you who are my truest companion, Ian, but rightly or wrongly I'm with Ollie, and you mustn't waste your life waiting for me*. It must have cost her a lot to let me go, but that was when she did, in Hampstead, over a sugar bowl, between the letters A and F. The new hairstyle (was it Ollie who had forced her?) made it easier for me. Shorn, she could have been anyone.

I wasn't surprised by what she said next.

'And you?'

'I'm OK.'

'Are you seeing someone?'

I told her I was, and had been for a while, but omitted to say that we were living together, for fear she wasn't ready for that. My instincts were right. I'd heard the rumble of jealousy in her question. And when I began to describe Em she cut me off, as if the thought of me being attracted to another woman was too painful.

'That's nice for you,' she said. 'God, is that the time?'

'I'll walk you home.'

'I'm getting the Tube.'

'To the station then.'

'Don't be daft. Stay and finish your coffee.'

She kissed me on the cheek, her coat buttoned to her neck, her handbag tight under her arm. I watched her go, stiff, short-haired, the antithesis of the Daisy I'd known. She could have had me once, in her prime. She could still have had me that day. But whether through cowardice or martyrdom, she missed the boat.

There's a games arcade near King's Cross and I played some slots while waiting for the train. When a drugged-up hooker came in and propositioned me, I ignored her, hoping she'd go away. But she kept bugging me and wrecking the game, even after I'd told her *Go fuck yourself*, and in the end I had to smack her round the chops. It wasn't a hard smack, more a slap to bring her to her senses. But my hand caught her off balance, and her heels were so high she teetered and fell. If I'd really smacked her there would have been blood but I saw none as she lay clutching her face. She was probably well known to the police and they would have thanked me. But when her groans turned into screams, I decided it wasn't worth the risk. I stepped over her and away, down the aisle of flashing machines. No one tried to stop me as I went.

Next day I proposed to Em.

A few months later, the four of us met up for the first time. And soon afterwards, Em and I were married. I'd had it in mind to ask Ollie to be best man but in the event he and Daisy couldn't come: the wedding clashed with a holiday they'd booked, cancelling which would have cost them thousands.

So they claimed, though I have always suspected that Daisy couldn't face the ceremony – not just because she was against marriage in general but because she was against *my* marriage in particular, having expected I'd always be there for her, the trusty sidekick and reserve.

As a guilt offering, they bought us a dining table and four chairs, delivered by furniture van the day before the wedding: it must have cost them as much as cancelling the holiday would have done, so I'm embarrassed to admit we barely use it, preferring to eat on stools in the kitchen or in front of the telly. We're just not dinner-party sorts – all that blahing about kids and schools, subjects we prefer to avoid. Still, whenever we do use the dining table I think of Daisy, and that day in the cafe, and the sacrifice she made to set me free.

I thought it was over between us. It *was* over between us. Until Badingley.

We had lived in a glare since Friday. Now clouds were gathering and it was England again, gloom-struck and drab. Daisy and Ollie fussed round the terrace, stacking the chairs, rushing the cushions inside, folding the large white parasol's wings. Milo told his girls to build an ark for their furry animals, before the heavens swept them away. The sky looked ready to crack. A few stray drops fell fat on the terrace. We were held in limbo, sultry and tense.

I sat in a deckchair with my eyes closed, imagining a shower of black ink, its rods and blobs erasing every trace of light. The end of the world, in an ink storm: it felt peaceful, imagining that.

'Tea?' Daisy said.

None of us wanted tea, or squash, or beer, only rain on our tongues.

Was it raining on Archie at his gig? To judge by the sky's

charred diagonals, it was raining on every village around. But it didn't rain on us.

Em had gone to lie down in the bedroom – she always gets a headache before a storm. My head, too, was tightening, as if sliced horizontally by cheese wire or squeezed by a circle of coil.

Get that in your thick skull, will you?

The girls, bored with playing Noah, demanded a game. Milo suggested Snap, and Daisy fetched some playing cards out to the terrace, since it still refused to rain. Milo asked if I would like to join in. For poker maybe, but I shook my head and wandered inside. No sign of Ollie: he was probably pushing his car into the garage or putting up its soft top.

The air was black, an angry scrawl overwriting the earth.

Upstairs, Em lay dozing under a thin sheet. Beside her lay a book, with a swooning woman in a long red dress against a backdrop of snow-capped mountains. Me, I don't read fiction any more: I had my fill of it at university. An actual person genuinely climbing a real mountain is more my thing these days, with accompanying facts and statistics. Tales of victory against the odds. Explorers, long-distance cyclists, yachtsmen, fell runners, potholers, adventurers in remote jungles: that's what I go for, late at night, when I've tired of websites. I'm not a driven person but I'm fascinated by men who are. Men like Ollie, that is.

'How are you, love?' I said, perching nurse-like on the side of the bed.

'So-so,' Em said, pulling me down beside her.

I stroked her forehead and kneaded her neck, careful in my ministrations. Close though I felt to her, the thought of sex alarmed me: both the disloyalty to last night's passion and the fear of being found out.

'What time is it?' she said.

'Sixish.'

'We could be home by eleven if we left now.'

'We've been through this.'

'I was watching you earlier, on the beach. You had a face like a funeral.'

'I'm fine,' I said.

'You looked worried – like something bad was about to happen.'

The bad thing was Daisy, and had happened already. I kissed Em's cheek in atonement. She kissed me on the lips in return.

'I'm glad you came up,' she said. 'I wanted to tell you. Daisy knows.'

'Knows what?'

'We talked. It all came out. She knows about the tumour.'

'When was this?' I said.

'Earlier. On the beach.'

Had she spoken to Daisy on the beach? I thought the figures arm in arm in the mist were Daisy and Milo.

'Christ. I told you not to tell her.'

'I didn't. She knew already.'

I sat down on the bed.

'Ollie told me she didn't know,' I said.

'Daisy can't understand that. Are you sure you heard him right?'

I replayed Ollie's remark on the fairway, the bit about being given his cards. Then the conversation in the pub garden: the crisps, the wasps, 'My Generation' pounding – and the terrible prognosis.

'I swear that's what he said,' I said.

'Anyway, the point is she does know and it's not as bad as Ollie says.'

'Of course it's bad. It's terminal.'

'According to the consultant, the tumour's low-grade and slow-growing. And there's a fifty-fifty chance that it's benign. They're doing more tests next week.'

'Ollie told me he was dying. Why would he lie?'

'He's in a panic. Anyone would be.'

'Stop sticking up for him,' I said. I stared at the window-pane, and the mummified fly in the spider's web. 'The lying fucker.'

'I thought you'd be pleased.'

'Of course I'm pleased. It's just . . . If he's not dying, why is Daisy marrying him?'

'What's that got to do with anything?' she said, feeling my brow as if I was the sick one.

'It must be a precaution. In case it *is* terminal. To keep things simple with the will and so on. And because she feels sorry for him.'

'You're being so weird about this,' Em said. 'It's like you *want* him to die.'

'Don't be stupid.'

'You're supposed to be his friend. He's frightened. He needs your support.'

It was true. I ought to be kind to him. But he had lied.

'I'm all sweaty,' I said, pulling my T-shirt off.

'That's how I like you. Climb into bed.'

'There's no lock on the door.'

'So?'

'Milo's kids are running around.'

'I thought you wanted to make love. What else did you come up for?'

'To see how you were. And change for dinner.'

'It's only a barbecue.'

'Even so.'

I pulled away. She shrugged, giving up on me.

'Put that nice green shirt on,' she said. 'No, not in the suitcase. The one hanging up.'

In my struggle to open the mirrored door, one of Em's dresses fell on the shoes in the bottom of the wardrobe.

'Not yours I take it?' I said, picking up a shrivelled black brogue.

'Yes, I saw those,' Em laughed. 'They'll be Mr Quarles's. His stuff is everywhere. I don't think he's touched anything since the accident. No wonder the place feels spooky.'

'You're not really spooked, are you?' I said, putting the shoe back and grabbing my shirt. 'We *could* leave, if you are.'

'I'd feel better if you got in bed and gave me a cuddle.'

Relenting, I slid in beside her. A cuddle was all I intended, but Em had other ideas. Her skin felt hot and the familiar scent had the familiar effect. She was my wife, for God's sake. Why feel guilty towards Daisy? Especially when the bitch was being so cold.

We were quiet in case the girls came up.

There can't have been much of me, after last night, but I came.

She smiled as I buttoned my shirt. That's when I knew she must be ovulating.

'I'd better go down,' I said. 'Ollie will be looking for me.'

'Be nice to him. Whether he's dying or not, he isn't well.'

The act might be over but when your foreskin's moist with cunt the act will be fresh on your mind. It was certainly on mine as I walked downstairs.

I'll be honest with you. Sex with Em hasn't been easy of late. Not for the past couple of years, in fact, since she started trying for children. We're rarely apart and sex is important to us both. It seems unfair, in the circumstances, that we haven't produced a child. Unfair on Em, anyway. To me what's unfair isn't failing to conceive but the damage to our sex life: the thermometers and 'impregnation-efficient positions' and the worry whether we're doing it too often or not enough. *It's no one's fault*, they tell us at the fertility clinic, but we've both suffered from a feeling of inadequacy. For Em it has been harder. She's a woman. And though the initial diagnosis was 'non-specific infertility', she naturally blamed herself.

Sometimes the pressure gets to us. A few days before Badingley she laid into me when I returned late after dropping off at the pub (less for a beer than for the slots and fruits).

'Childlessness suits you just fine, doesn't it?' she began. 'If you were a dad, coming home late every night would be more tricky. You're afraid of losing your freedom.'

'Don't be like this.'

'I'm being myself. This is me.'

'We've discussed it before.'

'Yes, but we never get anywhere, do we?'

For an answer I took her upstairs.

'Would I be doing this if I didn't want children?'

It worked, after a fashion. But Em still believes I'm holding out on her, as though willing us to remain infertile.

I'd be a liar if I said my performance hasn't been affected. Men these days are encouraged to be soft – except in bed, where we have to be hard. *Be gentle, be tough, kiss me, boss me, respect me, enter me* – the mixed messages are sometimes too much. I lose confidence, lose patience, lose desire.

Em blames herself, of course. She worries about putting on weight (not in the way she'd like to put on weight) and fears I'm no longer attracted to her. It makes life difficult for us both. None of it would have arisen but for the issue, or non-issue, of kids.

* * *

Ollie was next to the fireplace in the living room, a tumbler of whisky in his hand, inspecting the two crossed swords.

'I thought they were decorative,' he said. 'But feel that blade. They could do some serious damage. Want one?'

He meant a whisky, not a sword, and I nodded.

'Come through,' he said. 'There's a choice of malts.'

I had not been in the dining room since the first day and had almost forgotten it – easily done, since the door matched the design of the oak panelling in the corridor: once it was shut, you would never know the room was there. As a child, I'd loved adventure stories which featured secret chambers and used to comb our terraced house in search of one; now, decades later, I'd found it. An old drinks cabinet, with a mirrored interior and walnut surround, stood in the corner. Ollie pulled out a dining chair and gestured for me to sit down. The walls were a lurid violet and the brick floor smelled of mushrooms. But the room felt colder than the rest of the house, which was a relief.

'Thank you for being frank earlier,' Ollie said, closing the door. 'I can't be doing with evasions any more. It's all too late for that.'

Less of the too late, I thought. It was the moment to call his bluff, to say I knew, that Daisy had told Em, that his claim to be dying was a lie. But could Daisy be trusted? Suppose he *was* dying and she didn't want us to know. Or that she'd convinced herself he wasn't dying in order to feel less guilty about fucking Milo. If she was fucking Milo. The possibilities were endless.

The malt tasted good – a Glenmorangie, twenty years old, tanged with bitterness.

'You've set me thinking,' he said.

'Forget what I said.'

'Milo and Daisy are too fond of each other, you implied. What's the evidence?'

'I probably imagined it. Em says I have a dirty mind.'

'Imagined what? Stop protecting me, Ian. There's more to this.'

I swirled the whisky in my glass and thought of the malt-brown North Sea, how even the clearest sky can't turn it blue.

I looked at him and drew breath.

'I'll tell you, if it's bothering you, but I'm sure it's nothing. Last night, after you'd gone to bed, I took the dog for a walk, and when I came back Daisy was lying on the sofa, looking dishevelled. She seemed rather put out to see me.'

'Where was Milo?'

'I don't know. He probably heard me coming in and went off to bed.'

'Why would he do that?'

'They'd been talking. He'd told her about his marriage breaking up and how he planned to move to New York, and she was upset.'

'Daisy cries easily.'

'Yes, and she obviously had been crying. I fetched her some water while she straightened her clothes.'

'Why would her clothes need straightening?'

'No reason. I'm not suggesting she'd been up to anything.'

'What *are* you saying?'

'Nothing. Daisy loves you, not Milo.'

'You mean they're having an affair?'

'No way. She might have a crush on him but she wouldn't act on it. Not lightly. I should have kept my mouth shut. My dream life's disgusting.'

'What have dreams to do with it?'

'Well, that's the other thing. I shouldn't tell you, it's embarrassing – but after Daisy had gone off to bed I went through to see Rufus, and I was so tired I ended up falling asleep on the rug beside him, and next thing there were voices, as if

Milo had come back down, and then – sorry, this is ridiculous – I heard two people having sex.'

'Fucking hell.'

'No, but the point is it was only a dream. When I woke up and went through no one was there. I imagined the whole thing.'

'Maybe you overheard them in your sleep.'

'There'd have been evidence. Stains on the sofa or tissues in the waste bin. Trust me. Nothing happened except in my head. I apologise for bringing it up. Can I have another malt, please?'

You will think me a bad person, and sometimes I think so too. But it was true about the dream. So much had happened I'd forgotten it till then. After falling asleep next to Rufus, that's what I dreamt, the sweet memory of making love to Daisy coursing through me but with Milo in my place. I couldn't tell Ollie the whole truth. And if the dream hadn't come back at that moment, I would have refrained from telling him. But nor did I invent it. I'm not a monster.

Having said that, as we sat there in the cold little room I can't deny a certain satisfaction in seeing Ollie suffer. I've not spent my life in jealousy, but it did briefly poison my existence. And since Ollie was to blame for that, it was only right that he know how it felt.

I was avenging myself on Daisy, too. She might have been cold and aloof on the beach but she'd slept with me willingly enough the night before, and her eagerness, her sluttish enthusiasm, made me wonder how many other men she'd had before me. If Ollie now suspected her, that was only just. Suspicion is what she deserved.

'If it's true, I don't blame her,' he said, his back to me as he stood at the drinks cabinet.

'How do you mean?'

'I've not been easy to live with. It evens things up.'

I looked at him quizzically as he handed me the malt but he avoided my eyes, as if to say *Let's leave it at that*. Was he saying he'd had mistresses? Or that he'd made life difficult for her in other ways? I'd no time to digest it before he spoke again.

'Did I say when I showed you round?' he said, gesturing to the four walls. 'This is the room they brought my father to. Before they took him to the morgue.'

'Sorry?'

'Surely I told you about his death.'

'You told me he died when you were twelve. You never said how.'

'He drowned. While we were on holiday here. When they recovered the body, they brought him to this room and laid him out.'

He gripped the table edge, as if the solid wood between his fingers and thumb would somehow authenticate the story.

'God,' I said, playing along, 'how awful.'

'I remember my mother and me standing here. The oilskin they'd wrapped him in smelled of fish. There was a tiny strand of seaweed in his hair that made me think they must have dredged him from the seabed. But they found the body three miles out to sea. As if he'd set off to swim to Denmark and got into trouble. As if he'd been trying to escape us.'

I tried to remember when Ollie had first told me about his father dying. Before he met Daisy or after? Probably after. The word 'tragedy' would have made her feel sorry for him, just as his tales of Sandhurst made her think him brave. Hero and victim: no wonder she'd fallen under his spell. But to me he'd spoken only of a sudden death, as if from a heart attack or stroke, not a drowning. Of course, I wanted to believe he was telling the truth. But there was something opportunistic about it. Plagiaristic, too: only that morning Mr Quarles had described losing his family in the North Sea. I'd not been there but Em said it was the saddest story. Now Ollie in his usual way was trying to cap it.

'That can't be right,' I said, disputing the escape theory, not (as I should have) the entire story. 'You've always said he loved you and your mother.'

'He loved us but he felt trapped. They found a twenty-pound note in the inside pocket of his trunks. Why was that there?'

'By accident.'

'Or to start a new life.'

'You can't start a new life with twenty pounds.'

'My father could. I'd let him down, you see.'

'He was proud of you, you told me.'

'It was our last day – the bank holiday Monday – and we'd planned an early-morning swim. But when he came into my bedroom, I didn't feel like it and pretended to be asleep. He stood there saying my name then gave up and went alone.'

'If you'd gone you might have drowned too.'

'Rather that than him dying alone.'

'But if you'd died there would have been no Daisy in your life, or Archie, or a career or . . .'

Something bright – a sword-flash – lit the room from outside, then came an explosion to waken death.

'What the fuck?'

I heard the girls screaming outside, then adult laughter and the clip-clop of two doors being closed.

Rain at last.

Thunder was just the start of it. For the next two hours the house was a ship at sea, timbers creaking, deck sloshing, the horizon lost behind spray. Silver pitchforks flashed through the air then tossed us into darkness. You'd have thought a pantiled roof would be secure, but it drummed and rattled like a shanty hut, helpless against the chiding rain. A dozen leaks sprang from the eaves, the worst of them in our bedroom: I stuck a bucket underneath and let the drips slowly change their tune – ping, prang, sprong, shlung, sklish, shoosh – as the water rose towards the brim. Em was out of bed by then, coming down to watch the spectacle with the rest of us. What a picture we made, seven faces lining the windows while the terrace turned to rapids and the field ditch overflowed. I fixed my eyes on a plastic fertiliser bag – its neck open and its body slashed – as gusts bullied it about the orchard. Even the bales out in the meadow looked ready to take off. Under the French windows, sandbagged with towels, a pool seeped across the floor tiles. And still the storm bawled and tantrumed outside, our house the centre of its rage, the nails shrieking in the weatherboarding as the wind wrenched them like a crowbar.

I stood next to Daisy. One kind look would have cured me. But she refused to acknowledge me and disappeared upstairs.

It occurred to me that Milo was responsible for her moodiness – that when they were walking on the beach he'd upset her again and that, rather than be angry with him, she was punishing me. I decided to have a word with him, man to man. He was in the snug down the corridor, where Natalie and Bethany, tired of watching the rain, had unearthed a heap of board games. With no Em to deputise – her head was still bad and she'd gone back to bed – he was playing snakes and ladders with them. Pressed, I agreed to play a round or two. It was difficult to be candid when Natalie and Bethany were present, so for a while I gave myself up to the game and taught them the difference between 'die' and 'dice' ('you can have any number of dice but you can't have more than one die'), while my niftiness with the cup-shaker secured me three victories in a row. Bored of losing, the girls went off to find Rufus. It was then I seized my chance.

'I'm sorry to hear about you and Bianca,' I said, placing the counters for another game.

'It's for the best,' Milo said, after a pause. 'If we were going to break up, better now than later.'

'There's no one else involved, then?' An obvious question, I thought, but he seemed taken aback. 'If that's not too intrusive a question.'

He picked up the two dice and shook them in the cup.

'There wasn't. But Bianca's started seeing someone in New York.'

'And you?'

'I'm in no state. It's far too soon.'

'A good-looking bloke like you – you could have your pick.'

'The girls come first. All my energy goes into looking after them.'

'You're making a great job of it,' I said, though it was Em who'd looked after them all weekend.

'I do my best. Us breaking up is hard on them.'

'On Daisy, too,' I said.

'Daisy?'

'She told me about you moving to New York. It's unsettled her. She'll miss you.'

'And I'll miss her,' he said. Then, in case I got the wrong idea, which was probably the right idea, he added, 'I owe her a lot.'

I ran a finger down a snake. Blue eyes, long lashes, boyish cheeks, chest hair sprouting from his open collar: I wanted to slap him down, to crow that I'd had her and he hadn't. But what if he had?

'All I'm saying is be nice to her,' I said.

'I hope I am being.'

'Of course. But you know how sensitive she is. She feels rejected.'

'She shouldn't.'

'You can't be too attentive. She needs all the love she can get.'

The girls returned at that point, and demanded another game. But I'd said enough to get the point across. At the end of the game, which after my three earlier wins I didn't mind losing, Milo caught my eye and nodded, as if to say *Thanks, mate. That's good advice.*

To encourage him to pay court to Daisy went against the grain. But with any luck it might cheer her up.

In the living room, Daisy and Ollie sat in silence by the window, watching the rain. As I hesitated, wondering whether to join them, Em appeared, her headache seemingly cured.

'Poor Archie,' she said, taking my arm, 'out in this.'

'I'm sure they have tents,' Daisy said.

I squeezed Em's arm, as if to say *What parenting! If it were our child out in a storm we'd not be so laissez-faire.* But Daisy had a lot to take on board. Last night with me had blown her world apart.

'Drink anyone?' said Ollie, who had clearly had several.

'Just a small one,' I said, reluctant to put a damper on the evening.

No one felt like cooking. We were too tired, too lazy, too enthralled by the weather. And the drink we got through as we watched – even Milo's girls were treated to sips of wine – only increased our torpor. At 7.27 (a good time in my book) the rain finally stopped. Still no one talked about supper, till Milo's girls began to whine and he promised them scrambled egg if they changed into their nighties.

'While Milo's cooking for the girls,' Daisy said, 'I'll make something for the rest of us.'

'That'll be nice,' Milo said.

I could see Ollie clocking them both and wasn't surprised when he suggested a takeaway instead.

'You've done enough entertaining for one weekend, darling,' he said.

An ancient card was pinned to the noticeboard with a phone number for a restaurant called the Indian Pearl, and, unlikely though it seemed, someone answered immediately and took our order. The place was a twenty-minute drive, Ollie said. Since he was way over the limit I volunteered to do the driving. With Em and Milo absorbed in the girls, it was a chance for Ollie and Daisy to talk. Maybe he would confront her with his suspicions and Milo would be asked to leave.

Outside, the rain had eased off, not snare-drumming now but pinging like pebbles in a pan. I slammed the car door and was already turning into the drive when Daisy appeared, flagging me down.

'Ollie said you'd need a hand,' she said, climbing in beside me.

There's something I haven't told you which I ought to confess, even if it makes you think worse of me. It's about the debt Em and I were in. I say 'we' but we've always had separate accounts, so officially I was the one. I didn't tell her because it would have worried her and I thought I'd have the problem sorted soon enough. I've had such crises before. Something always turns up.

There's nothing wrong with gambling. People in the City are *paid* to do it and the money's not even their own. I've often envied them that power and freedom. With my head for numbers, I could have made a brilliant hedge fund manager. And I'd not have fucked up like the bankers and brokers in the City have done. Betting's the basis of our whole economy.

But you have to work to a system. And you can't take stupid risks when it's other people's savings you're playing with.

At least I've no one else's losses on my conscience. Still, I do feel bad about what happened. Back in January Em and I agreed to start saving for IVF, in case the traditional method for impregnation continued to fail. We gave ourselves a year: by putting aside a regular sum each month, we'd have saved enough for a first (and we hoped last) round of IVF by Christmas. The best way to proceed, I argued, was for Em to pay the household bills while I accumulated capital in my savings account. She had her doubts but in the end I talked her round. There was a principle at stake: I wanted to prove she could trust me. No more websites.

The plan worked like a dream. Free of domestic expenses – the gas, electricity, council tax, water and groceries – I saved over £400 a month. It's important to have some independence in a marriage and Em's not the kind of person to go looking at my bank statements (which I keep locked in a filing cabinet, just in case). But if she had looked she'd have seen not the usual fluctuations but steady growth. By the end of June, my account stood at £2,518.23.

Then the trouble broke at school. It's no excuse but when people are stressed they sometimes relapse. Not that I thought of it as a relapse at the time. The plan made sense. We had exceeded our monthly target, so where was the harm in rounding down the sum in my account and gambling the rest? The sum was modest, a mere £118.23. If I blew it, nothing was lost; if I got lucky, we could use the winnings for a holiday. I felt elated to renew old friendships: Mister Wheel, Mrs Fruit, Master Poker and Miss Slot. And to begin with I was – which you can be, believe me – a prudent gambler. Through skill and guile, I was up £500. But then my winnings went, through unbelievable bad luck, in less than fifteen minutes, late at night. In the old days I'd have had to wait till the banks opened before I could resume. It's not like that now, thanks to credit cards, debit cards and the Internet. Four hundred pounds, a month's savings, which I could soon make up, seemed a reasonable extra outlay. I had no intention of gambling the other £2,000. But. What more can I say? You know the rest.

Frankly, I despise myself at times.

If I tell you that by late August my debts stood at £9,700, I am of course including the £3,200 towards IVF treatment that would and should have been in my savings account by then: on paper, my various overdrafts and IOUs amounted to only £6,500. That still sounds a lot to you, I dare say. It does to me, too. But there are always people out there who'll lend you money, at a price. I'd been thinking of resorting to them but thanks to Ollie's impulsive bet I now didn't need to: £10,000 was in my grasp. The neatness of it – down to the £300 surplus I could gamble with – seemed preordained.

Perhaps then you can understand why, despite the shame and guilt swirling through me that Sunday evening, I also felt optimistic. 1–1, with tennis to come, and Ollie the better player, didn't look promising. But since we'd first agreed to the bet, several things had changed. First, if Ollie was dying he wouldn't need my money. Second, even if his tumour was benign, Daisy might decide to leave him and if she did, and we were living together, she would settle the debt for me. Third, more immediately, Ollie was drinking heavily: at this rate, he'd be in no condition to compete.

I had those three reasons to feel hopeful, plus one more. If Ollie won, he would be too much of a gentleman to insist I pay him; and if he lost, he would be too much of a gentleman to wriggle out of paying me. Till the weekend, I'd feared losing everything – my house, car, computer, job and wife. Now I stood to secure them again. With luck I might even upgrade them.

I left the Indian Pearl with two large brown bags, goo soaking through the bottom. Though the roads were still wet, the sky had cleared to the west, and behind, in the wing mirror, the dusk turned from salmon to tangerine. Daisy was sleeping, or pretending to, as she had on the way, her hunched body turned towards the nearside window. I knew she had come reluctantly, at Ollie's insistence, because – stupidly jealous as he now was – he didn't want her being around Milo in the kitchen; since she'd got in the car, we'd barely spoken. I felt cheerful, nonetheless, as if restored to her favour. Whether as a friend, lover or future husband didn't matter so long as I was somewhere in her life.

The rain began again as we left the main road, sloshing across then pounding at the windscreen – like the rinse cycle of a washing machine. I turned my headlights on and upped the tempo of the wipers, to no effect. The road became a river, the banks either side our only guide. I could imagine the engine dying and a tide rising high between the hedges, the car surfing over them on the crest of a bore and riding out through the meadows to the sea. Love for Daisy flooded through me. I felt elated rather than scared.

She sat up. The Indian meal had steamed up the windows and she rubbed her sleeve to make a porthole.

'Ollie told me about his tumour,' I said, sensing cancer was a safer topic than love.

It was a while before she responded. 'The consultant thinks it's benign.'

'Why did Ollie tell me he was dying, then?'

'You know what he's like. Without a certain level of hysteria, he can't function. Tension energises him and panic keeps him sane.'

'Telling people you're dying when you're healthy isn't sane.'

'He believes it. He really does. I could sit him down with his X-rays and scans tonight and show him the prognosis is good, but tomorrow he would still be convinced he's dying. It's how he is. A hypochondriac and a stoic rolled into one.'

I kept my eyes on the road but sensed her looking at me. The coldness was melting.

'He also told me you didn't know,' I said.

'Of course I know. It was me who made him see a doctor in the first place, because he was getting headaches.'

'So why did he say that?'

'I've no idea. Are you sure that's what he said?'

'Absolutely.'

'Maybe he thought it was the best way to stop the subject coming up – he hates talking about it.'

I slowed the car. Though I feared upsetting Daisy, I couldn't hide my dismay with Ollie.

'First he tells me he's dying when he's not,' I said. 'Then he tells me you don't know when you do. I think he enjoys telling lies. That story of staying at the farmhouse in 1976 is obviously bollocks too.'

'They did stay, I'm sure of it. Ollie has photos somewhere.'

'And the MGB being his dad's. And how he was head boy at school. And how he went to Sandhurst but then packed it in after a year.'

'That's right – he had some sort of breakdown. Of course it's true. It's all true. How can you even ask?'

'And his father drowning. He told me that this evening. I'd never heard the story before.'

'Don't be daft. He told you at university. Don't you remember the three of us discussing it? He certainly told me.'

Her gaze briefly fixed on me then swung away, like a lighthouse beam. Despite her anger, we were getting on again. Why couldn't she see we were meant to be together?

'You've such a weird take on Ollie,' she said, still protective despite no longer loving him. 'When you talk about him, it's as if he's someone else. Can't you see he's going through a bad patch? It's why he asked you for the weekend.'

'So it was his idea, not yours?'

'Don't be so touchy, Ian. I hoped it would take his mind off things. I remember how it was at university. The two of you were inseparable.'

'It was you he wanted to be with, not me.'

'We were a trio.'

'You were a couple. I was the hanger-on.'

'I'm the one who used to feel left out,' she said, leaning forward to clear the windscreen again. 'I still do sometimes. Em, too, I expect. We sit on the sidelines while you two go off.'

'Em enjoys your company.'

'Em makes me feel trivial. When I listen to her talking about her work, mine seems so pointless.'

'She respects what you do. We both do. Seriously.'

Seriously not. But I felt sorry for Daisy – something I'd rarely done before.

Over the last mile, the rain eased off and the river road dwindled to a stream. As we puttered like a barge along the drive towards the farmhouse, Daisy said: 'I'm sorry for what I said on the beach. Last night should never have happened. But I know you must have been drunk. We both were. And I do still want us to be friends.'

If she had apologised earlier, I wouldn't have suspected her and Milo. Nor would Ollie have got the wrong idea about them.

'Daisy,' I said, parking the car and cutting the engine.

'What?' she said.

'There's something . . .'

I reached for her hand but she was too quick for me. She'd already opened the door and was stretching for the paper bags on the back seat.

'What?' she repeated, impatiently, when all I wanted was to warn her of Ollie's suspicions.

'Never mind,' I said.

Daisy was right about Ollie's hypochondria. It seemed an odd affliction, in someone so physically strong. And for a time at university I failed to see it, because he worked so hard to appear tough. For instance, one Saturday during the second year he was badly trampled in a rugby maul and came home with a black eye, swollen lips and bruised cheekbones. Not once did he complain. When he groaned through the bedroom wall that night, his injuries weren't the cause, but Daisy.

Minor ailments could send him into a panic, though. Was that mole on his body cancerous? Could the temperature he was running be due to Lassa fever, rather than flu? And he didn't just worry on his own behalf. One night we were eating together at the house – a rare evening without Daisy. He had cooked us both steaks. They were meant to be fillet steaks but mine was tough – no doubt the butcher, taking Ollie for a clueless toff, had palmed him off with a cheaper cut. A lump of meat stuck in my gullet. This wasn't the first time such a thing had happened and I knew the only remedy was to wait: the gathering saliva made breathing a struggle but there was no danger of me choking to death. It was Ollie who panicked. He thought the meat must be obstructing my windpipe and dialled 999. A manic phone call ensued, with him demanding that an ambulance be sent and me protesting it was unnecessary. When the operator hung up, thoroughly confused, Ollie dragged me outside, intent on driving me to hospital himself. By then his hysteria had begun to affect me: I was panicking and gasping for breath. But as the night air hit us on the doorstep, the steak-lump suddenly loosened and slipped down.

He'd been a good friend that night. But perhaps at some level he was also willing me to die, so as to re-enact the defining trauma of his childhood: as I struggled for breath, my mouth filling with salty fluid, I must have reminded him of his father drowning. That's if the story of the drowning was true, of course. As I sat in the car outside the farmhouse, with Daisy's words still ringing in my head ('Of course it's true. It's all true'), I tried to persuade myself it must be.

Ollie was my oldest friend, the brother I'd never had: why doubt him? But my faith was weak. He had lied to me too many times. If I trusted him, I'd be at risk. He might even destroy me.

'Dessert wine?' said Ollie, who had meanwhile opened another red.

'Not for me,' Milo said.

Rather than eat in the poky dining room, we'd dragged the metal table in from the terrace, and were sitting by the living-room windows watching the rain. The ruins of the Indian takeaway lay before us – spilled rice grains, torn-off ears of nan, silver trays with saffron-orange sauce. Em sat opposite me, with Daisy facing Milo, and Ollie at the head of the table. Natalie and Bethany were sound asleep and, washout though it must have been, Archie was still at his gig. All was peaceful.

Except Ollie, who, having dozed during the meal, had now sprung to life again, full of mischief.

'Don't be feeble,' he said, filling Milo's glass.

'Whoa. I'm not much of a drinker. It goes to my head.'

'That's why you need it. It'll inspire you. You're an artist.'

'I *trained* as an artist. Now I barely get time for my own stuff.'

'That's not true,' Daisy said, turning to Em. 'You should see his work. It's wonderful.'

I avoided Em's eye, knowing she hates gushiness as much as I do. We don't hold with enthusiasm in Ilkeston.

'I'm sure Milo's a genius,' Ollie said. 'But drink will raise him to even greater heights.'

'Shut up, Ollie,' Daisy said. 'You don't know what you're talking about. When have you ever taken an interest in art?'

'I go to openings with you. I see the portfolios you bring home. If Milo's art is something I'd enjoy, here's to him.'

Ollie smiled and clinked glasses with everyone.

'I'm not sure you would enjoy it, if you like figurative stuff,' Milo said. 'To me figurative art is about duplicating, and I don't see the point. The world exists already – why copy it?'

'But that's what people want, isn't it?' Ollie said. I nodded in agreement. 'For artists to portray things they can recognise.'

'To me that's no better than ventriloquism. Here's a voice we know. Here's a landscape we know. And here's a copy. What a dull mechanical exercise! Art should be something more.'

'OK,' Ollie said, 'you're not figurative. But I assume you could be, if you chose. I mean, if we asked you to do a sketch of the five of us sitting round this table, you could knock one off.'

'I don't know about knock off . . .'

'Call it what you like, if we gave you a pencil and paper you could draw us, right? And any sketch you came up with would be markedly better than anything the rest of us could come up with?'

'It's not the way I work.'

'Come on,' Ollie said. 'You're a professional artist and designer. Don't tell me anything I did might be equally good. There must be a sketch pad round here somewhere. Let's have a competition. We'll take a sheet each and a pencil and all get cracking, then fold the finished sketches up and pass them round and see if we can guess which one is yours.'

'Shut up, Ollie,' Daisy said, 'you're being a pain.'

'It's a bit of fun. So Milo can prove a point.'

'He doesn't need to,' Daisy said. 'He's saying that representational accuracy isn't the way to judge art. I agree.'

Were they playing footsie? Was his hand on her knee? I knew that Ollie must have his suspicions.

'Unless Milo can do the figurative stuff,' he said, 'why should we trust the rest?'

'It's not a matter of trust.'

'But how can I judge it when I don't know what I'm looking at?'

'Take no notice, Milo. When Ollie's had a drink or two he likes to argue. It's his training as a barrister.'

'Exactly my point, sweetie. Because I trained as a lawyer, I've the knowledge and skills to practise as a professional. That's what people pay me for, because they know what they're getting. Whereas –'

'Whereas people pay me because they *don't* know what they're getting,' Milo said. 'I'd be a failure otherwise. It's like Matisse – when his Russian patron commissioned him to do a painting of a blue room, he did it in red.'

'So much for the patron.'

'The patron was delighted. Even if he hadn't been, the painting was a triumph. It's not the job of an artist to make people feel comfortable. They're comfortable enough already.'

'Do you think the people I represent are comfortable?' Ollie said. 'The man falsely accused of murder? Or the girl raped by some thug?'

'Of course not,' Milo said, suddenly sheepish. 'Your work must be very distressing at times.'

'Don't apologise,' Daisy said. 'Ollie loves playing the gladiator.'

'It's not about play,' Ollie said.

'Art is, though. I think that's the nature of our disagreement,' Milo said, smiling and leaning back in his chair. 'You're demanding the same earnestness from my work that you bring to yours. There's your error – art should be fun.'

Ollie, sipping his wine, seemed chastened, vanquished, stuck for words. But as Daisy stood up to ask who wanted coffee and who herb tea, he said: 'It certainly seems to give you and Daisy a lot of fun.'

'Sorry?' Milo said.

'I barely see Daisy these days. And when I do it's Milo this and Milo that all day long.'

'You're being ridiculous,' Daisy said, embarrassed at being caught out or at Ollie making a spectacle of himself. 'I'll put the kettle on.'

'I'll clear these,' Em said.

'I need a pee,' Milo said.

I put my hand over the glass as Ollie tried to pour me dessert wine but consented to the red. He filled his own glass at the same time, then half emptied it in one swig. Marooned at the head of the table, he looked lost, as if – with only me there – the purpose of the evening had slipped away. Female murmurs came from the kitchen where Daisy would be complaining that Ollie was impossible and Em consoling her that all men were as bad.

'Take it easy, Ollie,' I said, as he swigged again. 'That wasn't funny. It's too near the bone.'

'Ah. So you admit something *is* going on.'

'His wife has just left him. He's feeling vulnerable. It's no time for jokes.'

'It wasn't a joke. I know now. I've seen.'

'Seen what?'

'The tissues. With dried sperm on them. In the waste bin.'

'No, Ollie,' I said.

'Just like your dream.'

'No, you mustn't think –'

But before I could disabuse him Milo was back.

'That was quick,' Ollie said. 'Prostate in good order, then.'

He seemed set to renew his attack. Perhaps literally: the knives we'd been using were steak knives, sharp enough to penetrate a heart. I'd never known Ollie be violent. But nor had I seen him so pissed and self-deluding. The prostate reference showed how he was thinking: he'd be onto Milo's penis next and where he might have inserted it. I readied myself for mayhem. But for once my good counsel prevailed.

'More red?' was all he said, backing off.

Relaxing, relieved, as if he'd imagined the earlier insinuation, Milo smiled and shook his head.

'I should get to bed. The girls wake up early.'

'Don't be a wimp. Just the one.'

'Who's being a wimp?' Daisy said, carrying in the tray: herb teas for her and Milo, coffee for Ollie and me, nothing for Em.

'Milo's talking about going to bed.'

'I don't blame him. It's been a long day.'

'But we've not had our sketching competition. So he can show us up.'

'For fuck's sake, Ollie, leave it alone.'

'Well, OK then, darling,' Ollie said, pronouncing his words with a pedantic accuracy that betrayed him more than if he'd slurred them, 'let's play Scrabble instead. Or Monopoly. Or have a debate about something. Politics. Religion. They always get people going. You choose, Daisy. No? Milo then? Em? Ian? OK, good idea. Let's talk about sex. More specifically, the problem of sustaining a sex life when you've been with someone for ten years or more. Isn't that why marriages break up?'

'Ollie, for Christ's sake.'

'I'm not being personal, sweetie, just making a general point. It's obvious: the need for sex brings people together, but once they're together the need wears off. There's something faintly indecent about it, like having sex with the family pet. And it's so routine it scarcely registers. Ian and Em, let's take you. We're all friends here, you can be honest. When was the last time? Last week? Last month? Last year? I bet you can't remember. That's fine. I can't remember the last time, either. Sex isn't for people over forty. It's for kids, or for having kids, not for us lot.'

I looked at my reflection, upside down in a dessert spoon, with candles flickering over my head. I didn't dare look at Em, who if she wasn't yet tearful soon would be. Even her hands, on the table, seemed reproachful: *We should have told them about our problem. If we had, Ollie wouldn't have said what he just did.*

'Shut up, Ollie,' Daisy said, 'you're embarrassing everyone.'

'Only you, my love,' he said, back on track. 'I'm trying to explain why even the best of people can stray. Because they're trying to recapture a lost excitement. Hence love affairs, and fuck-buddies, and dogging, and all the rest. I don't sit in judgement. What I'm saying – this is important – what I'm saying is that I *understand*.'

Daisy passed me the coffee pot as if he wasn't there. I didn't blame her. Alcohol had mugged him and scarpered with his brains.

'Milo? Daisy? Anything to contribute? No? Let me make my other point then. When two people have been together a long time, they might not make love as often as they used to. But that doesn't mean they don't love each other. Take Daisy and me. We're solid as rock. She might have her head turned now and then. But she won't ever leave me. Tell them, sweets.'

'Tell them what?' Daisy said. 'That you're drunk? They can see that for themselves.'

'Me, drunk? This is my right hand and this is my left hand, I can stand well enough and speak well enough – what's drunk about that?'

Defiant, he poured himself another.

'I think I ought to go,' Milo said.

All he meant was go to bed, but Daisy heard it differently.

'You're not going anywhere,' Daisy said. 'Ollie doesn't know what he's saying. In the morning, when I remind him, he'll apologise to us all, and if he doesn't then *I'll* go.'

'Tell you what,' Ollie said, not so out of it as to miss the chance of a barristerial flourish, 'since no one seems to appreciate my presence, let me be the one to go. Night-night.'

Smiling and nodding, he grabbed the edge of the table with both hands, a manoeuvre that pivoted him into a standing position but also jerked the table. Several glasses tipped over. The wobble sent him lurching backwards but he steadied himself on the wall behind and, with great deliberation, like someone avoiding stepping on cracks, made his way across the room and down the corridor.

'I'm sorry,' Daisy said, once he was out of earshot. 'He gets like this sometimes. He won't remember any of it in the morning. It's nothing personal, Milo.'

Milo, nervously sipping his herb tea, looked unconvinced.

'When he's drunk, he misjudges his tone,' Daisy said. 'I should have stopped him earlier.'

'He wasn't implying . . .' Milo said.

'Of course not. He'll be mortified when I tell him tomorrow.'

'I'll get to bed, then.'

Milo wandered off in a daze, his bare feet printing the damp tiles. If he knew what was good for him, he'd clear off before Ollie woke. Good riddance: his presence had all but ruined the weekend. Not that the fault for tonight's debacle was entirely his. In being attentive to Daisy, he had simply been polite – as everyone except Ollie could see.

Once he was gone, Em burst into tears.

'Don't tell me Ollie's upset you too,' Daisy said, reaching for her hand. 'What is it?'

While Em sobbed, unable to speak, I too reached for her hand, my fingers closing on Daisy's as I did, the three of us locked together at the table, the two women in my life and me.

'Tell me, love,' Daisy said, drawing her hand away though I could sense she longed to keep it there.

Between us Em was a heaving mess.

'Let's get you to bed,' I said.

'What upset you?' Daisy said.

'I'll take her upstairs.'

'What was it Ollie said?'

'She's in no fit state.'

'I know you want to tell me, love.'

'Bed's the best place.'

'*Fuck it, Ian, leave her where she is*.'

So I left her where she was and she told. The works. With me there to hear. I suppose I could have left them to it.

I wasn't *made* to stay. And Em was protective of me, up to a point, describing the problem as 'our problem'. But in other respects she didn't spare me at all, complaining that I had been slow to seek help and slower still to see that IVF was the only option. Her description of our sex life as 'normal and healthy' was especially unfortunate: it must have suggested to Daisy that I still wanted Em, when I'd told her I didn't.

Since half the conversation was conducted in whispers, with Em in Daisy's arms on the sofa and me banished to a wicker chair, I wasn't close enough to hear every word nor sober enough to retain them all. I confess that's true of the evening generally: because my hearing's bad, and I was drinking heavily, I may have occasionally got things wrong. For instance, I could have sworn that it was Ollie who chose sex as a topic for debate, yet Em later complained that it was me. If so, I wasn't thinking straight, failing to see where it might lead. But it's just not true that I 'egged Ollie on' or that I kept topping up his glass in order to 'make trouble'. Sometimes Em completely misses the point.

I must have nodded off as I sat there because next thing Daisy was the one wailing.

'Where's Archie? He ought to be back. What time is it?'

'It's 12.13,' I said, trying to hide how ominous that was, twelve and thirteen being two of my least favourite numbers.

'If he's out there in the rain, he'll be catching his death.' Daisy scanned her mobile for a message. 'No reception again. What if he's been trying to call? We should never have let him go.'

I offered to take Daisy in the car and look for him. But Em said I had drunk too much and that she would. They left me to clear up – to dump the silver curry trays in the bin, wash the plates and cutlery, gather up the bottles and wipe the rice grains and curry blots from the table. It was past two before they got back, without Archie, and rather than come through to the living room, where I sat waiting in the dark, they went straight upstairs. Not ready to follow, I bullied Rufus outside for a tour of the orchard. The air was black and soupy, fine rain swaying in it. Cries of pain – prey and predator – echoed from the fields. Finally, around three, I headed upstairs, climbing in beside Em's moist body and wishing Daisy was there too or instead.

Monday

I was woken by shouting below. In the dark I couldn't find my watch but a hint of lemon behind the curtain suggested dawn. It was easy to guess what was happening. Milo, waking early or not having slept at all, had packed, dressed, shushed his daughters from bed and – hoping to make a quick getaway – urged them downstairs. Only to find that Ollie was waiting or had heard him descending and gone in pursuit. The shouts were muffled; they seemed to come from outside, Milo having stuck his luggage in the boot, and his key in the ignition, before Ollie confronted him. Would Ollie use only his fists? The alcohol that had sedated him at the dinner table would have worn off by now. There were knives in the kitchen, swords on the wall, pitchforks in the outhouse. Was that a little female voice I could hear, frightened and protesting? I felt sorry for Natalie and Bethany, forced to watch. Milo might be younger and fitter, but the adrenalin of righteousness was pumping through Ollie. The violence would be severe.

I was tempted to leave them to it. But the sound of that other voice – a woman's not a girl's – made it impossible. It was one thing for Ollie to chop Milo to pieces; that had a certain justice. But I didn't want Daisy getting hurt as well.

Shoving a T-shirt on with my boxers, I crept downstairs to find the front door closed. The shouts weren't coming from outside but from the living room. I ran along the corridor and turned the handle, expecting sweat, panic, pools of blood. Even the best of men sometimes forget themselves and Ollie had been pushed beyond endurance.

There he was, sure enough, in pale blue pyjamas. And Daisy, with a silk dressing gown pulled loosely over her nightie. Both in a rage. But not with each other. They were shouting at the person between them: Archie.

I can't deny a sense of anticlimax.

'And now, on top of everything, you've woken Uncle Ian,' Ollie shouted.

'Don't mind me,' I said. 'What's going on?'

'Archie just got back.'

'We've been frantic,' Daisy said, her face pallid and her eyes red. 'Why didn't you tell us where you were, Archie?'

Archie's hair hung in rats' tails. Mascara had run down his cheeks. His trainers were slurried with mud.

'We've been through this, Mum.'

'I've still not had a proper answer. I called you at 1.15 and got a ring tone. Why didn't you pick up?'

'I was with people. It wasn't cool.'

'Not cool to speak to your own mother? Just to tell me you were OK?'

'I called you back.'

'When? Em and I waited in the car for twenty minutes.'

'Then I texted.'

'I didn't get a text.'

'I sent one.'

'There's no reception here. You know that, Archie.'

'Yeah, and that's why I didn't call earlier.'

I'd been right about it being dawn. The light was poor, with rain pocking the panes, but the birds were in full chorus.

'So where were you?' Daisy said, renewing the attack.

'The gig got rained off so we went back to someone's.'

'Someone's?'

'Jed, I think he's called.'

'You *think*. You told us you were with friends from school.'

'I was. Then I met some new people. There were a lot of us there.'

'Doing what?'

'Hanging out.'

'Taking drugs, you mean.'

'No, Mum. I'm clean.'

'And how did you get home?'

'Walked.'

'On your own?'

'Yeah.'

'You're soaked.'

'It's raining, in case you haven't noticed.'

'Don't get smart with me.'

'You're not my keeper.'

He had said the same to his father on the tennis court. Perhaps that's why Ollie now weighed in.

'Until you leave home you're our responsibility and we don't want you wandering round alone in the middle of the night.'

'Or in the middle of nowhere,' Daisy added. 'Why didn't someone give you a lift?'

'Dunno. Too busy.'

'You could have got lost. You could have been wandering round till morning. You could have . . .'

Archie's face was so wet and blotchy it took a while for me to realise he was crying. It was impossible for Daisy to cradle him while standing up, so they dropped to the sofa, where she held his face to her breasts as he sobbed about a fight at the house and having to leave and being given directions to Badingley but missing a turning and floods and strange sounds from the fields and a car crawling by with a staring man in it and how he *had* phoned and *had* texted but there was no fucking reception was there so what was the fucking point. While he sobbed into the V of her dressing gown she gave Ollie a look that said *Don't you dare say a word – let him cry all he likes*. I doubt Ollie would have spoken anyway. Archie might be overdoing it, as he had when the tennis ball hit him, but even Ollie seemed touched, and plonked himself the other side of Archie, stroking his hair and rubbing his back. I too was moved – by Archie's head shamelessly nuzzling his mother's breasts, as I'd done, on the same sofa. He was her son. He'd every right. But I felt usurped.

Mouthing goodnight, though it was morning, I left them to it, slipping back along the tiled corridor and up to bed.

Some minutes later I heard footsteps on the stairs, then two doors closing, one after the other. Archie, exhausted, would be asleep at once. Not so Ollie and Daisy, who had outstanding business from last night. Though their voices didn't carry, it was easy for me to imagine the row. Arms folded, her hair swirling angrily around her, Daisy would be giving Ollie hell.

How dare you treat a guest like that! How dare you imply that something's going on between me and Milo!

Ollie, unfazed, indeed annoyed with himself for not speaking more plainly at dinner, would have his answer ready.

Why do I think there's something going on? Because you dragged him up here when we're on holiday. Because you've been all over each other all weekend. And because of the tissues.

She would shake her head at that point, bewildered.

Which tissues?

The tissues in the waste bin.

What about them?

You know what I'm talking about.

I haven't a clue what you're talking about.

I'm talking about you and Milo having sex.

Hearing which, outraged, Daisy says: *If you believe that of me, you can forget about the wedding.*

Fine, Ollie replies, *since I can't trust you any more, I don't want to marry you anyway.*

Then I'll marry someone who does want me.

Who, Milo?

Not Milo, Daisy says, *someone else.*

I listened as they argued in my inner ear, knowing Daisy would be too discreet to mention what had happened between us. That could come later, when she confessed (to herself as well as to him) that she was in love with me. For now all that mattered was to get through the weekend.

Someone else? Who?

None of your business.

Slipping from bed, I crept to the bathroom in the hope their voices might breach the lath-and-plaster partition. I put my ear to the wall tiles as I pissed: nothing. But as I pulled the chain, the sound of Daisy laughing carried through. Laughter wasn't in the script. Perhaps I'd imagined it. But as I crossed back to the bedroom, a second laugh, Ollie's, floated along the landing, and then Daisy's voice saying: *We should never have invited him*. Or if not those words exactly, something very like them.

They're talking about Milo, I thought, climbing back into bed. But why would they laugh about it, after the tensions over dinner last night? Then an ugly thought struck: that it was me they were talking about; that Ollie had used me to justify his suspicions; that Daisy had mocked me when he did. The dialogue was easily reconstructed.

It was Ian who put the idea in my head.

Ian! Why would anyone listen to Ian, you know how jealous he is.

Jealous of who?

You, me, Milo, everyone. I know he's your friend –

Your friend too.

He's not my friend, not after this weekend.

Why? What's he done?

You don't want to know.

Tell me.

Put it this way: we should never have invited them. Em's all right. But he's a nightmare.

Laughter from Ollie: *I know what you mean.*

Incidentally, do you know what Em told me about him? Well . . .

So that was why they were laughing at me. I lay on the sheet, sweatily reviewing the finale of the night before. While I'd been there to listen, Em had described our fertility problem as a mutual one. But then the two of them had gone off in the car. In my absence, there was nothing to stop her telling Daisy the truth. The full works. Every shameful detail. Now Daisy, in turn, was telling Ollie. Hence the laughter, as he delighted – they both delighted – in my humiliation.

I didn't expect them to understand. No one does. If you say you're infertile, people assume you can't get it up. Daisy knew that was untrue. But she could hardly tell Ollie *how* she knew. All she would have told him was what Em had told her. That I'm deficient. A sub-prime sperm producer. That I shoot blanks.

It didn't seem that way when we first visited the clinic. The doctor spoke of 'non-specific infertility' and it was Em – less physically fit than I am – who did the initial tests. They showed she was ovulating normally. More from pride than fear, I stalled on my tests, allowing her to think I'd done them when I hadn't and, then, worse, when I *was* tested, lying to her about the results. I now knew it was one in ten million she'd get pregnant through 'unassisted intercourse'. But I'd had outside bets come home before and I kept on plugging away. Eventually the clinic had us in together and the truth came out. Em felt too sorry for me to be angry for long but she bemoaned the delay: if I'd been honest, we could have begun saving for IVF six months earlier. In penance, I agreed to start saving up – from now on we'd put a hefty sum aside each month. But as I've confessed already (by now you know every sad truth about me), the savings are no longer there.

To Em, my condition is a medical fact, not a matter for shame. Many times in recent months she has urged me to 'talk to someone', and maybe I will one day. But the thought of Ollie and Daisy knowing the truth, and laughing together in bed about my inadequacy, stirred memories of past suffering at their hands. As I lay there with my head under the pillow, I told myself to calm down: I mustn't let my mind run away with me. But I couldn't now unhear what I thought they'd said.

Storms are supposed to clear the air. Afterwards should be like the morning after a death – clean, formal, lucid, empty, fresh. Global warming seems to have changed all that. Or perhaps it was Badingley's microclimate. At any rate, when I got up a second time that day, around nine, the air was slimy and rank, a cold sweat across the windowpanes, the sky a soiled grey sheet. Leaving Em to doze, I made myself tea and opened the French windows for Rufus. Outside was breathless and clammy. To judge from the beaded grass, the silvered rose bushes, the eucalyptus leaves like laundry dripping from clothes pegs, it had been raining all night. When Rufus returned from his tour of the orchard, he looked like the hull of a boat, tar-blackened halfway up. He shook himself out, hosing the terrace and my bare feet.

I brought a cane chair out and sat with my mug in the soupy light. The garden was spectral. I gazed at it through empty sockets. Bird calls echoed through my skull.

I remembered Ollie saying that the house had no foundations. The fissured earth would be awash now, and if the water pooled, then froze when winter came, surely the bricks would move, the flint crack, the walls give way, the whole ramshackle structure come down.

You build your life on a handful of principles – trust, reason, fairness, love and friendship – and when you find they're an illusion you collapse.

'Up already?' Ollie said, behind me.

'This is late for me,' I said.

'More tea?'

'If you're making it.'

'Anyone else about?'

'No.'

Perhaps Milo had made an early start and gone home. Two wooden tennis rackets lay twisted on the lawn, where his girls had left them. There'd be no tennis played with them again. By the look of the sky – bulging like a ceiling after a flood – there'd be no tennis for Ollie and me, either.

'Sorry about the performance,' Ollie said, handing me tea. I was surprised he could remember any of it, and was about to say so – till I realised he meant Archie's, not his own. 'He never cries like that. He was really shaken up.'

'Useful lesson,' I said. 'A shock to the system will do him good.'

'Do you think?'

'We all need discipline, Ollie. Surely Sandhurst taught you that.'

'Parenting's not like the army. Daisy and I try to be flexible.'

'There's your mistake. Why do you think Archie stopped going to school? Because he knew he could get away with it. That there'd be no comeback.'

'There were other factors. It's complicated.'

'You're making excuses for him.'

'Am I?'

'I know it's not easy,' I said, backing down. 'You've had a tough few months. I'm sure he'll be fine in the end.'

Had Em been there, she'd have urged Ollie to be more loving and affirming as a father. Though I stopped short of such soppy nonsense, I tried not to make him feel criticised. We were leaving today. I wanted to depart on good terms.

Swallows chizzled overhead, like wires short-circuiting. Occasional swifts, too, on their long fuse. The air crackled, as if charged. It would rain again any minute.

'It doesn't look good for tennis,' I said.

'It'll dry out later.'

'Em and I ought to head off before lunch.'

'And miss our decider?'

I expected him to protest at length but he shrugged and sipped his tea.

'We'll have to think of an alternative,' I said, humouring him.

'Anything to win the bet, eh?'

'I couldn't care less about the bet. I'm just trying to honour our deal.'

The leaves on the eucalyptus tree rattled in a sudden gust. Ollie's indifference shocked me. Was he tired? Hung-over? Afraid of losing? Or after Daisy had told him about my fertility issues did he think me not man enough to be worth taking on? The fucker. I would show him. We'd shaken hands on it. I'd not let him weasel out.

If tennis was impossible, a board game would do. Even better, I had some cards in my suitcase – my own special deck. I was about to suggest I fetch them when a car pulled up in the driveway.

'Who the hell's that?' Ollie said, marching off like a squire to evict the trespassers.

* * *

For what it's worth – one last word on the subject – my sperm count is perfectly normal: four million spermatozoa per gram of testicle per day. The problem's not numbers, but movement. Motility: the ability of sperm to move by flagellate swimming. Mobility, if you prefer. Where your average sperm goes off like an underwater missile, making straight for the target, mine amble around in circles. They're clueless, work-shy, undirected – like teenagers who won't stir from bed. The doctor at the clinic put it more kindly, describing my sperm as 'hyperactive' rather than idle: they thrash around, in wildly gyrating patterns, unaware of their purpose. Either way, it's a judgement. My sperm are just like me.

I'd been wrong about Milo disappearing to London. He'd got up early and driven to Frissingfold with the girls, in search of goodies; his was the car we heard coming up the drive. 'My contribution to breakfast,' he said, carrying in croissants, Danish pastries, orange juice, eggs, bacon and marmalade, along with flowers for Daisy and a bottle of whisky for Ollie. The obsequiousness of the gesture – when his only contribution until then had been to ruin the weekend – was transparent. And his knee-crooking gratitude 'for a wonderful break' renewed my suspicions: if his relationship with Daisy was innocent, he should be confronting Ollie, not appeasing him. I was surprised Ollie couldn't see this and appalled to hear him apologising ('Fear I drank too much last night. Hope I didn't say anything out of order'). As for Daisy, the flowers made her coo and simper: 'You shouldn't have.' Indeed he shouldn't. It was high time he fucked off.

(It's true that Em had also wanted to buy our hosts a thank-you present, till I dissuaded her. If Ollie and Daisy wanted flowers or whisky or suchlike, they would buy their own, I said; it wasn't as if they were short of the wherewithal. Only an outsider like Milo would resort to empty tokens. Real friends knew better.)

Though the sky was black as a Pennine graveyard, Ollie insisted on everyone having breakfast outside, as if we'd suffocate if we stayed indoors. He wasn't far wrong. When I went in, to help Daisy take the croissants from the oven, it was as though I were drowning in lava, hot slurry closing over my head. This wasn't the moment to discuss our future so I stuck to small talk instead. I was just saying something about the weather forecast when we heard a high-soprano scream. Both of us rushed outside.

Em and Milo were already in attendance, Milo pulling Bethany onto his lap while Em asked her where it hurt. She was crying too hard to speak but pointed to her arm. We huddled round, as if for a baptism: a screaming infant with a wet head cradled by a solemn adult. The wasp sting looked minuscule – a pinprick – but Bethany was enjoying the drama too much to calm down: an audience of grown-ups, raptly attentive, and she centre stage. Ollie, in a panic, rushed off to fetch ointments, sticking plasters, antihistamines. The only sensible one there was Em, who tried to squeeze out the sting. What is it with kids and pain? You'd think, from Bethany's screams, no human had ever been stung by a wasp before. *Come on, boy, walkies*, I said, to get Rufus away. Exposure to screaming brats is bad for dogs. They're sensitive animals.

Ten minutes' tantrum later, Bethany calmed down. After that, no one except me felt like croissants. But the episode had a happy outcome, persuading Milo it was time he headed home.

'Do you *really* have to?' Daisy protested. But after last night she had more sense than to push it. The girls ran off to help their dad fetch the bags.

'Making a run for it, is he?' I said, sitting next to Ollie.

'Yes, to beat the traffic,' he said, missing the point.

'Nasty bugger.'

'Yes, it must have been a big wasp, the poor girl got quite a shock,' he said, missing it again.

Ten minutes later, we gathered in the drive. There were kisses all round, but Milo, to avoid suspicion, gave Daisy just a peck on the cheek. As we stood waving them off, I watched her for signs of emotion. Was that a tear in her eye? It didn't matter now. One less rival, I thought, as Milo's Saab turned out of sight.

'Game of cards?' I asked.

Ollie shook his head and suggested a walk by the sea instead. I muttered about having to leave soon.

'There's time. I'll have you back within the hour.'

I'd no great enthusiasm for the idea, but with a long journey ahead of us, it made sense to give Rufus some exercise.

'Let's take swimming trunks, in case,' one or other of us said.

Em, upstairs packing and not best pleased, declined to come, as did Daisy, who was already making us sandwiches for the journey. With Archie asleep after his night wanderings, that left just the two of us, as Ollie doubtless intended.

The weather wasn't MGB weather. But Ollie, resurgent, had the hood down before I could protest, and Rufus, his head hanging out the side of the car, appreciated the open ride. Hills and hedges went by while Ollie rattled on. It could have been university again and him driving us to a golf course or country pub. Mostly he talked about his father: that last holiday and the fun they'd had before the drowning. I kept my eyes closed till we reached the sea and he cut the engine. I wanted to love him, as I'd always loved him. But he had made himself a stranger with his lies.

The beach was the same one we had cycled to. But under cloud, in the seeping light, the place looked unfamiliar. Those tar-black wooden huts housing oily winches – had they been there the previous day? And the fishing boats tilted to one side? And the concrete blocks thrown like giant dice in the dunes, the gaps between them too narrow for German tanks to pass through – shouldn't such fortifications have been removed by now, seven decades on? A roar came from the tideline, where the water was kicking up a storm. Rufus scuttered off into the marram grass, puppily excited by the scent of other dogs, though there were none to be seen, no humans either. The light was weary and the beach smelled of decay, but I marvelled at the emptiness. On this overcrowded island, on the last weekend of summer, we had the coastline to ourselves.

I knelt down to unlace my trainers, while a barefoot Ollie headed off towards the dunes. The mist keeping us under wraps was partly fog and partly sea spray. To the north, just visible through the haze, were a stripy lighthouse and red-brick houses tumbling into the sea; to the south, a grisly power station and a comical water tower; in between, unpeopled dunes and shingle. Even the gulls had deserted the place, off for richer pickings out at sea.

We followed Rufus along the ridge of the dunes. There was nothing to stop us descending to the beach – no wartime barbed wire or vertical drops. And a walk by the shoreline, over flat white stones with clumps of sea cabbage, would have been easier than slogging through sand. But we kept to higher ground, as if a view of the sea put us in command. Not that the sea looked dangerous, not exactly. But its animation was surprising, each fresh collapse shuffling the stones. Last night's storm had died from the wind but was living in the water – in the waves, grinding the shingle, and the black, capricious depths beyond.

'I love this place,' Ollie said. 'If I'd time, I'd look for a house here.'

'Make time,' I said. 'Ring some estate agents.'

'That's not what I meant.'

We were sitting in a sandy hollow looking out to sea. I couldn't let it pass again.

'You don't have cancer, Ollie. I've talked to Daisy. I know.'

There was a clump of marram grass beside him. He yanked at it till a blade came free, which he brandished like a sword.

'I've tried telling Daisy. She won't listen.'

'You told me you *hadn't* told her.'

'I asked you not to bring it up, that's all.'

'She says there's probably nothing wrong with you.'

'That's what she wants me to think.'

'It's what the consultant says. It's the truth, Ollie.'

He stood up, looming over me.

'Whose side are you on?' he shouted.

We were alone in a peaceful hollow at the edge of a long beach, not a soul for miles, the sea stretching blackly to the fogged horizon. And there was Ollie, shouting, a spear of marram grass in his hand.

'It's not about sides,' I said, grabbing the spear from him, aware how absurd we must look, though there was no one to see.

'You just accused me of lying!'

'A man close to death can't ride a bike like you did yesterday.'

He paused a moment, then reached down to touch my shoulder and said, in a softer voice: 'It's because you're my friend that you don't want to believe the worst, Ian, and I appreciate that. Come on. Let's hit the beach.'

We scrambled down the sand cliff to the shingle, where Rufus had found a dead cuttlefish, which he brought over and dropped at my feet like a bone. I threw it in the sea for him to swim for and stood at the tideline, letting the waves slide froth-tipped to my feet. Ollie's stubbornness didn't surprise me. He hated losing arguments or being caught out. I felt better for confronting him, nevertheless, purged and refreshed. The closer to the waves I stood, the wetter the waft of sea spray on my face. There was a breeze, too – the energy of pounded water – where the dunes had been windless. A good blow, my mother would have called it. I felt sorry for Ollie, exposed as a fantasist and denied the finale of our bet. But I was pleased I'd had my say.

One plunge into the water was enough for Rufus: he dropped the cuttlebone, shook himself out and ambled off. The froth swirling round my feet was feathery and brownish white, like the dead owl I'd found. The waves looked taller than they had from the cliff – but choppy, irregular, not surfers' waves. Above them, through the mist, a fishing trawler was heading in, gulls flying from it like pennants. The sea must have been rough when the crew set sail at dawn, but here they were, safely returning.

'Fishing boat,' I shouted, but Ollie, twenty yards off, couldn't hear because of the waves, so I pointed and gestured instead. Behind him, over the dunes, the sky was splitting up, a blue-black crack – the colour of agapanthus – breaking the monotonous grey.

'What?' he shouted, at my side.

'There's a fishing boat. See?'

'I thought you meant the buoys.'

He pointed left and right offshore. Beyond the breakers, a hundred yards apart, two white heads were bobbing, like the buoys we'd seen on the other beach.

'Who'd moor a boat here?' I said. 'Unless the buoys are to warn against rocks.'

'There are no rocks.'

'Why are they there, then?'

'To denote safe bathing.'

'It doesn't look safe,' I said.

'Of course it's safe. I remember swimming here with my father. They're probably the same buoys as then – white, see. All the modern buoys are orange.'

The story seemed a typical Ollie story. I held my tongue.

Rufus scurried between us, in the water. I looked at my watch: 12.13 it said, which should have told me.

'So, did you bring your trunks?'

'Shit. I left them in the car. Did you?'

'Who needs them? There's nobody around.'

'You're not serious?'

'I will if you will.'

'Go on, then.'

We began stripping off.

'We must be mad,' I said, trying not to look at Ollie's cock. I was still undressing when he stepped into the violet water.

'Anyway,' he shouted, wading in past his knees.

'Anyway what?' I shouted, dropping my boxers on the cairn of clothes.

By the time I looked up, I'd already lost him in the breakers. It seemed amazing he had got out so far in such a short time, all the more so when I tried to follow. The shallows were knotty as a mangrove swamp, with rips and swirls I had to hack through. The shingle sharpened as it fell away, slashing my feet, till my soles found a shelf of sand. Cold swirled round my balls and chest. My body wasn't up to this. I thought of retreating. But the tide was dragging me out, and surrender seemed the easiest course.

I let go and pushed off, through the foothills towards the peaks. It was impossible to swim straight out – the rip tide pulled diagonally – but by gripping the water and hurling it behind me I crawled to where I'd last seen Ollie.

After the struggle to reach them, the breakers, when they came, were quickly surmounted: a few slaps round the head and mouthfuls of water, and I was through.

Behind the break point I found Ollie, in a trough of calm.

'It'll be easier now,' he said.

'Liar,' I gasped, but it was true: the first buoy was only twenty yards away, and the swell looked steady and benign.

We were bobbing alongside and looking in each other's eyes. I can't remember who spoke first.

'Let's settle it then.'

'What?'

'We'll start from one buoy and race to the other. Winner takes all.'

'Swimming's not my forte.'

'Nor mine. We've an equal chance.'

'Which stroke?'

'Any. Freestyle. Are you on?'

'Sure.'

We shook hands as we bobbed there.

The waves swept across us from behind. Floating on our backs to conserve strength, we drifted towards the first buoy, the start line. I felt calm, energised by the cold, ready for action. But then, just as we reached the buoy, Rufus appeared. It was stupid to have assumed he wouldn't follow us. If I'd said 'Sit, wait' back on the beach, he'd have sulked and whined but obeyed. But I'd forgotten the magic words.

'Rufus, good boy,' Ollie said. He seemed less bothered by his presence than I was and suggested we let him paddle with us as we raced. But I didn't want the distraction or the worry. This was no place for dogs. Rufus had to go back.

A thin black branch was floating nearby and I hurled it for

him to pursue. It died a few yards away, and he quickly retrieved it. With me beside him in the water, he seemed to find our fetch game enthralling. But after cursing and shoving him shore-wards several times, I finally showed him who was boss. Defeated, he turned his baleful eye from me and paddled back.

'Ready?' Ollie said. We were by the first buoy, him with his right hand pressed against it, me on the other side with my left.

'Ready.'

'Go.'

I can't honestly claim to have been expecting a 'Steady' in between, but the speed of Ollie's getaway caught me unawares. He was only doing breaststroke, and by opting for crawl I should have drawn level, but even flat out I failed to close the gap. As it widened I consoled myself that he'd gone off too fast. The second buoy was still a good distance away, with the waves – sweeping diagonally to the shore – more against than behind us. But though the conditions were the same for both of us, Ollie was coping far better. When he turned and took in how far behind I was, I thought he might let up. But winning wasn't enough for Ollie. He wanted to humiliate me.

His sleek head ottered away through the tide. I should have realised: with his big hands and long legs, he had the perfect physique for swimming. Whereas I fought to stay afloat – the waves flogging my back, the salt acidic on my skin – he moved smoothly over the surface, like a black billiard ball rolling over baize.

The waves weren't high but I was shipping water and sinking.

'Ollie,' I cried, the race forgotten, terrified I was going under. But my shout died in the waves' throat. We were past halfway now, and I was ten yards behind.

Hyperventilating from cold and exhaustion, I wondered if it would be better to die than to live through the days ahead:

the £10,000 I'd have to find; the disciplinary hearing; the emotional fallout from making love to Daisy. Panic ought to have meant an adrenalin surge, but the gap between Ollie and me remained the same, whereas the gap between him and the finish was closing fast. I flung my arms out in a last effort, even managing half a dozen strokes of butterfly, before subsiding to a weary doggy-paddle.

Resigned to defeat, I closed my eyes to protect them from the burning salt. When I opened them again there, miraculously, was Ollie, just a couple of yards ahead. For a crazy second I thought I'd been rewarded for my efforts, but then I saw that he was treading water: if the gap between us had narrowed, it was only because he'd come to a halt. I thought of the story I'd read at university all those years ago, about the man who goes to prison for fifteen years to win a bet, then throws it all away at the last minute. Perhaps winning no long mattered to Ollie, either – because he thought he was dying; or because, having come within yards of victory, he had proved his point. The sight of him bobbing there enraged me nonetheless. Worse still was his patronising 'Are you OK, Ian?' when my arms were balsa and my legs pure lead. The sea wasn't deep here – ten or twelve feet at a guess – but whereas he was in his element I felt anchored to the ocean floor.

'OK?' he shouted again, his back to the waves.

'No problem,' I shouted, swallowing more seawater.

'You had me worried there.'

'I'm fine,' I gasped. 'There's the finish line. Let's go.'

Thumbs up, he grinned and swung round, Ollie as I'd always known him, desperate to stay ahead. The wave that broke over him as he turned wasn't huge, but it was bigger than any we'd faced till then and the force of it knocked him back. I was luckier, having seen it coming, and dived below, into the marble undertow, like a boxer ducking under a hook. When I resurfaced Ollie was right next to me. Buffeted back by the first wave, he was ready for the second, which we swam through almost side by side. After those two, the worst seemed to be over. We were paddling alongside each other in a trough. The white buoy appeared farther off now, but would be easily reachable once we got our breath back. Ollie looked tired, like me, allowing the swell to carry him over the next few waves. Dangling there like frogs, we dared each other to make the first move. When he began to thrash, I followed, eyes closed, heading for the buoy. The sea was flatter now, hard and smooth as a butcher's slab, no glassy gulfs to overwhelm us. I closed my eyes, driving forward, almost home.

It must have been the rip tide that dragged us into each other without warning. Or perhaps, as we pushed ourselves, Ollie veered naturally to the right, and me to the left. Either way, ten feet short of the finish we collided like competing boat crews, not sufficiently to capsize but with a violent thud, Ollie's arm hitting my ribs like a wayward oar. I kicked out to get free and accidentally caught him in the balls, or so I guessed from his angry scream. 'Sorry,' I cried, but he came back at me, clutching my arm. Since I was now the one nearer the buoy, I thought he'd done it to pull me back, and I shoved him away. That he might have been winded or in trouble didn't occur to me. The shove wasn't meant to be forceful but it sent him down, and when he didn't re-emerge I stopped for a second, to check whether he was all right. When he lunged upwards, I saw it had been a ploy. His eyes looked bright, eager, desperate – desperate, I thought, to win. He grabbed my arm again, his fingers like the suckers of an octopus, his mouth a rictus grin. I tried to shake him off but his arms snaked round me, the left gripping my shoulder while the right circled my neck. As we struggled, whiteness bloomed about us, a feathery line of bubbles drifting away. Still he wrapped himself round me, like bindweed, dragging us both down. As well as his grip, there was the weight, his body roped to me like a corpse. I wanted to shout at him to stop messing around, that no bet was worth risking death for, but my mouth was shut against the water. Changing tack, I let my body go slack, in the hope he'd do the same. It didn't work: we sank like two white statues through the green. Surely even Ollie can't hold his breath much longer, I thought. But he kept on going, down into the blackness, my body tied to his. I punched him in the face but the water deadened the blow. I kneed him in the stomach but my knee rebounded. I remembered him saying he had no feelings any more. That love and friendship no longer counted. That he'd reached a place beyond morality where nothing got through.

With the last dregs of strength, I forced my hand under his chin, pushing till his neck tipped back to horizontal, our bodies tilting in a slow arc till he was underneath me. Useless till then, my legs now had my weight behind them and kicked a path along his thighs to his chest so that I could tread him down. I trod him like grapes. I trod him like earth. I trod him till his hands slipped, the noose slackened and he floated away, trodden under, trodden down.

Back up top, I coughed and gasped, my eyes salt-scorched, my lungs exploding in my ribs. For a time I lay there with my head tipped back. Below me, the water felt cold and hard, like a stone slab. Slow clouds drifted above.

Once I got my breath back and the blood stopped pounding in my ears, I swung myself upright. Where had Ollie gone? And when would he resurface, grinning at his prank? It briefly occurred to me he hadn't been fooling, that there had been more to his arm-wrestling than winning the race. But it seemed more likely he'd pop up and sneakily pip me to the post. Taking no chances, I paddled the last few yards and touched the buoy with the fingers of my right hand.

Looking round, exhausted and triumphant, I could still see no sign. 'Joke's over, Ollie, where are you?' I shouted. A black shadow seemed to flit below. It could have been nothing. It probably *was* nothing. But I took a deep breath and prepared to dive down.

It was then that Rufus broke water, ten yards away, nosing up from the depths like a seal. 'Here, boy,' I said, as he frantically paddled my way. Almost at once he went under again. Where Ollie and I had swum, the waves had broken between us and the shore. But Rufus, closer in, had been battered by them and now he was paying the price. His black snout broke the surface again, just feet from me, then disappeared. Normally dogs are good swimmers, but Rufus was in trouble and the sight of him struggling was more than I could bear. Reaching below, I grabbed him by the collar and hauled him upwards. I had little strength left after my own ordeal. And Rufus was hard to manoeuvre, a dead weight, his sodden fur dragging him down. But by keeping his head above water with one hand and paddling with the other, I managed to steer us both towards the shore. Close in, where the waves broke, I nearly lost him again. But at last my feet touched bottom and, with what little strength remained, I pushed him to the safety of the shingle.

Only then was I free to swing round and scan the sea. Surely Ollie would be visible by now. But between the two buoys was green and white water. Nothing else.

I swam out again and searched for him as long as I could, floating on my back at the end, useless, brain-dead, thrashing in circles. Near the second buoy, my hopes rose as a large black shape appeared. But when I closed on it my hands met wood. Ten minutes passed, maybe twenty, maybe more.

I kept expecting Ollie to bob up, against the odds. He'd grab my leg as I clambered through the breakers. He'd tap me on my shoulder as I put on my clothes. He'd leap from a sand hollow as Rufus and I shivered through the dunes. He'd be the one taking the car keys from his trouser pocket. The one in the driver's seat of the MGB. The one making the 999 call from the telephone box. The one pulling up the drive. The one breaking the news. The one holding Daisy as she howled. The one saying he'd done all he could. The one who'd got home safely. Who'd pulled through. Who'd triumphed. Who'd lived to tell the story as it was meant to be written, not the story I'm telling you now.

November

One thing they don't tell you when you're young, or if they do you fail to listen, is that getting older doesn't make you any wiser. If life were arranged more fairly, the loss of youth would be offset by knowledge and self-confidence. You would know who you are and where you're going. But, till lately at least, that is not how it has been for me.

The other thing they don't tell you about is depression. Apparently researchers have found that the worst age for depression is forty-four. Not fourteen, when you're a tortured, self-mutilating adolescent. Not seventy-four, when half your friends are dead and you think you're next. But forty-four, the age I am now. At forty-four, so I read in a recent article, people feel exhausted by their kids (I have none), or suffer the loss of their parents (mine are still going, worse luck), or become aware of their own mortality (I've been aware of mine since I was five). The article made no mention of what makes people *truly* depressed at forty-four, which is realising that the life they're living is the only one they'll ever have. What hits you at forty-four is that the person you imagined being, and promised yourself you could still become, isn't going to emerge, that you're stuck with who you are till you cease to be. Unless – an even worse prospect – a diminished version of yourself (drunk, drugged, disabled or demented) takes over.

Apologies if I sound miserable. But seeing the light sometimes begins with a plunge into darkness.

Before Badingley, I thought I had all a man could reasonably hope for: career, marriage, home, health and sanity. Afterwards I saw things differently. What had made my life tolerable till then was that it seemed provisional: a book I could lose myself in but return to the library whenever I chose. Now I realised it was becoming the opposite: fixed, fated, the only story I would ever have. I'd got by until then because I felt needed. But necessity is the enemy of invention. And work and marriage were killing what inventiveness I had.

The weekend away was intended as a brief escape. I didn't expect it to bring me freedom. That was pure luck – the bonus ball.

It might seem tasteless to talk of luck in the wake of what happened. Ollie was my friend and his death devastated us all. More than once I've picked up the phone to call him for a banter or wind-up. The desolation I feel replacing the handset is hard to describe.

When tragedy strikes you go over it time and again, as if by doing so you can avert it, turn the clock back, derail the runaway train. As I see it the key factors were these:

– Ollie was bipolar and/or having a breakdown.
– He deluded himself he had cancer when his tumour was benign.
– He wrongly suspected Daisy of having an affair with Milo.
– He feared Daisy would leave him.
– He had these suspicions before I carelessly mentioned my own, which confirmed them. (I used to berate myself for putting the thought in his head; now I realise it only stuck

because he mistrusted Daisy already. Jealous people don't need a cause, they're jealous because they are jealous.)

- He felt guilty about his failure to parent Archie successfully.
- He hoped that a family holiday would put everything right.
- He also hoped that by renting the Badingley house he could relive the happiest time of his childhood.
- That time was in reality the unhappiest, because his father had drowned there. So Ollie claimed or believed. (I still have serious doubts. When I googled 'Moore, Drowning, East Anglia, August 1976', nothing showed up. And I can't ask Ollie's mum for confirmation because she's gaga. I sometimes wonder whether Ollie's parents didn't just divorce – whether his father isn't still out there somewhere.)
- So powerful were Ollie's memories of that summer that he created a kind of bubble – a time warp, lost domain or parallel universe – into which we were all drawn. I'm a level-headed bloke but believe me there was a weird psychic energy around Badingley. Mr Quarles, for instance: was he for real?
- In reliving (and he hoped exorcising) the trauma of 1976, Ollie planned to use me as his stooge. Winning our bet would be redemptive, with Badingley a site of triumph rather than loss.
- All would have been well but for the storm on Sunday night, which washed out tennis the next day.
- Though physically powerful, Ollie was not a strong swimmer.
- His heart wasn't strong, either. Though the coroner recorded the cause of death as misadventure (death by drowning), a medical student I got talking to in the pub the other night said a heart attack could not be ruled out.
- From the way he fought me off, I seriously doubt

whether Ollie wanted to be saved. He had developed a death wish.
– In those last moments, he thought he had become his father or that the two of them were about to be reunited.
– That's why he was grinning just before he went under for the last time.

A large number of contributory factors, then. I agree they might seem muddled. How can anyone have a heart attack and commit suicide at the same time? But it's malicious of Em to suggest that my compiling of the list above, in a notebook, is 'an act of guilt and desperation'. I'm desperately sad to have lost a good friend, yes. But what do I have to feel guilty about? I might have been kinder to Ollie, Em says. But kindness was never our way; we liked to taunt each other and josh around. I needn't have accused him of being a liar, she says, as I did on the dunes immediately before our swim. But he took it well and we made up. I could have refused to go into the sea, she says. But Ollie would have felt I'd let him down. I *should* have refused to go in, she says, because I knew how dangerous the currents were. But the currents were the same for both of us. As for sleeping with Daisy, that was wrong, I know, but they weren't married and Ollie never found out so it's irrelevant.

Em did find out, which is partly why we're not together now. It was I who told her. Not from shame or self-abasement. Not because I wanted there to be no secrets between us any more. Not to save our marriage. On the contrary, I told her so she would throw me out and I'd be free to live with Daisy. I know I should have left voluntarily rather than waiting for Em to make me go. Since I'd already decided our marriage was over, why did I stay another two months and endure the tears, fights, silences and abortive reconciliations? (And also endure the continuing saga of Magda, who, thanks to Em's efforts, ended up keeping her baby.) Em called me cruel, and perhaps I was, not for sleeping with Daisy but because I made no effort to atone for it; if I had, she would probably have swallowed her pride and forgiven me. 'I suppose you have some woman lined up,' she said, in the middle of our last row. 'You wouldn't have the guts to live on your own. Men never do.' I shrugged: if we were separating, what right had she to know? Then a cloud crossed her face: 'Not Daisy? You don't seriously think Daisy would have you. My God, you do, don't you? You're even crazier than I thought.'

To tell the truth, I'd had little contact with Daisy since the funeral, and the day had been a blur for all of us: the sea of flowers, the pews heaving with mourners, the shouldered coffin floating down the aisle. Back at the house, among friends, Daisy seemed remote, closed off behind her veil of grief. I touched her arm and whispered condolences, but it wasn't the moment for anything more. She needed time. And I needed to sort my life out.

I left Ilkeston with a handful of possessions and no regrets. My stake in our existence there had always been small. The fish pond had been bequeathed to us by the previous owner. Every object in the house and plant in the garden had been chosen by Em. I hadn't lived my life, I'd simulated it. Easy come, easy go. 'Off to your tragic lodgings, then?' Em said, not teasing any more, but angry, mocking, contemptuous. I closed the door behind me, saying nothing. The bedsit in Heanor is comfortable enough, as a temporary base. The only drawback is that they don't allow pets; I miss Rufus terribly but for now he has to stay with Em.

When I told Daisy, over the phone, that Em and I had separated she was tearful. 'It's one grief after another,' she sobbed. I hoped her upset would pass once we met in person. My plan was to go down to London one Saturday: grave, dignified, but ecstatic to be together at last, we would sit by the tall sash windows, with drizzle darkening the decking outside. Unfortunately, when I called her again to fix a date she said the house was being redecorated. No problem, I said, picturing stepladders and paint tins in the background. Fresh paint for a fresh start, I thought, and wondered how it would feel to move in with her, among the bookcases, Chinese carpets and leather sofas. Surely she knew that was what I wanted. Surely that was what she wanted too.

While she rabbited on about Archie, who was doing well in his new school it seemed, I nerved myself to say the words.

'I've been talking to Em,' she said, before I could. 'We had a good chat.'

My plans had not allowed for that. I'd imagined Em hurling abuse at Daisy.

'You're making a big mistake,' she said. 'Em's lovely. And you're so good together. You'll be lost without her. Go back and apologise. Beg. Plead. Tell her you can't manage on your own.'

'I don't intend to be on my own,' I said.

'Em and I talked about that, too.'

'Em's angry with me. But it can't be helped. I . . .'

I heard the click of a cigarette lighter and an intake of breath. Daisy never used to smoke. Obviously I was making her nervous. I took it as a good sign. The same with her hair, which (she'd already told me) had been cut short again: disappointing in one respect but a sign that she was ready for change.

'I know what you're going to say, Ian, and I don't want to hear it. Em was furious with me at first. But when I explained about the past – what happened at university and so on – she calmed down.'

'You told her about that?' I said.

'We should never have hidden it from her. Now it's in the open, she's willing to forgive me. She knows I was totally drunk that night.'

'Come on, you wanted it.'

'I kept saying no but you wouldn't listen. At the time I was too shocked. I couldn't believe it of you. But since talking to a counsellor, I realise what you did.'

'You feel guilty because it's tied up with Ollie's death.'

'I don't feel guilty. I feel unclean. You raped me, Ian. Think what Em would feel if I told her. Or if I went to the police.'

'I wanted you so much. I love you.'

'Well, I don't love you. I don't even want to see you unless it's with Em. How much clearer can I be?'

No clearer. I would have liked to defend myself: for her to use the word rape was ridiculous. But I knew she'd hang up on me if I protested. As her silence smouldered in my ear, I realised the chance was gone, that it hadn't been there in the first place, that the likes of me never stand an earthly with the likes of her, that the Daisies will always choose the Ollies of this world and banish the Ians to the outer darkness. I was sitting by her hall of residence again, on the outside looking in.

'You want children,' I said, after a long pause, 'is that it?'

'What's that got to do with anything?' she said, in bewilderment. Em had not let on about my immotile sperm, then.

'Or perhaps you're seeing someone.'

'How can you say that? Ollie's only been dead three months.'

'Is it Milo?'

'Milo's in New York.'

'One of your other artists, then.'

'I've just been widowed.'

'All the more reason.'

'For what?'

'For you to be fucking someone.'

'You disgust me, Ian. You're off your head. I don't want to speak to you ever again.'

I've been watching a lot of horror films lately. Most films seem to be horror films these days – you see an ad for some innocuous-seeming western or detective story, only to find, once you're at the cinema, that you can't watch for fear of throwing up. It's lucky I keep my eyes closed, or the violence might have rubbed off by now and I'd be telling this story from prison. As it was, rather than travelling down to London, smashing Daisy's skull in with a marble ashtray and having sex with her blood-smeared corpse, I accepted that I'd handled things badly. Best wait a while before I pressed my suit again. She was still in shock.

It didn't occur to me, at that point, to ask her for the ten thousand pounds I'm owed by Ollie's estate. But I've since sent a couple of letters suggesting she pay up. In the most recent, I gently pointed out that she was dishonouring the memory of Ollie, who would want to do right by his old friend. He and I had put nothing on paper, of course. But the agreement was a gentlemen's agreement, and she knows I'm honest. It's not as if she can't afford it. Ten grand is a drop in the ocean to a woman like Daisy. Whereas to me it's a small fortune and would allow me to pay off half my debts. Many men in my position would charge interest as well. Perhaps when Daisy stops grieving – if she *is* grieving, not putting it on – she will see sense.

When the divorce comes through, and Em sells the house or pays me my share of it, I'll be in the clear. But for the present my debts are mounting. After rent, electricity, food, drink, etc., there's not much left and the little there is I spend on websites. The wheels have been spinning against me lately, the wrong cards falling from the deck. But once I've mastered the new system I'm using, my luck is sure to turn.

Meanwhile I have my salary, which the local authority continues to pay. I had every hope the disciplinary hearing would exonerate me over Campbell Foster. But in the event the hearing didn't take place. Ollie's death was widely reported the day before: 'TOP BARRISTER IN SWIMMING TRAGEDY', 'LEADING LAWYER DIES ON HOLIDAY', 'FATAL DROWNING IN NORTH SEA', etc. (Excuse my pedantry, but – as to the last – when is a drowning not fatal?) On the day of the tribunal itself, the local rag also ran a story: 'ILKESTON MAN'S HOLIDAY DRAMA: A local teacher was recovering yesterday after a desperate struggle to save his best friend in ten-foot-high waves.' Journalists have a bad name, but the young chap who came to see me (and with whom I've since shared the odd pint) made a decent fist of telling the tale. I would not myself have used the word 'heroic' of my actions but it can't have gone amiss with the governors. They decided that the disciplinary hearing would be 'inappropriate' at such a time and would have to wait till their next meeting after Christmas. In the interim I am excused all teaching duties and 'suspended on full pay'. As I've been telling people, what they've effectively done is to grant me compassionate leave. If they won't have me back, no worries. To be frank, I'm sick of the place – of Mrs Baynes, my colleagues, the kids, the parents, everything. So I'm hopeful the local authority will find me a post in a more congenial environment. A place where my talents can flourish, until I make the move to London. As the young journalist was saying the other night, it would be scandalous if the governors found against me. He is ready with his story

– 'OUTRAGE AS SCHOOL SACKS SWIMMING HERO' – if they fail to do right.

I do sometimes blame myself. That's natural – a displacement of my grief and loss. I miss Ollie and wish I could rewrite history. But an overdeveloped sense of responsibility is debilitating. You have to move on.

To have no home, no wife, no job or possessions is strange but also bracing. It has made me a new animal, determined and full of hope. I sometimes think that's what went wrong for Ollie. That what made him go under was the prospect of futility: the waves breaking pointlessly over and over, nothing ever changing, the same wasteful charade for all eternity. He had wanted to make a difference in life and the waves told him he hadn't and wouldn't: *You're nothing. Accept your fate. Be at peace with us.* The light in his eyes was the joy of surrender. Water was his medium. He entered it joyfully. He'd had enough.

He was my friend and I loved him but he wouldn't have thanked me for rescuing him. He asked me there to help him on his way down.

The news on the television tonight was lacking in drama – no terrorist outrages, no murdered schoolgirls, no celebrities entering rehab. All I noticed, belatedly, was the date. 27 November, exactly five months since Ollie called that Sunday night and exactly three months since the Friday we turned up at Badingley. That's three 27s, the sort of coincidence I appreciate, and in this case an unusually significant one, since 2 plus 7 makes 9, and three 9s make 999, which I dialled that day from the telephone box in hope of saving Ollie. A painful memory, needless to say, so I was relieved just now, when midnight struck, to know the third 27 has gone and the sequence is over. From tomorrow I will make a new start. Surprise is the best strategy, I've decided. I can see it already

– my finger on Daisy's doorbell, her puzzled face as she opens up, then the smile, the hug, her apology, my proposal, and our lingering kiss in the stained-glass hall. It might turn out differently, of course. But, if it does, I'll think of something. Defeat's not in the script. I'm a survivor.